"I'd love to go to

Blue blinked as if sur
"Really?"

She laughed, although she felt somewhat annoyed.
"Why did you ask if you expected me to refuse?"

"Because I'm worried. I don't want to see anything
happen to you or the girls."

Her annoyance fled, replaced with gratitude for his
concern. "Blue, you're a good man."

She watched, surprised, as he turned pink beneath
his tan. She chuckled. "Not used to hearing
compliments?"

He merely shrugged.

Blue seemed to truly care about her safety and that
of the girls. Like she'd said, he was a good man. *He
should really remarry. He has so much to offer. He—*

Not knowing where those thoughts came from, she
slammed the door on them right quick.

If Blue Lyons chose to marry or otherwise, it was
none of her concern. She had her own issues to
worry about. There was no room in her life for
wondering if Blue would ever consider taking
another wife.

So why couldn't she stop wondering what it would
be like to be married to a man who treated her like
an equal and yet showed tenderness and concern?

Linda Ford lives on a ranch in Alberta, Canada, near enough to the Rocky Mountains that she can enjoy them on a daily basis. She and her husband raised fourteen children—four homemade, ten adopted. She currently shares her home and life with her husband, a grown son, a live-in paraplegic client and a continual (and welcome) stream of kids, kids-in-law, grandkids, and assorted friends and relatives.

Books by Linda Ford

Love Inspired Historical

Christmas in Eden Valley

A Daddy for Christmas

Montana Marriages

Big Sky Cowboy
Big Sky Daddy
Big Sky Homecoming

Cowboys of Eden Valley

The Cowboy's Surprise Bride
The Cowboy's Unexpected Family
The Cowboy's Convenient Proposal
Claiming the Cowboy's Heart
Winning Over the Wrangler
Falling for the Rancher Father

Visit the Author Profile page at Harlequin.com for more titles.

LINDA FORD

A Daddy for Christmas

HARLEQUIN® LOVE INSPIRED® HISTORICAL

Recycling programs for this product may not exist in your area.

 ™ LOVE INSPIRED BOOKS

ISBN-13: 978-0-373-28330-9

A Daddy for Christmas

Copyright © 2015 by Linda Ford

www.Harlequin.com

Printed in U.S.A.

But God commendeth His love toward us, in that, while we were yet sinners, Christ died for us.
—*Romans* 5:8

Christmas is a special time made more special
by sharing it with those I love.
This book is dedicated to you.
Thank you for filling the day and my life with such joy.

Chapter One

Edendale, Alberta, Canada
December 1882

The church door clattered open. A cold breeze skittered across the floor as two little girls rushed into the room from beyond the partition of raw wood that separated the entryway from the main part of the partially finished church. They skidded to a halt, staring at him with wide eyes.

The peace twenty-eight-year-old Blue Lyons sought so desperately shattered into fragments as tiny and elusive as the sawdust at his feet.

"We need help," the bigger girl said, an unfamiliar child with hair the color of caramel candy sticks and heavily lashed eyes as dark as night.

"Something's wrong with Mama," the second girl said. This one had sunny-blond hair and blue eyes.

At the fear he saw in their expressions, Blue felt cracks begin to form in the barrier he'd erected around his emotions. Then he tightened his self-control. Part of the reason he'd asked to work here, making pews for the new church in town, was to avoid contact with children. Back at Eden Valley Ranch he was surrounded with them—smiling, laughing, chasing, playing, happy children continually threatening the fortifications he'd built around his memories.

But these two little girls were alone and frightened. "Whoa. Slow down. Where's your mama, and what does she need?"

The pair gasped for air, then closed the distance to his side, apparently unafraid of him as a stranger. Or were they so concerned about their mama they would seek help from anyone?

The girls caught his hands, one on each side, and tugged at him. He let them drag him forward as the memory of other occasions burst from the locked vault of his mind. Two other children—a boy and a girl—pulling on his hands, eager to show him something. Sometimes it was a new batch of kittens. Sometimes a flower peeking through the snow. Once they'd discovered a baby rabbit hidden in some grass, and the three of them had hunkered down to watch it.

The two girls who had burst into his serenity hurried him toward the door. Then, suddenly, one of them halted.

"Stop. You need your coat. It's too cold to go out without it." The older one had suddenly grown motherly and concerned. She spied the coat hanging from a nail and dropped his hand to point at it. "Best put it on."

He hesitated. He'd like nothing more than to get back to the peace he'd found in his work. But how could he until he made sure everyone was safe? So he obeyed and slipped into his warm winter coat.

The girls rocked back and forth, their little faces wreathed in concern and urgency.

His nerves twitched at the impatience of the girls, but he would proceed cautiously. "We haven't met. My name is Blue Lyons. I'm going to be working here for a few days, making pews. Do you have a name?" he asked the older child as she twisted her fingers in her worry.

"I'm Eleanor. I'm the oldest. I'm eight."

The little one piped up. "I'm Libby. I'm seven, so I'm just about as old." She gave her sister a challenging look.

Eleanor's dark eyes flashed. "Are not."

Little Libby's chin jutted out. "Am, too."

Blue did not let the argument escalate. "What's your mama's name, and where is she?"

"Mrs. Weston," said Eleanor with a degree of triumph that she had spoken first.

"Clara Weston," Libby added, not to be outdone.

Reminded of their mission, they again grabbed his hands. "Come on."

He let them pull him along, as curious as he was concerned. "Where are we going?"

"To Mama," Libby said. "She fell down."

His heart lurched. He tried to still it, but it refused to obey. "Is she hurt?"

"I don't know." Libby's voice wobbled.

Oh, please don't cry. Please don't.

Eleanor must have had the same thought, though likely for an entirely different reason. "Libby, don't blubber. We gotta get back to Mama."

She sounded so grown-up. *The responsible one of the pair.* Now why would he think that? He knew nothing about them. He slammed shut the quaking doors of his heart. All he had to do was make sure their mother was safe.

They trotted onward, both girls latched on to his hands as if afraid to let go. Their fear and concern knotted in his stomach. What if their mother—

No. He would not think the worst.

Though nothing could be as bad as what he'd seen two years ago. The fire. The—

He would not, could not, think of it.

They headed for the river. A dozen possibilities rushed at him, none of which he hoped to find.

"There she is." Eleanor pointed. With a cry, she broke free and rushed to the figure facedown on the ground.

Blue's heart flipped over. His breath stuck in his chest.

Libby stopped, pulled Blue to a halt. "She won't wake up," the child wailed as she turned and pressed herself to his side.

He couldn't move with her clinging to him. But he must check on the woman.

"Eleanor, see to your sister."

Eleanor stepped back and pulled Libby to her. The pair stood with their arms around each other, eyes as wide as moons as they watched him.

He knelt at Mrs. Weston's side and pressed his fingers to her neck to check for a pulse. Good, she was alive.

Seeing no sign of injury, he rolled her over. "Mrs. Weston, wake up." No response. He patted her cheeks. She felt cold. So very cold.

"Clara." He spoke louder. It wasn't right to use her Christian name so freely, but if it got her to wake up, she'd surely forgive him.

She stirred, tried to raise her eyelids and failed, then mumbled something.

He bent closer. "What did you say?"

He made out the words. "My girls."

"They're here. They're fine." Then she stilled, and he could get nothing more from her. "Gather up your things," he told the girls. "We're going back to the church." He considered his options for about two and a half seconds. What he was about to do seriously crossed the boundaries he had built around his life as well as overstepped rules of proper conduct. But he didn't see what other choice he had. He scooped Clara Weston into his arms and trotted back to the church. The two little girls tried to keep up but were burdened down with carrying their bags. He didn't wait for them; he rushed into the building.

He began to lower Clara to the floor, then realized it was bare and cold. His bedroll was nearby, and Blue kicked it toward the stove and used his boot to spread the bedding. He'd expected he might see some cold weather, so he had brought a supply of furs. Now he saw how right he'd been in thinking ahead, though never in his wildest imagination did he think he might need them to warm up a sick or injured woman.

He lowered her to the padding just as the girls entered, yelling for their mama.

"What's wrong with her?" Libby demanded, her hands on her hips as if she held Blue responsible.

Eleanor hushed her and knelt by her mother's side. "Mr. Blue, is she gonna die?"

He wanted to assure them otherwise, but he'd never offer false hope when their mother lay before them so still, her skin so pale it was transparent. "I think the first thing we need to do is get her warmed up. Why don't you two bring me some more firewood?" Eddie Gardiner, owner and operator of Eden Valley Ranch where Blue worked, was always organized and had put a supply of firewood inside, near the back door, so Blue would have dry wood to last him a few days.

The girls hustled over and filled their arms. Two chunks of wood each was about all they could carry. He could have done three times that in one trip but that wasn't the reason for getting them to help. The girls needed to be kept busy.

He knelt at Clara's side. My, wouldn't she be offended at the familiar way he thought of her and addressed her, but it was hard to be proper and formal when the woman looked ready to expire. "Mrs. Weston. Clara." He rubbed her shoulders, held her icy hands. Why was she out in this weather without adequate clothing?

He pulled one of the furs over her and threw some of the wood the girls brought into the stove.

"Has your mama been sick?"

Libby began to say something, but Eleanor grabbed her hand and jerked it. She spoke for the pair of them. "She's not been sick."

He knew everyone in town and the surrounding area. These people were new. Must have been dropped off from the last stage earlier today. Petey, the driver, had immediately headed back to Fort Macleod with four important British investors of one of the nearby ranches.

"Is your papa coming for you?" Likely he was one of the many new settlers in the area.

"Got no papa," Libby said. "He died." Her words

carried a weighty sorrow that he felt in the pit of his stomach.

"Libby, remember what Mama said."

At Eleanor's warning, Libby clamped her hand over her mouth.

Blue nodded. "Were you planning to meet someone?"

Silence from both of them.

"Where are you going?"

His question was met with more stubborn silence, though Libby dropped her hand and looked about to speak. Then she glanced at Eleanor and thought better of it.

"Do you girls have a secret?"

Eleanor scowled. "Mama said not to tell strangers our secrets."

He gave them a faint smile. "That's something to remember most days, but right now your mama needs to get someplace warm and safe, so I think it's okay if you tell me where you're going."

Eleanor's face crumpled in what he could only think was confusion. "We can't."

They were making this difficult. "I already explained about secrets."

"It's not a secret." Eleanor sighed expansively. "We don't know where we're going."

Perhaps their mother hadn't given them the information. "Who is meeting you?"

The girls shook their heads.

"You don't know?"

More head shaking.

This was getting him nowhere. He turned back to Clara. She still lay motionless, her skin tinged a faint blue. He touched her cheek. Still icy cold.

"Mrs. Weston, wake up. Open your eyes."

The girls knelt beside him. "Mama, wake up."

Libby's voice broke, and Eleanor wrapped an arm about her shoulders. "Libby, 'member what Mama said. God will take care of us."

Blue kept his opinion to himself. But he didn't see God taking care of these people. Blue was doing it, and he sure didn't consider himself God. Or even godly. If he had a fraction of the power God had, he would have quenched the fire that had consumed his house and killed his family. At the very least, he would have gotten there in time to pull them from the inferno. He'd never forget the leaden weight of his legs when he saw the smoke, saw it was his house and ran until his lungs nearly exploded as he tried to get there to rescue them.

Tried and failed.

"I—I know." The words stuttered from Libby. "But I asked God to send us food, and He didn't and I'm so hungry."

"Me, too," Eleanor whispered and shot Blue a look that seemed to warn him she didn't mean for him to hear.

He sat back on his heels. "When did you last eat?"

Eleanor's expression grew stubborn, but Libby hung her head and sighed dramatically. "We had supper yesterday. Some biscuits Mama found. And some cold bacon."

Eleanor grew thoughtful. "But Mama didn't have any. She said she wasn't hungry. Lots of times she said she wasn't hungry, but I think she was."

He considered this latest information. They obviously had no funds. The girls didn't know where they were going or who was meeting them. He was beginning to think no one was.

So Clara might be suffering from hunger as well as cold. He wrapped the furs more tightly around her and added another piece of wood to the fire. The heat was enough to make a man sweat buckets, but she was still like a block of ice.

"Clara. Open your eyes."

The girls patted her cheeks. "Mama." Eleanor's voice caught.

Libby laid her head on the furs and sobbed. "What if she never wakes up?"

Clara's eyes fluttered.

"Lib. Lib." Eleanor nudged her sister. "Look."

Libby lifted her head. Both girls grinned when they saw their mother had opened her eyes.

"Where am I?" Clara's voice was so faint he almost wondered if he imagined it.

He scooted closer so her eyes found him. "You're at the church. You'll be safe now."

Clara sighed deeply and closed her eyes again. Her color had improved. The warmth of the fire had done that. She needed one more thing before she'd be on her feet again—food—and he knew where to get some.

"Wait here," he instructed the girls. "I'll be back in a few minutes. Watch your mama and make sure she stays warm." He dashed out the back door and trotted over to Bonnie and Claude Morton's. The couple ran the business of feeding travelers and providing baked goods for Macpherson's store. He burst through the door.

Bonnie glanced up, a startled look on her face. "You're early for dinner." He planned to take his meals here while he was working on the church.

He snatched off his hat and turned it around and around in his fingers. He realized he was nodding while she waited for his answer.

He pushed the words from his brain. "Would you have anything ready at the moment?"

"I suppose the soup could be served anytime. The bread isn't ready yet, but there are biscuits. There's always biscuits. Macpherson says he can't keep enough of them in the store. Would that suit you?"

"Yes, fine."

She reached for a bowl and put it on the table. She thought he meant to eat here.

"Ma'am, could you put the soup in a container so I could take it back to the church?"

"You're welcome to eat here."

"I know, but I need to take it to the church." He would tell her why but not until he had a chance to talk to Clara. For some reason, he felt he had to protect her until she said otherwise.

"Very well." She reached for a pint jar.

"You got something bigger?"

Her hand went to a quart jar.

"How about that one?" He indicated a half-gallon jar.

With a little chuckle, she filled it. "You are hungry today, aren't you?"

He nodded. "And I'll take a bowl." He scooped four from the shelf and tucked them in his pocket, hoping she wouldn't notice. From the way she watched him, her eyes narrowed, he guessed she had.

"I suppose you want half a dozen biscuits?"

"Yes, please. I'll pay you extra for this." Bonnie and Claude meant to feed him as part of their contribution to the church project, but this was more than one man would eat.

He hurried out before she could demand to know what was going on. It wasn't like he could answer her. What were Clara and her daughters doing here? Where were they going? Most of all, how had he managed to get himself involved?

Warm furs ensconced Clara. She'd glimpsed the girls hovering over her, then closed her eyes to stop the dizziness that made her queasy. She should say something to ease their minds, but she couldn't dredge up enough energy to do so. She forced her eyes open and stared at the ceiling. Why did it shimmer and shift as if driven by a wind? Perhaps she was dreaming. If so, she didn't want the dream to end. She wanted to keep floating on the warm bed.

"Mama?" Eleanor's voice came from a long way off.

Clara pushed at the edges of her mind, blinked as she tried to find her children. "Eleanor? Libby?"

Two sweet, smiling faces floated in front of her, so close she felt their warm breath.

"Where am I?"

"We're at the church," Eleanor said. "The one we saw on our way to the river."

"Mama, we was so scared. You fell down and wouldn't get back up."

Clara pushed harder to escape her dream. Then she remembered. She'd been by a river. Had wanted to get a drink. That was the last she could recall. "How did I get here?"

"Mr. Blue carried you."

"Mr. Blue?" Were they imagining such a person?

Clara thought the strong arms and comforting voice had been part of her dream.

"We talked to a stranger," Libby said.

"You aren't mad at us, are you?" Eleanor's voice quivered.

"No. Not this time." If she was to be angry at anyone, it would be herself. She should have made more of an effort to find food. Begged if necessary. *Please, God, provide a way.*

Clara collected her thoughts.

She had managed to get to Edendale only to learn the stagecoach wouldn't be going north for at least a week. Maybe two. The stagecoach driver had been rather nonspecific in his answers to her questions. He had no set schedule for the hundred-mile trip to Fort Calgary and only went when it was necessary. Right now, he said, he had to make another run back to Fort Macleod. It was a pressing matter. After that, he'd take her north.

It had never crossed her mind that transportation would be so uncertain.

She needed to get to Fort Calgary. A newspaper story had said there was a shortage of women in the area. There'd even been an ad from a man wanting to hire a housekeeper to care for his three young children. She'd sent a letter saying she was willing to do so. Now she wondered if the letter still sat somewhere, waiting to be delivered. Just as she waited to get there.

Fort Calgary was in the middle of nowhere. Which suited her perfectly. No one would expect her to go to such a remote place, especially her father. He thought twenty-eight-year-old Clara was unable to take care of herself in a city full of conveniences, let alone look after herself and two little girls in the primitive west.

Edendale was equally as remote, but she had seen no opportunities for work in the little town. And she had to prove she could manage herself and her girls.

The girls sprang up. "He's back."

Clara closed her eyes. How was she to face a man who had carried her in his arms? Something else came to her thoughts. He'd called her by her Christian name. Highly improper, but she could hardly protest. Her name on his lips had pulled her back from the valley of darkness.

She heard the sound of boots clattering on the wooden floor. The smell of winter and leather grew closer. A movement of air signaled his nearness.

"Mrs. Weston?"

Oh, yes, she was Mrs. Weston now. She'd combined her married name of Westbury and her maiden name of Creighton in the hopes her father wouldn't be able to find her. She reasoned that way she wasn't really being deceitful by combing her maiden and married names. Hopefully, it was enough to put her father off her trail for a time, at least.

"Are you awake?" the man at her side asked.

Slowly, she opened her eyes and looked straight into gray ones that held her gaze so firmly she couldn't blink. It was like looking into deep, still waters and finding herself reflected back from the depths. *What a strange thought*, she realized.

"You're awake. Good." He turned aside. "I brought food for us all."

He twisted a lid from a jar, and the aroma of something savory—tomato and beef, if she didn't miss her guess—made her empty stomach tighten like a fist.

Metal rang against glass. Was he serving soup into bowls?

"Thank you," the girls chorused.

She imagined them eating eagerly, their complete attention on the food. She knew nothing but gratitude that their empty tummies would be warmed and filled, but she didn't want to owe this man.

Although she already did.

The need to accept help and the desire to take care of herself warred for but a minute. She was not in a position to refuse this man's kindness. As soon as she felt stronger, she would return to her plan.

Plan? For a moment, she couldn't remember what the plan was. *Oh, yes, take care of the girls. Keep them from Father and wait until the stagecoach driver saw fit to make the trip north, where I expect to find employment.*

She tried to sort out the details of the past few hours. "You know my name."

"Your girls told me. Allow me to introduce myself. Blue Lyons."

"I believe you rescued me. Thank you."

"Your girls are very persuasive."

She didn't know if those words should please her or alarm her. Before she could decide, Blue's hand slipped around her shoulders, and he raised her head. She thought to protest the familiarity but couldn't dredge up words.

"Eat this." He held a spoon to her lips. Not even stubborn pride stopped her from opening up like a little bird. He tipped the spoonful of soup into her mouth. Her taste buds exploded at the succulent flavor. She couldn't begin to describe the pure pleasure of hot food; she simply enjoyed the first decent meal she'd had in days. He held another spoonful to her lips and then another. She consumed it greedily.

The warmth filled her stomach and spread throughout her body.

She shifted so that she sat upright without his supporting arm. The fur around her shoulders slipped to her lap as she reached for the spoon. "I can feed myself."

He yielded the spoon to her but continued to hold the bowl. She scooped out a bit of the mixture. When she tried to raise the spoon to her mouth, her hand shook so much she lost the contents.

He took the spoon back. "Think it might take a little longer for your strength to return."

She didn't want to feel helpless, but he was right. "I feel like a baby," she murmured.

"'Cause Mr. Blue is feeding you?" Libby asked.

"Yes."

"She's not a baby, is she?" Libby demanded of Blue.

Clara darted a glance at him under the curtain of her eyelashes.

"Nope, she's a mama." Blue continued to feed her as if it were an everyday experience.

She looked directly at him, matching him look for look, silent assessment with silent assessment. "I perceive you've had practice at this. You must have children."

His hand paused midair. He stared into the distance, then shifted his attention back to her. "I once did. Once had a wife, too."

Once? He spoke as if they were gone now. It could mean nothing else, and her insides wrenched with the thought of his loss. "I'm sorry."

"It's the past." The words came out flat, as if he felt nothing.

A shiver crossed her shoulders. She knew it wasn't something that left a person immune.

He mistook her shiver. "You're still cold." He tossed the last of the gathered wood into the fire.

"I'm not cold." *Any more than you aren't sorrowful.* She shifted again and reached for the bowl and spoon. She managed to eat the rest of the soup without spilling it. He handed out biscuits, and the girls sighed blissfully as they bit into them.

Clara couldn't blame them. The biscuits tasted fine and went a long way toward filling the emptiness in her stomach. Though she'd fed the children whatever food she'd found the past two days, she'd no doubt they were still hungry. She watched as they ate with glee.

Blue sat cross-legged facing her. "Ma'am, if you tell me where you're going, I'll see you get there."

She studied the half-eaten biscuit in her fingers. Felt his waiting and the watchfulness of the girls. She had to say something and settled on a portion of the truth. "I'm waiting for a ride from someone."

When he didn't say a thing, she looked at him. She wished she hadn't when she saw the way his expression grew hard. He glanced at the girls, then back at her. He leaned in. "This person is going to come today?" He was so close his breath brushed her cheeks.

"I'm not certain when to expect him." Petey, the stagecoach driver, had made only one thing clear about his return.

"Ye'll know when I'm back in town," he'd said. "Won't likely stop long with winter weather to contend with. So be here and be ready if you want a ride. 'Twill be the last trip I make north for the winter."

"So you're stranded until this person shows up?" Blue asked. "What if he doesn't?"

She sat up straight and tipped her chin. She had no intention of telling this man her plans. "I'm trusting God to take care of us. He will provide."

He sat back. "Exactly how long are you planning to wait for that to happen?"

"As long as it takes." It sounded foolish, simplistic, even childish, but she had no one else to turn to but God, nor did she trust anyone else. Anyone could reveal her whereabouts to a seemingly concerned person asking after her, and that bit of information could be relayed to her father. She managed to control the shiver racing through her. If Father found them…

"In the meantime, are you planning to sleep in empty buildings? Faint from hunger and cold? What about—" His gaze darted to the girls and back.

This was not a conversation she wanted her daughters to hear. "Girls, you can go play quietly."

"Where, Mama?" Libby's surprise was expected. Where could they go but to a different corner of the big room?

Eleanor took her sister's hand. "Come on, Lib. They want to argue, and we're not supposed to hear."

"We aren't going to argue," Clara called as they marched away. She faced Blue squarely. "I can take care of the girls with God's help."

His eyes never flickered. His expression never changed. "It's none of my business, but seems to me you need a better plan than sitting around waiting for something to fall from the sky."

"I trust God." She knew she sounded as stubborn as Libby often did, but she clung to her faith.

"Well, that makes it easy."

She waited, wondering if he believed what he said or mocked her. When he didn't say anything more, she got her feet under her and stood. "Thank you for the food. I will pay you back someday." She would continue to trust Him even though her plans had fallen through. *Not fallen through*, she amended. *Only delayed.*

"Mrs. Weston, I don't want repayment. The only reason I helped was because of your girls. I lost two children who would be about their age now." He turned away as he spoke, and his voice again grew flat, emotionless. He was hiding, she knew, hiding emotions so deep and raw that he didn't know how to face them. "I could do nothing to save them, but helping your girls was something I could do."

"And I thank you for that."

Libby and Eleanor chased each other up and down the length of the building, laughing and squealing.

She smiled. Her heart overflowed with love. They trusted her to take care of them.

How was she to do that? It was too cold to sleep outside and not safe, but there was no hotel in this little town even if she could afford a room. If she had a warm place to spend the night, then she could devote time to finding a way to feed them. But where? She glanced about. The church would make good shelter. Her gaze settled on the bedroll upon which she had so recently lain.

Blue obviously spent the nights here.

That eliminated the only option she'd been able to

discover in this tiny pioneer town. There had to be
something somewhere.

God could not fail her now.

She set her feet going toward the door.

"Wait a minute."

At his words she paused without turning around.

"I can take you someplace safe and warm."

Why had he used the word *safe*? Did he suspect she
was running from someone?

Chapter Two

Blue analyzed everything she'd said and wondered if there truly was someone coming for her. And if so, when? One thing was certain. He couldn't let a woman and two little ones manage on their own in winter weather without any sign of shelter or home. Never mind that it triggered memories he had sworn to bury and never resurrect. He could forget them again. He was good at forgetting.

"I could maybe send a messenger to let your party know you've arrived. Or take you there myself."

"Thank you, but that's not necessary. Come on, girls." She signaled them.

The pair had been racing around the room and now skidded to her side.

"Mama, where we going?" Eleanor asked, her joy of a moment ago swallowed up in worry. "Back to Grandfather?"

Clara's shoulders stiffened enough for Blue to understand she didn't care for the notion. "Certainly not."

Libby's expression grew stubborn. "But it's warm here."

"We're going." Clara hitched one bag over her shoulder and tucked another under her arm and marched for the door.

Blue watched. Did they plan to return to the river? They'd freeze to death. He groaned. He couldn't allow it even if every minute increasingly threatened the fortress he'd erected around his heart.

"You need to reconsider. My boss at Eden Valley Ranch is Eddie Gardiner. His wife, Linette, often has people staying there." Linette would soon have a baby, and Eddie had imposed limits on how many people she could take in. Still, Blue allowed himself a tiny smile. He couldn't see Linette turning anyone away if she saw a need, even if Eddie didn't approve. "It's twenty minutes' drive away," he added. "You'd be most welcome."

"Thanks, but no. We need to wait here."

He strode across the room to stand perilously close to the trio. The girls looked up at him, their expressions full of hope, silently begging him to help them.

Clara, on the other hand, kept her back to him, her shoulders rigid.

He scrubbed his fist over his chin. "Ma'am, you can't wander around in the cold."

She shrugged.

Whether it meant defeat or resistance, he couldn't say. "If God is looking after you, surely He means for you to accept help."

She spun around to face him, her eyes flashing. "We've already accepted your help."

The girls sighed as if realizing she meant to say no.

He couldn't allow it.

"Ma'am, don't let your pride be the cause of putting your children in the way of danger." He hoped his words would make Clara rethink her decision without alarming her daughters.

"It's not pride." Then she clamped her mouth shut.

"You need help. Why not admit it and accept it?"

He watched a war wage behind her eyes. For some reason she hesitated to accept help. Why? If not pride, was it independence? Fear? He guessed he saw flickers of all three in her struggle. And it brought a rush of emotions to his heart. He appreciated a person's need to take care of herself, but of what or whom was she afraid?

Resignation filled her expression. "I must stay in town."

He wished he knew why, but it seemed futile to ask her. She kept her reasons to herself.

"Then stay with someone in town."

Hope flared in her eyes. "Do you know of someone needing help for a few days? I could work for food and lodging."

He considered everyone in town. None needed help this time of year. If it had been summer, the Mortons could have used someone to assist with meals.

That gave him an idea. The Mortons had a shack on their property, one where Cassie had lived before she married the ranch foreman, Roper Jones. It was better than sleeping in the open and at least there was a stove. "I have an idea. Stay here while I check it out." Blue didn't wait for her agreement or otherwise. He grabbed his coat and rushed out the door and across the space between the church and the Mortons' place.

He swallowed hard and slowed his breathing before he stepped inside.

Bonnie chuckled. "Back so soon? Wanting more food?"

"Not food this time." Again he twisted his hat. "Would you be willing to let someone use your little shack?"

She gaped at him, then shrugged. "Guess it would depend who needs it. You? I thought you meant to stay at the church."

How to explain his predicament? "Not me. I'll be fine at the church. Closer to my work." He saw Bonnie's confusion. "It's for this lady and her two girls. Mrs. Weston. Her girls are Eleanor and Libby. They're seven and eight."

Bonnie leaned back on her heels and grinned. "A woman and two girls. Where did you find them?"

"They're waiting for someone."

"I see. Who are they waiting for?"

He curled his fingers around the brim of his hat. "They didn't say. I offered to take her to the ranch, but she says she has to stay in town and wait."

Bonnie chuckled. "Why, Blue Lyons, how did you manage to get yourself involved with a woman and two children? I've always thought of you as a loner. Someone who avoids people."

"Yes, ma'am." That was him all right. "I just happened to be the one who stumbled upon them. That's all."

She nodded, but judging by the way her mouth tipped upward in amusement he guessed she wasn't agreeing.

"About that shack?"

Bonnie shook her head. "We've been storing things there."

"So they can't use it." *Now what?* He reached for the

door handle. *Maybe... No, it wouldn't be proper to stay in Macpherson's store or the livery barn.* Blue was out of suggestions.

"Wait." Bonnie stopped him. "How long would they need the place?"

"I can't rightly say." Clara had been unwilling to reveal any details.

"I suppose we could fit them in. They would be crowded, but if they don't mind…"

"I'll bring them over." He hurried back to the church.

Clara stood where he'd left her.

Eleanor and Libby sat on their bags, their elbows resting on their knees and their chins in the palms of their upturned hands. Their expressions were dejected until they looked up and saw him. Then they smiled, so trustingly, as if convinced he would solve their problems. He hesitated. He didn't want anyone trusting him to take care of them. Didn't want the concern and fear that came with it.

He shifted his gaze to their mother. "I found a place for you."

She didn't move. "I will only go where I can take care of our needs myself. I won't accept charity."

Seemed to him she was long past that. "It's just a shack mostly used for storage. It's no castle, but there's a stove in it and the owner said you were welcome to use it."

Still she stood there as stubborn as a long-eared mule.

"Why not have a look at it and then decide?" he suggested.

"Very well." She hitched her bags higher and stepped out of the church.

He reached out to help, but she shrugged away and gave him a look that made him drop his hand in haste.

"I thought she was going to say no," Eleanor whispered to Libby as she got to her feet.

Libby sighed and rose more slowly. "Sure glad she didn't."

He led them to the Morton place. The path skirted the edge of town but wasn't exactly invisible. Soon enough Macpherson would know of Clara's presence. Soon enough everyone would. He couldn't say why it mattered if they did, except that he preferred no one linked his name with hers.

Bonnie had been quick enough to jump on that thought. Made a man glad there weren't a whole lot of people in the area, though the population had certainly swollen greatly in the two years he'd been working at the ranch.

Libby dropped her bag on the ground and plopped down on it. "I'm tired."

"Come on, Libby," Clara said, her voice full of patience. "We might as well see what's ahead."

Libby shook her head. "I don't care. I'm not going anymore."

Blue waited. The sooner he got them safely into a shelter and got back to the church and the peacefulness of his own presence, the better.

Eleanor and Clara studied Libby.

"Are you coming?" Clara asked.

Libby shook her head. "No."

"Very well. Come along, Eleanor." She turned to Blue. "Lead on."

Blue jerked back. "You're going to leave her here?"

"She'll come once she sees we're leaving."

"No, I won't." Libby stuck out her chin.

Blue carefully considered his options. He could take Clara and Eleanor and hope Libby would follow. Or he could stand here and wait. Or he could—

Oh, for goodness' sake. He scooped up the child. "Now let's get this done."

Libby grinned. "I knew you wouldn't leave me."

Clara sighed. "Libby, you don't need to be carried."

"Yes, I do." She settled into Blue's arms as if it was the most natural thing in the world.

What he had gotten himself into?

Clara wanted to snatch her daughter from Blue's arms. She'd taught Libby better than that, and normally her youngest was shy around strangers. But not Blue, and that had Clara's nerves twitching. Libby could be stubborn to the point of exasperation. Having her decide Blue was someone she could trust was dangerous. He already knew far too much about them. Should anyone ask, he had no reason not to say what he knew. At every stop, on every train, buggy and stagecoach, she had kept her head down and instructed the girls to do the same. She had changed her way of dress. She had changed her name. The girls had been told not to tell people anything about who they were or where they were going. She didn't dare hope they had outrun her father. Not yet.

If only the stagecoach would whisk them away. Fort Calgary offered her a place to live and work and take care of herself. To prove to one and all she could provide for her girls.

Until then she had little choice but to wait.

But if she arrived there too weak to work, her plans

would fail. She made up her mind. She would accept this shack for now. Find a way to provide food for her daughters and be prepared for the trip north.

She followed Blue along the pathway as Libby glanced over his shoulder, a triumphant look on her face.

Clara hated to admit it, but it was time she reined in her younger daughter.

They turned into a neat yard bordered by trees. She spied a pathway that led to the river. To their right lay the store and other buildings of town that she'd seen upon her arrival and where she'd asked if they had need of someone to help.

A woman waited at the tiny shack at the back of the yard. Wooden walls rose to shoulder height, then gave way to canvas nailed to slats. Blue was right about one thing. It was no castle.

He introduced Bonnie Morton to them.

"Blue told me you needed a place to stay." The blonde woman greeted them. "This is nothing fancy but you're welcome to it." She glanced at the girls, seeming somewhat taken back by the sight of Libby in Blue's arms. "You're more than welcome to share our house."

"I'm sure this will be fine." Clara was weary to the point of falling over again. All she wanted was to rest.

"If you're sure." Bonnie opened the door and indicated Clara should step into the building. Clara pushed past a stack of wooden crates and into a space barely big enough for herself, Eleanor and Blue, who had followed still holding Libby. There was a table with a lamp on it, two chairs and a tiny stove by way of furniture. A trunk stood in one corner, and on it were stacked more boxes.

"It's fine."

"I like it," Libby announced from her perch in Blue's arms.

"Me, too," Eleanor added. "Can we light the stove?"

"Of course," Bonnie said. "There's plenty of firewood stacked outside. Help yourself. The well is out there, too. Water's free to anyone who needs it."

Blue put Libby on her feet and went to the stove. "Let me check the pipes first and make sure they aren't plugged. Wouldn't want a fire."

"But we do want a fire," Libby protested.

"Only in the stove, little one. Only in the stove."

Clara's throat closed off at the tenderness in his voice. No one but herself had ever shown anything but disinterest in her girls unless they had something to gain. Her dead husband, Rolland—a much older man her father had arranged for her to marry—had only spoken to them if he had to and always in a brusque tone. Father had ignored them except to tell them to smile pretty or sit nicely.

"I'll leave you to it," Bonnie said. She stopped in the doorway. "I see you don't have supplies to make meals, so please join us. I feed people. That's what I do."

"Thank you." Clara meant for the use of the shack. She wouldn't be taking any free meals. Surely in all this array of stuff she could find a pot and make her own meals.

Out of what? Could she snare a rabbit, catch a turkey?

Never before in her life had she felt such resentment at the upbringing that had left her unprepared to take care of herself. No, that wasn't completely true. She'd proven she could manage without a man. Could look after her girls, too. They'd escaped her father's domain in Toronto and had traveled the many miles to Edendale. She'd run out of money days ago except for the amount she hoarded to secure passage to her destination. She'd washed dishes in a dining room, hung laundry at a boardinghouse and dusted shelves in a store. Until they headed north from Fort Macleod. Since then she'd been unable to find anything but dust and icy snow.

"I'll check the pipes outside." Blue stepped past Clara.

In a minute the stovepipes rattled and soot puffed into the room; then he returned with wood in his arms. When he started to build the fire in the stove, she sprang into action.

"I can do that."

"I expect you can." He continued anyway.

She could hardly elbow him out of the way, so she stood aside, all of three feet away, which was as far as the room allowed.

He closed the lid and turned around. "There you go. You'll be crowded but warm."

"It's fine. Thank you."

He nodded, went to the door and stopped. Slowly, as if reluctant to do so, he turned around to face them. "I don't know what your story really is, or who you think is coming to get you, but you're safe here for as long as you need." And then he was gone.

What a strange man.

"He's nice," Eleanor said. Then as if her mother's words had finally resonated, she asked, "Mama, who are we waiting for?"

Clara hadn't told the girls her plans. If they didn't

know, they couldn't tell anyone. And that's how she wanted it.

"Someone we haven't met yet."

"If we haven't met him, how do you know it isn't Mr. Blue?"

Why were the girls so ready to accept Blue as their friend and helper? So ready to trust him?

"I know it isn't him because this isn't where we're going."

Libby crossed her arms over her chest. "Then where are we going?"

"You'll have to wait and see. Now let's get ourselves organized."

They pushed the table and chairs into one corner and shifted some boxes so they could put their bags on them. There was room enough for them to stretch out on the floor at night. She thought of poking through the boxes for a pot, but it seemed intrusive and she couldn't bring herself to do it.

"Do you want me to read to you?" she asked the girls when they grew restless.

She pulled her Bible from her bag, trailed her fingers over the cover. This book had been her comfort for many years. A kindly servant girl had given it to her just prior to her marriage. "Let's read Exodus."

She explained that it was the story of the Israelites fleeing Egypt.

"Just like we're fleeing Grandfather," Eleanor said with more insight than Clara expected.

She read about how the pharaoh wanted to kill the boy babies but let the girl babies live.

"Good thing we're girls," Libby said. "Pharaoh would have let us live."

"Mama?"

Clara turned to Eleanor.

"Did our father wish we were boys?"

"Of course not. He thought you were precious."
Though he gave them barely a passing glance, she admitted to herself. He seemed to share her father's opinion that girls were useless objects.

She returned to the story, her daughters listening intently.

After a bit, Libby interrupted her. "Mama, are we going to a land flowing with milk and honey?"

Eleanor sighed. "I miss having milk."

"Remember the sweet cakes the cook made? Mmm."
Libby rubbed her tummy. "Wouldn't I like one right now."

Eleanor licked her lips. "I'd like a dozen of them."

"Girls, we aren't going back to your grandfather's."
She should have never gone back in the first place, but after Rolland had died a year ago, she had been too shocked to resist her father's insistence that she must move home. For a year she'd turned a blind eye to how her father treated her like a brainless, helpless female. But when she'd heard him telling the girls they didn't need to attend their lessons because all they needed was to learn how to smile and be pretty, she'd confronted Father. He administered the money left to her by Rolland, and when she'd asked for funds to get her own place, Father had flatly refused. He'd made it clear that she couldn't manage on her own. Told her he was arranging another marriage for her.

She shuddered at the thought. She had no desire for another husband handpicked by her father. He must have read the resistance and rebellion in her expression for he'd bent closer at that moment.

"And if you think you can take the girls and leave, or perhaps think you might throw yourself on the mercy of one of your friends, you best reconsider. I would not hesitate a minute to gain custody and forbid you to ever see them again."

That's when she'd made up her mind to slip away without his notice. Not that she thought he would simply let her go. He would follow her to the ends of the earth if only to prove himself right. Tension snaked across her shoulders, and she glanced around, half expecting to see him poke his head through the door. But of course he wasn't there. He'd expect her to go to a city and find comfortable lodging. It was why she had chosen the opposite. The move might have bought her some time, but sooner or later he would realize she'd gone west, and he'd find her. She could only pray by then she would have proven she could manage on her own.

She settled her nerves. God had led them this far. She'd trust Him for the rest of the journey. "We'll have a home again soon," she said. "I promise. I trust He'll provide us with good things, too."

"Like this little house?" Libby asked.

Clara nodded. "It suits us just fine for now, but it isn't where we'll be staying."

"Will we have a new home in time for Christmas?" Eleanor asked. The girls studied each other a moment as if sharing a secret, then regarded Clara.

"I hope so."

They smiled widely.

She wanted to warn them not to get their hopes too high. She couldn't guess what accommodations they'd find in Calgary. *Please, God, let us have a home by Christmas.* She wished she could plan a bountiful Christmas for the girls, but this year would be vastly different from previous years. No china dolls or satin dresses or fur muffs. However, having a home would be the best present she could offer them.

Eleanor looked thoughtful. "I think Mr. Blue is a good thing, too."

Clara smiled. "He might not appreciate being called a thing."

"Mama, I'm hungry. Are we going over to eat with that lady?"

"No, Libby. We already ate, thanks to Mr. Blue. But I'll find something for us. I promise."

"But, Mama—"

"Girls." She cut off Libby's protests. Eleanor kept her thoughts to herself, but her expression said she didn't care for Clara's decision any more than Libby did. "Hasn't God taken care of us so far?"

They nodded.

"He won't fail us now."

They studied her intently.

"What will God do?" Eleanor asked.

"Why don't we ask that nice man for help?" Libby added.

"We don't know that he's a nice man."

Libby nodded stubbornly. "I know he is."

There was no point in arguing with a seven-year-old who saw things as she wished they were.

"Mr. Blue is nice," Libby persisted. "He has a good face. Didn't he, El'nor?"

Eleanor grinned. "I'd say so. I liked the color of his hair. Kind of red but not brick red."

"Sandy red," Libby said with the degree of certainty only an innocent child could portray.

Eleanor nodded.

Libby got a dreamy look on her face. "He is very handsome, isn't he?" she asked her mother.

Clara stared. "I'm sure I didn't notice." Which wasn't entirely true. She'd noticed his eyes and had been impressed with his kindness. That was all. "I'm surprised you did."

Eleanor sighed. "Grandfather said she was precocious." She stumbled over the word but Clara knew what she meant. Father had said the same thing to her, and he hadn't meant it as a compliment.

"Your girls should be learning to mind their manners," he'd growled.

He meant they should be seen and not heard. Seen as pretty things with vacant heads. How well she remembered the frustration of dealing with Father's disapproval at any sign of the ability to think for herself.

She returned to reading aloud to the girls, but it was soon obvious their minds wandered and she left off.

The afternoon hours dragged. Her stomach lurched at the smell of food coming from the nearby house.

"Mrs. Weston?" Bonnie called from the other side of the door. "Supper will be served in a few minutes."

"Thank you, but we won't be coming."

Bonnie spoke again. "The food is ready. I'll just have to throw it out if you don't come."

Clara closed her eyes. Being independent was so hard. "Thank you, but we'll manage on our own."

"Mama!" Eleanor protested in a shocked whisper.

"Hush." She waited for the woman to depart. "Girls, we can't accept help from everyone."

Was she doing the right thing? Was she trying to prove she could manage on her own when she obviously couldn't? Was she punishing her girls in order to prove something?

God, what is the right thing for me to do?

She thought of the chapters she'd recently read. God told Moses he would deliver His people. He would bring them out. He'd promised to put words in Moses's mouth. Could He not just as easily put food in her children's mouths?

But by what means? If she accepted the offered meal, how could she repay the woman's kindness?

Seemed she was stuck between two failures. If she accepted charity, it would prove that she couldn't manage. Yet if she didn't accept help, the girls would suffer and again prove she couldn't manage.

She had no doubt Father would use either against her.

A knock sounded on the door; then Blue burst in without waiting for an invite.

"Clara Weston, are you so prideful that you would starve rather than accept a meal offered by that good woman out there?"

She stared at him. He thought it was pride that compelled her? Pride meant nothing. At the darkness in his eyes and the tightness around his mouth, she shivered.

What did he intend to do?

Chapter Three

Blue stood stock-still as Clara stared at him, her eyes wide, her lips parted. Her wheat-blond hair had been smoothed back into a tidy knot at the back of her head. He noticed such details with only a portion of his mind as he hovered in the doorway. Did she think he threatened her?

He sucked back air and forced calmness to his voice. "Bonnie said you refused to join them for supper."

When Bonnie had told him that, Blue had stomped over to the shack and burst in without considering his actions. All he wanted was to see this trio safely taken care of so he could go about his business without worrying about them. How could he do that if she holed up in this tiny shack and starved herself and her girls to death?

"Do you think that gives you the right to burst in here roaring like a madman?" Her voice quivered just enough to confirm that his action had frightened her as much as annoyed her.

The girls peeked out from behind her.

"Do you want us to leave so you can argue?" Eleanor squeaked.

"We aren't going to argue, are we?" He smiled; he guessed it looked as if it required a bit of effort, which it did. Why must she be so prickly when all he wanted to do was help her so she'd get out of his hair?

Clara sucked in air as though she'd forgotten to breathe for a bit. "That is entirely up to you."

"Me? I never wanted to argue in the first place. Why don't you just come along quietly and enjoy the nice meal Bonnie has made?"

"Mama," Libby began.

"Hush." Clara held up a hand to silence her little daughter.

Blue's smile came more easily when he saw Libby tip her head and glance at the ceiling as if seeking patience from someone up there.

"Very well. But after tonight, I must find a way of taking care of us without…without accepting charity."

"You mean without accepting help." He thought to say more about the trouble this stubborn pride would cause her, but she hustled the girls into their coats, grabbed her own and gave him a challenging look. "Well?"

"Well, what?" What was wrong with the woman?

"Are you going to stand there blocking the door?"

"Course not." He stepped aside, feeling as if he'd lost the ability to think rationally. He ground his molars together. The sooner he got this troublesome woman out of his hair, the better.

He followed her across the yard and into the Mortons' kitchen, then stopped dead as he realized he'd just insisted they sit at the same table as he. He grunted, bringing Eleanor's attention to him.

"What's wrong, Mr. Blue? Somethin' hurting you?"

"No. I'm fine." He could hardly tell this innocent beauty that what was hurting was his way of life. He was a loner, and she and her sister and mother were tromping all over his plans to remain that way.

He had left the ranch to work at the church so he could be alone and shut his mind to everything but the task at hand. Summer was easier as he always asked Eddie to send him to the farthest line cabin and he spent weeks alone with the cows and wildlife. Winter was harder as he had to be at the ranch, where most of the men were hunkered down for the winter. Too many talkative cowboys. Too many cowboys with wives who liked to talk.

"I'm delighted you chose to join us." Bonnie took Clara and the girls' coats, then led Clara to the table. "It really bothered me to think of you cramped up in the crude little shack with nothing to eat." She chuckled. "Though that's where Claude and I spent the first few weeks we were here." She indicated the girls should sit on either side of their mother, then turned to Blue. "Join us."

He shed his coat and stared at the place Bonnie indicated. Right across from Clara. He shrugged. *So what?* In an hour or less, he'd return to the church and finally find the solitude he had come in search of.

Claude joined them and said a quick grace. Bonnie passed around a platter of roast pork, a bowl of mashed potatoes, cooked carrots and thick slices of fresh bread.

"Oh, Mama." Libby stared at her plateful of food. "This is like eating at Grandfather's."

"Better," Eleanor added. "We're allowed to sit with the grown-ups."

"Girls, mind your manners." Clara spoke quietly, and Blue thought she seemed tense.

Libby nodded. "I know we're not supposed to tell people our business, but that was okay, wasn't it?"

Clara smiled. It seemed a bit forced to Blue. "Just eat your meal." She turned to Bonnie. "This is very good, and we're most grateful."

Bonnie looked pleased. "I love cooking, but there haven't been many travelers through here of late. So nice to have you folks with us." She paused thoughtfully. "Where are you planning to go? Is someone coming for you?"

Clara shot the girls warning looks before she answered. "We're waiting for someone."

Bonnie's eyebrows went up with obvious curiosity, and Clara quickly added, "I'm afraid I can't say anything more."

A startled silence filled the room.

Claude cleared his throat. "Glad you're going to make those pews, Blue."

"I'm looking forward to it." He couldn't wait to get back to the church.

They ate in strained silence for a few minutes.

Bonnie tried again. "Do you girls have enough to occupy yourself over there?"

"Mama's reading to us from the Bible," Libby said, edging forward on her seat as if eager to talk about what Clara read. "It's the story of the Israelites. They're running from—" She turned to Eleanor. "Who are they running from?"

"From Egypt." Eleanor watched her sister as if amused at her intensity.

Libby nodded. "Just like we're—"

Clara's hand came down on Libby's shoulder, making her swallow the rest of what she meant to say.

Blue studied the child. Libby merely sucked in a deep breath and started talking again. "I like your house," she said to Bonnie. "It's nice. I like the one you lent us, too. It's—" Again she consulted her sister. "What is it, El'nor?"

"Cozy and warm."

"Yes, warm. Mama, where are we going to sleep?"

"I explained that already. There's plenty of room on the floor for our bedrolls." She turned to Bonnie and then Claude. "I'm so grateful for your generosity. Is there something I can do to repay you? Help with meals, do laundry…?" Her voice trailed off as a glance around the room proved Bonnie didn't need any help.

Bonnie touched the back of Clara's hand. "If we were busier, I would gladly accept your help. But as you see, we aren't busy. No, you accept the use of that little shack as long as you need it. You'll be doing us a favor."

Clara's eyebrows rose in frank disbelief.

"Yes. You see, when we first came to these parts, I was so sick I couldn't go on."

"I was very worried about her," Claude said.

Bonnie smiled gently at her husband. "Cassie—she's Mrs. Jones now—had just built this house after spending many weeks in that shack you're in. With four children if you can imagine it. Of course, it was summer and the children could run and play outside." She smiled around the table. "She let us use that shack until I was strong enough to continue. So you see, you are allowing us to show our gratitude by extending the same courtesy to someone else." Bonnie beamed as if the idea pleased her.

Blue saw by the set of Clara's mouth that she was somewhat less pleased.

When the meal ended, Clara began to gather up dishes. "Let us do the washing up at least."

Bonnie hesitated. "Very well, if it will make you feel better. I'll go ahead and set the bread dough."

Clara hustled about, carrying dishes to the pan of hot water that Bonnie had prepared. She handed drying towels to the girls, and they carefully wiped every dish as she washed it.

Blue wanted nothing more than to hustle back to the church and settle down in his own little world, but first he'd make sure Clara and the girls were safely back at the shack and the fire was banked for the night.

Clara hung the towels and dumped the dishwater in the bucket.

"Thank you again." She looked at her hands, then toward Bonnie.

"Is there something you need?" Bonnie asked. "If so, just ask."

"Could I borrow a pot to boil water in so I can wash the girls?"

"Why, of course." Bonnie drew one from the bottom cupboard. "I apologize for not thinking of it myself. You'll need a bucket, too." She handed one to Clara.

Clara slowly raised her hand to take it. Pink stole up her cheeks.

Did she think help came with strings attached? Out here in the west, lending a helping hand to friends, neighbors and strangers alike was the way life was lived.

She stammered her thanks. "Come along, girls."

As she prepared to leave, Blue grabbed his coat and followed.

Outside the door she turned her back and headed for the shack.

He knew she meant to dismiss him, but he followed on her heels. "I'll get some more firewood for you."

She spun around. "No need. I can do it."

He didn't stop until he reached the woodpile and began to load his arms. "You remind me of a two-year-old. *I can do it myself.*" His son, Beau, especially had been so stubbornly independent.

Blue straightened and stared into the dark trees. He had this woman to blame for making him think of his boy toddling about, refusing help.

Clara grabbed an armload of wood. "I could cook for us."

"What would you cook? It appears you have no food, no supplies, no money. Nothing but a huge amount of pride." He sighed impatiently. "Don't let your pride make you stubborn."

She was close enough that even in the dusky light he could see how hollowed out her eyes grew. "You keep accusing me of pride, and it's not that at all."

"Then what is it? What are you running from?"

"Not what." The words crept from her throat, soft yet full of anguish. "Who."

"Who?"

She flung him a dismissive, angry look. "I've said far too much." She spun around again and stomped to the shack. The girls chased each other through the shadows.

Blue followed her inside, dumped the wood in a pile by the stove and lifted the lids to check the coals. He strategically added several pieces of wood and adjusted the damper.

She studied him, her arms crossed over her chest, her mouth set in a fearsome scowl. "I can do that, you know."

"I expect you can." Satisfied the fire wouldn't burn too hot during the night, he turned to face her. His sudden movement filled her eyes with surprise, but to her credit she did not back away. "But I never take chances with fires."

They considered each other unblinkingly. He couldn't say what she thought she saw in his eyes, but he guessed he saw a couple of things in hers—her constant guardedness underlined by fear, a strong dose of protectiveness. Then she blinked, and he knew she thought she'd learned something about him.

He edged past her and hurried out the door. He'd revealed far too much of himself this day. Far more than he meant for anyone to know about him. He couldn't pull back the words that had spilled from his mouth. Couldn't even say why they had. For two years he'd never mentioned his children or the fire that had taken them, yet in a matter of hours he'd said enough for Clara to begin putting the pieces together.

From now on he would say no more. He could only hope she would soon be on her way to wherever she was going and leave him to forgetfulness.

Clara stared at the door as it closed behind Blue. *My, what a strange man. So cautious about fires.* Yes, it paid to be careful, but he acted as if he expected the place to burst into flames.

She shuddered and glanced at the canvas roof overhead. Was it likely to ignite? She looked at the crates between where she meant to sleep and the door. Blue had her all nervous. Perhaps that was a good thing.

The girls hadn't come inside yet. Their voices rang out in the growing dusk. While they were gone, she'd rearrange things. She pulled the boxes from near the door. At least if there was a fire, she could get out. Then she took the bucket Bonnie had lent her and went to the pump to fill it with water. She placed it on the table within handy reach.

Maybe she should thank Blue for making her so conscious of the danger. She pressed her hand to her chest in a futile attempt to slow the pounding of her heart. Or she should scold him for alarming her.

Her daughters dashed in and skidded to a stop.

Eleanor looked around. "You moved stuff. How come?"

"It's a little more convenient this way."

"Where's Mr. Blue?" Libby asked.

"He's gone."

Libby drooped. "But, Mama, I thought he'd stay."

"Of course he can't. Why would you think such a thing?"

Libby sank to her bedroll. "No one ever stays." She made it sound as if she were alone in the world.

"I'm sure I don't know what you mean."

"Our father died."

"That's not the same. He was sick and wasn't going to get better."

"I know. Then we left. I miss Mary."

She meant the gardener's little daughter. At her father's, Clara had often taken the girls outside to play, and they had become friends with the girl.

"I know you miss her. I'm sorry. But not everyone leaves. I'm not leaving."

Libby gave her a look of disbelief. "Of course not. You're our mama."

Clara laughed. It was good to know Libby trusted her so implicitly. "Soon we'll find a place where we can stay and settle down." *And be safe.*

Libby nodded. "For Christmas. Right?" She gave Clara a trusting look, then turned toward Eleanor. "God will answer our prayer for a new—"

A silent message passed from Eleanor to Libby, and the younger child clamped her mouth shut.

Clara pressed down alarm at Libby's trusting expectation. *God, please don't let me fail this child.*

Eleanor turned to Clara. "Did God send plagues to Grandfather?"

"Why on earth would you think that?" Maybe she'd quit reading Exodus. The girls took it so literally and applied it to their situation.

"'Cause Grandfather said he would never let us go. Just like Pharaoh."

Clara tried to think how to respond. How could she explain the situation to them without giving them cause for alarm? Without saying things that Libby would inadvertently blurt out at the most inopportune times? "I'm your mother. I'm the one who decides what's best for you."

Eleanor nodded, seemingly satisfied with the answer.

"I'd like to see Grandfather's house full of frogs." Libby pressed her hand to her mouth to stifle a giggle.

"Girls, it's time to get ready for bed." She'd earlier filled the borrowed cooking pot from the borrowed bucket and it heated on the borrowed stove in the borrowed shack.

Borrow. Borrow. Borrow. The word went round and round inside her head. Father would surely see it as failure and use it as proof she couldn't provide for her children.

She washed the girls as well as she could and heard their prayers. They whispered and giggled for a bit once they lay on their bedrolls. She caught the word *Christmas* several times, and every time the weight of it increased. Only a few weeks until the day they both looked forward to. Would she be able to keep her promise and provide them a home in time?

Only with God's help. She'd about run out of opportunity and strength to do anything on her own.

Later, after the girls fell asleep, she explored her options. Bonnie and Claude fed her and provided this place of shelter. She must find a way to repay them.

And she just might be able to do it.

If Blue didn't prove difficult.

The next morning, she was ready to go to the house for breakfast when Bonnie called. She cautioned the children before they left. "Now, girls, don't eat too much. And for goodness' sake, don't chatter too much."

Blue crossed the yard as they exited the shack.

Libby rushed up to him. "Carry me."

He looked surprised for a moment, then swung her into his arms.

"Libby!" She hadn't thought to warn her daughter against that.

"It's okay, Mama. Isn't it, Mr. Blue?" Libby grinned from her perch.

"She's not heavy."

Clara wasn't concerned that he might find her too much of a weight. She was worried that Libby had attached herself to this man so completely after bemoaning the fact that everyone left. Or they left everyone. Libby should be prepared for leaving Blue soon.

They reached the house, and he set Libby on her feet.

Clara wanted to say something, warn him not to encourage her daughter, but now was not the time.

Claude asked God's blessing on the food, and then they dug in to the generous breakfast—biscuits fresh from the oven, canned peaches, oatmeal porridge. A very satisfying meal.

Blue rose as soon as he was done. "I've got work to do." He paused and looked at Clara. "Do you need anything?"

She narrowed her eyes at him. Must he continually treat her as if she couldn't do a thing on her own? "I'll be sure and let you know if I do."

Her sarcasm wasn't lost on him. He blinked and then a slow, teasing grin filled his face. "Yeah, I'm sure you will." He jammed his hat on his head and, chuckling, left the house.

Claude followed on his heels.

Bonnie stared after the pair. "Well, I'll be." She shook her head. "I believe that's the first time I've heard Blue laugh. He's a real loner, you know."

Sure couldn't prove it by her, Clara thought as she

turned to wash the dishes. Wouldn't a loner leave her alone? And Blue didn't.

She finished the dishes, hung the towels to dry and bid Bonnie goodbye. Time to proceed with her plans.

Chapter Four

Blue cut the piece of lumber. The smell of the wood filled his senses. As his mind consumed it, he felt himself drowning in the present. That was his way of forgetting the past and ignoring the future. Later he'd sweep up the sawdust that fell at his feet and burn it, enjoying yet another scent. He shifted his mind to the process necessary to complete a pew. Measure, cut, fit, secure, sand, polish. Each step held comforting details to occupy his thoughts.

The outer door clattered open. *Now what?* Who'd have thought being alone would be so difficult?

Eleanor and Libby rushed into the room, bringing with them a cloud of cold air. Clara followed.

Blue leaned back on his heels and studied them. He saw the determination in Clara's face and stiffened his spine in preparation for whatever complaint she meant to voice.

"I've decided." She nodded as if to persuade herself.

His eyebrows went upward. What had she decided? And did she plan to tell him? He guessed she did or she wouldn't be there, facing him with such a fierce look.

"I'm going to help you."

His mouth fell open, and he snapped it shut.

She held up her hand. "Now before you try and dissuade me, listen to my reasons. I cannot continue to accept charity. It makes me look weak, and that's not something I can allow. I expect you're getting paid for the work."

It wasn't exactly the case. He drew wages from the ranch. Eddie had allowed him to take on this job off the ranch because it suited everyone to get the church done as quickly as possible.

"I'm not asking much, but I will help, and you can pay me from the pay you receive. All I need is enough to buy my meals from Bonnie."

Well, if she didn't take the cake when it came to expectations. "What do you know about woodworking?"

"Nothing. But how hard can it be?"

He snorted. "I learned woodworking from my father." Back in Texas. He hadn't seen Pa since he married Alice and moved to Wyoming, where he'd started a little ranch of his own. He slammed the door on the intrusion of memories. He could blame Clara for this constant struggle to keep them at bay. "Pa said woodworking is like playing a musical instrument. Those who do it well make it look easy."

"I couldn't say. I've never seen anyone make something from wood."

"Yet you expect me to hire you to help?"

The fierceness in her expression faded, leaving her uncertain. "Couldn't you teach me to do something?"

He considered the idea. He didn't need help. Didn't want it. Most certainly didn't fancy the idea of having Clara and the girls underfoot day after day. But wasn't she moving on? Soon, if he didn't misread her intentions.

If he agreed to let her help, at least he would have the assurance she wasn't starving herself out of pure foolish pride.

"Fine, but I can't pay you. All the work done on the church is on a volunteer basis."

The wind went out of her so quickly he thought she'd collapse.

"But the Mortons feed me as their part in the work. If you're helping here, they'd expect to volunteer meals for you just as they do for me."

She lifted her chin. "Fine. Then I accept."

She accepted? As if she did him a favor? He laughed outright. The sound rumbled from his chest. He stopped. Blue never laughed anymore, and yet he'd done it twice in one morning.

She held out her hand. "Agreed?"

"Agreed." He slowly brought his hand up to hers and shook. He drew back so suddenly he almost pulled her off balance. But he hadn't touched a woman in two years. It felt strangely pleasant.

"Now show me what to do."

"You certainly are bossy."

The girls had been dragging their boots through the sawdust, leaving little trails, but they looked up at his comment.

"You called Mama a bad word." Libby sounded affronted.

"What bad word did I say?"

"You said *bossy*. Mama says we aren't to say that to people. But you did." Poor Libby looked so shocked Blue rushed to apologize.

"I'm sorry. I didn't realize it was a bad word." He glanced toward Clara. She grinned as if she enjoyed his discomfort. Which was hardly fair seeing as he'd never before considered it a bad word.

"It's okay." She patted his arm. "Libby will be sure and straighten you out if your language gets too rough." She laughed, a sound so pure and sweet he could only stare.

He quickly came to his senses. "You're enjoying this a little too much." He tried his best to sound aggrieved.

"Sorry. But the look on your face was priceless."

It was time to get things back to order. He hunkered down in front of the sections of a pew he'd cut. "This is what I have so far. The wood is oak. One of the finest woods they make, in my opinion. Look at the beautiful grain."

She ran her fingers over the wood. "It is nice."

"Nice?" He took a beat of silence. Did he expect her to see the beauty of the wood just because he did? "Of course, it isn't finished yet. By the time I run my plane over it a few times, it will be so smooth you won't believe it."

Libby squatted at his side. "Like Mama's skin?"

Clara blushed bright red.

Blue grinned. It was her turn to have Libby cause her problems. "You keep your mama on her toes, don't you?"

Libby studied her mother's feet. "No. She's not on her toes."

Eleanor sighed. "Lib, it's a saying. It means you make her pay attention."

"To what?"

"To what you are going to say or do next."

Libby stood up and held her hands in the air in a gesture of confusion. "But how can she know? Even I don't know."

Clara rolled her head back and forth. "And that's a good portion of the problem."

Blue returned to his full height. His eyes caught hers, and they laughed as they silently acknowledged how this child had embarrassed them both by turn.

She'd done something more, he realized. She'd put them both a bit more at ease.

But was that a good thing or not?

He jerked away and led Clara to the sawhorses. "You can help me measure each piece." He showed her the plans he'd drawn. "This is what we're going to make."

She studied the drawings, then nodded. "Looks simple enough."

"It is. All I have to do is make sure each cut is exact, the grain is always going the right direction and everything fits together perfectly."

"Don't you mean all *we* have to do?"

"We'll see." He had a whole wagonload of doubts about how much help she'd be.

His plans seemed a vague dream at the moment.

He positioned a length of lumber on the sawhorses. "First, we measure. Hold the end of the tape there." He showed her and took the first measurement. "Hold it firmly. Even a fraction of an inch can have a bearing on the finished product."

"I have it."

The girls stood close by, watching.

He measured several different places where he would have to cut. "Now I'll measure again and make sure they're all correct."

"Again? Did I do something wrong?"

"No, but the rule is measure twice, cut once. It's the safest way."

"Hmm." She held the tape as he repeated the process.

"Okay." He rolled the tape and stuck it in his pocket. "Now I'll cut." With long steady strokes, he cut the pieces for the end of the pew. Two for each pew and one for the middle.

Patiently, he allowed her to help him measure each piece needed for the rest of the pew. "Now I need to plane them smooth."

She blushed as if remembering Libby's earlier remarks.

Ignoring her reaction, he slid the planer over the wood. Paper-thin curls of wood peeled off.

The girls knelt beside him. "Can we have those?" They pointed at the curls.

"Don't see why not."

They gathered up the bits and carried them to the corner, where they were soon busy playing some game.

Blue returned to the task, concentrating on the sound of the blade and his movements.

"Can I do that?" Clara's voice startled him from his thoughts. "It looks like fun."

He stared at the planer. He enjoyed the work. But if he didn't let her do enough to qualify as help in her eyes, who knew what she'd do? He turned over the piece meant to be the seat so she could work on the bottom, where her mistakes wouldn't show. "Push down just enough to start it shaving. Then keep the pressure firm and continue clear through to the end." He let her take the planer.

It caught. It stuttered. There would be cross lines at every stop.

"You made it look so easy." She sounded annoyed, as if she blamed him for her failures. Then she clenched her teeth and started again. Stalled again.

He saw her problem. "Steady pressure. Like this." And before he could think to stop himself, he placed his hand over hers on the planer and showed her how to do it. A thousand sensations rushed through him. They threatened the boundaries he had so carefully and solidly built. And yet there was something about them that filled him with comfort.

He jerked back and let her do it herself.

She grinned as the shavings peeled from the wood.

For some strange reason, he grinned, too, pleased at her success.

Then he wrenched his attention away. He had work to do here and put his mind to building pews until the morning passed.

"It's time for dinner." He grabbed his coat and was halfway out the door before he stopped himself. Like it or hate it, he couldn't hurry away and leave them to walk across on their own.

Clara fairly bubbled with excitement as she traipsed across to the Mortons' for dinner. She'd never seen a piece of furniture under construction before, never dreamed she might have a part in the process. Yes, it was a small part. But hopefully one the Mortons would deem worthy of a meal for her and the girls.

Bonnie flew to Clara's side as they entered the room. "I was worried about you. I went over to invite you to join me here. I know the shack is small and thought you might like to visit. But when you weren't there…" She fluttered her hands.

"I'm helping at the church."

Bonnie stared at her. Claude came to her side. "Are you helping Blue?"

"Yes."

"Why, I think that's a great idea." Claude squeezed his wife's shoulders, and they gave each other a glance that seemed full of secrets.

Clara wouldn't look at Blue to see his reaction. But she sensed if he thought the pair saw romance budding between them he would run for the hills and never return. But he needn't worry. One thing she did not want or need in her life was a man. And she meant to prove it. To her father, to anyone who might voice a concern and most of all to herself.

She wondered how to broach the subject of receiving the meals in exchange for help at the church when Claude spoke up.

"Our contribution is to provide meals to those who work on the church. Clara, that includes you, so sit down and enjoy the food Bonnie has prepared."

"Thank you." For the first time since she'd stepped off the stagecoach at Edendale, she felt as though she could achieve at least part of her goal. *Why, was that just yesterday?* It seemed so much longer.

God had provided in a way she could not have imagined, and she ate the meal with gratitude. When she offered to help wash up, Bonnie waved her away. "I have all afternoon to do it. You go on back and help Blue."

Blue had departed a few moments earlier and now Clara and the girls followed his footprints back to the church.

Clara suspected he might wish she'd change her mind about helping him, but he'd soon learn she wouldn't.

Eleanor went to Blue. "Mama says we must do our share. What can we do?"

He straightened and met Clara's eyes over the girls' heads.

She gaped. She had not meant for the girls to feel they, too, must earn their food. Parents provided for children.

Libby teetered back and forth on the balls of her feet. "Mama says we should owe no man nothing. She says that's in the Bible."

Blue's eyebrows rose, and his lips twitched. "Is that a fact?" His gaze rested on Clara.

"If Mama says it's true, then it is." Eleanor spoke with utmost loyalty.

Clara could almost believe she saw a twinkle in Blue's eyes.

"Glad to see you girls listen to your mama."

The pair nodded their heads as Clara floundered for a way to explain that although she'd said the words, she'd meant them for herself, not the girls.

Blue leaned back on his heels. "And now you want to help?"

More nodding.

"That's a very noble thing. Let's see." He looked around the room.

Clara did, too. It might be good if the girls had something to do that made them feel useful, but what on earth could two little girls do that wouldn't put them underfoot?

"Well, you could always make sure there are three pieces of firewood by the stove. You could keep the stack by the door neat. When I'm not sawing, you could clean up the sawdust and put it in that coal pail." He pointed. "And I think you could keep those buckets full of snow. I melt it for my water. You think that's enough?"

"Yes," they chorused and sprang into action, grabbing the buckets and heading outdoors to find snow. There was plenty from a previous snowfall along the north side of the church and in the trees.

Clara waited until the door closed behind them. "Thank you. That's most generous of you to give them useful tasks."

He picked up a board and carried it to the sawhorse. "Children should feel useful and appreciated."

"I certainly agree. Even if they're girls."

He put the board down and stared at her. "What difference does it make if they are boys or girls? Each child can contribute something."

Not wanting to meet his gaze, she stared at the board between them. "Some people don't value girls the same way."

"Well, that's just plumb foolish."

She wondered if he truly believed it or only thought he did. "You said you had two children. Were they girls?"

"One of each." His answer was curt, and she glanced at him. His eyes had grown cold and distant.

"Did you treat your daughter as you did your son?"

He grabbed the tape measure. "I have no idea what you mean. Here, let's measure this."

She took the end of the tape and held it where he pointed. She understood his reluctance to talk about his losses and would not press him even though she was a bit curious. But that was all. What events had shaped his life mattered little to her. Just as her life mattered little to him. They'd been thrown together by accident, and only temporarily. Not that she wasn't grateful for a warm place to sleep, good food to eat and a job that allowed her to earn her own way.

He tossed aside the tape measure as if it had offended him. Then he grabbed it and stuffed it in his pocket. "Would you like to see how the pews are going to look?"

"I'd love to. You know, I never considered the workmanship that goes into furniture making." She ran her hand along the smooth finish of a piece of wood ready to assemble. "But it's kind of fun."

He nodded, his eyes again alive with feelings. "Wait until you see the finished product. You'll be amazed at how much pride it gives you to know you had a part in making it." He stood up a piece of wood cut in an angled L shape. "Hold this."

She did so as he stood up a matching piece. The girls skidded in at that moment, snow dusting their coats, their faces rosy from being outside.

"Who'd like to help put the pew together?" Blue asked.

"Me," the girls cried in unison and shed their coats.

"Hang them up," Clara reminded them.

They did so, then hurried to Blue's side. He showed them how to hold the other upright and picked up another piece. "This will be the seat." As he worked, he explained everything he did.

He screwed the seat into place. Clara helped him with the back and let herself glow with pride to realize he would have struggled to do it on his own.

"There is our first pew." He stood back, hands on his hips, grinning. "Who wants to try it out?"

The girls didn't need any more invitation. They sat down and folded their hands primly as if attending a service.

"It's very nice," Eleanor said.

Libby ran her hands along the seat. "It's so smooth. Just like Mama's—"

"Libby!" Clara could not let her again mention her smooth skin. She'd already been embarrassed enough.

Blue chuckled.

Clara remembered what Bonnie had said about him. That she'd never heard him laugh. Seems her girls had restored his ability.

She sneaked a glance at him. Did he appreciate it or resent it? She couldn't tell from his expression.

"You and Mama should try it out, too," Eleanor said.

Clara hesitated. She didn't care to sit next to the man on a church pew. She tried to assess her feelings. They'd bent over the same piece of wood, he'd guided her hand when she tried to plane the wood that now made up the seat of the pew, she'd walked across the yard with him. Why would sitting side by side on the pew make any difference?

It didn't.

Aware the girls watched her curiously, she sat down next to them.

Blue faced them. He eyed the spot beside her.

She almost laughed at the wary expression on his face. So she wasn't the only one who found this a bit awkward.

"Mr. Blue," Libby said. "It's a nice bench."

"I'm sure it will hold all of us." Eleanor paused. "Won't it?"

"Of course it will. I made it strong." He took the two steps that brought him to them and sat down, perching as if ready to run for the hills at any moment.

The idea so amused her that she couldn't contain a chuckle. She tried to cover it with a cough.

He turned and regarded her with narrowed eyes. "Are you laughing at me?"

She nodded. "But no more than at myself. I was just as leery about sitting here, though I have no idea why."

He sucked in air and slowly relaxed until he sat against the back of the pew. "Nor do I." He shifted a little. "The pew is quite comfortable."

"Yes, it is."

The girls got down and hurried over to the sawdust with broom and dustpan.

Blue and Clara remained on the pew. For a pair so reluctant to sit they showed no sign of being in a hurry to get up.

Clara told herself it was simply that it felt good to rest for a few minutes. When was the last time she felt so relaxed? She tried to think. Certainly not since she'd left her father's house. Not while she was living there, either. Maybe when she'd lived in the house Rolland had provided. Her own little domain. Would she ever have such a thing again?

Blue shifted to glance at her. "That was a mighty big sigh."

"I didn't even realize I sighed."

He continued to study her.

She met his eyes and saw the questions and uncertainty there. Likely he hoped she would explain what she was doing in Edendale. But she dared not. She suspected that if Father showed up, Blue would feel it his duty to turn her and the girls over to his authority.

She sprang to her feet and hurried to the piece of wood on the sawhorses. "I'll help you measure this."

He pulled the tape measure from his pocket and handed her one end.

She ducked her head and concentrated on the task, giving it far more attention than it required.

For a moment, she'd let her guard down. It must not happen again. If she didn't keep her wits about her, keep her goal firmly in mind and her senses tuned for danger, she could end up losing her daughters.

A tiny groan escaped her lips. She felt Blue's silent question but would not look at him. Good thing he was a loner. Equally good she didn't want anything from him but a chance to feed herself and the girls until she could leave this town.

Chapter Five

Blue ignored Clara's groan. He wouldn't let her problems be his concern. He reminded himself that he only allowed her to help in order to make sure the girls got regular meals. He'd want people to do the same for his kids if they'd lived.

He bent over as if to pick up something off the floor, but it was really to stop the pain that grabbed his gut.

Eleanor and Libby had stacked the woodpile neatly and now played with bits of bark from the firewood. He caught bits and pieces of their conversation. Something about Christmas and a new—

But he never caught the word and refused to dwell on the subject. Christmas had meant nothing to him since the fire.

The two girls were pleasant enough. Their mother seemed a nice woman. But he didn't welcome them into his world.

He straightened. Only one way to make this afternoon pass quickly, and that was to keep his mind on work. And hope whoever Clara waited for would arrive quickly. Like right this minute.

But of course nothing happened. No wagon or buggy rattled into town. No rider came looking for a young woman.

Did she really have a plan, or was she hoping for something to fall from the sky?

A bit later, he glanced out the window at the fading light. "It's quitting time," he announced. He'd succeeded in keeping his mind on measuring, measuring again, cutting and using the plane. Well, almost. At every move, Clara had been at his elbow, reaching to help, holding the tape, insisting she could use the plane.

"I love doing this," she said as thin shavings peeled from the wood. "Am I doing a good job?"

He admitted she did. "I've never seen a woman doing woodwork before, though my pa said he knew of one and said she did a good job. Said she had a light touch, which he recognized in all her work."

Clara sat back on her heels. "Maybe I could make furniture." She sounded as surprised as he felt.

"Why would you want to? Won't you remarry? Seems running a home and raising kids is work enough."

She came to her feet, her eyes flashing like lightning. "What you are saying is I require a man to take care of me and all I need to do is sit around and look pretty." She spit out each word as if they were the pits of sour fruit.

He held her gaze without flinching. He knew she resented what he'd said and couldn't understand why. "From what I've seen, running a house and looking after the children doesn't allow much time for sitting around. My wife worked very hard, as I recall. Most of her days were longer than mine."

Slowly, the fire faded from her eyes. "I have no use for sitting around being ornamental."

Nor did he, but why should she think such a thing? He took in her blue eyes, her hair with varying colors of blond that reminded him of finely grained wood. She was a beautiful woman. Why hadn't he realized that when he'd first seen her? No doubt she'd pitch a fit if she knew what he thought. Nevertheless, he finished his assessment of her. Skin so pure that it was no wonder that Libby used it as a comparison. Shapely hands that had proven to be capable of working with wood. A grin came unbidden to his mouth. "Seems to me you'd have a hard time not being ornamental."

Her mouth fell open, and she sputtered.

He continued to grin, pleased he had left her speechless. "We best head over for supper." He gathered up his coat. The girls followed suit.

Clara made a sound of exasperation, then grabbed her coat. "It's far more important to be useful," she muttered as they left the church.

"No reason a woman can't be both." He spoke airily, knowing most women would have welcomed the compliment. But she only huffed toward the Morton place without offering any explanation.

Libby slowed her steps. "I'm awfully tired after working so hard." She gave Blue a sad look.

"Don't suppose you'd like a ride?"

"Oh, yes, please." She practically threw herself into his arms.

He shifted her to one side. "How about you, Eleanor? Maybe you'd like a ride, too?"

Eleanor shot her mother a look, but Clara steamed on ahead of them and didn't glance back.

Eleanor nodded, and he swung her up in his other arm.

The two of them were a load, but he didn't mind. He could spare them a little extra attention once in a while.

Just as he would have for Beau and Nancy.

Sorrow dripped its bitter poison into his veins.

Libby touched his cheek. "What's wrong? You look sad."

He nodded. "Sometimes I am."

She didn't ask for more explanation but pressed her head to his neck in a way that offered comfort.

And he let her. For the first time he accepted it from someone. Somehow it seemed fitting it should come from a child.

Over the meal, Bonnie chattered about everything under the sun. Claude added a comment or two, asked a question of Blue that he answered in as few words as possible. Clara seemed equally indisposed to conversation, though the girls more than made up for their mother's lack.

When the meal was over, Clara offered to help clean up. He rose and left but paused outside the little shack. If he went in, she would object to the intrusion. But if he didn't, he'd worry all night about the safety of the stove. He'd sooner endure her wrath than his worry and stomped inside.

The first thing that hit him was the scent of something sweet. Perhaps a perfume or a scented soap. Or perhaps it was simply the way a space with three females would smell.

The furniture and boxes had been rearranged so the open space where they would sleep was closer to the door, farther away from the stove. He had no idea why she'd placed things so, but it eased his mind to know they wouldn't likely be trapped by a fire.

Three dresses hung from hooks on one wall. Two small ones and one larger. He stared at them for a moment as a flood of memories assailed him. Hadn't Alice and Nancy hung their dresses in a similar fashion? His and Beau's shirts had hung side by side, too. He'd often thought it was an indication of what was to come…the child growing until the garments became the same size as the parent's or even larger.

Only his children would never reach adulthood.

He drew a long breath into his starving lungs and turned his back on the clothes and his attention back to the task he'd come for.

He shook out the ashes and took them outside, then built a fire in the stove. One that would burn slowly and steadily. No sudden flaring and overheating. Then he returned to the church.

The winter days were short, requiring him to light a lamp. He settled comfortably on his bedroll with one of the books he'd brought with him from the ranch.

His mind wandered from the story. Working with Clara triggered so many memories. Some he didn't welcome. But he let his mind go back to Texas and the days he'd worked with his pa. When was the last time he'd written home?

Not since he'd notified Pa of the death of Alice and the children. Why? He leaned back on the rolled-up bedding and thought of his reasons. Mostly, he'd shut his mind to anything but the moment before him. He allowed no thoughts of the past. Not even of his pa. Poor Pa must be worried about Blue, especially as he didn't even know where he was or how to contact him.

He bound to his feet, grabbed his coat and strode down the street toward Macpherson's store. It would be closed and locked up by now, but Macpherson lived in the same building.

Blue banged on the door until Macpherson threw it open.

"Blue, what's all the racket about? I'm closed for the day."

Blue knew he opened the door for business whenever it was required. Travelers came at odd hours, especially in the summer when daylight lasted long into the evening.

"I need to purchase something."

Macpherson stepped aside and let Blue inside. "And it couldn't wait until morning?"

Blue didn't want to wait. "I'm working during the day."

Macpherson gave him an odd look. "What is it you need?"

The words stuck in Blue's throat. His request was going to sound mighty odd to Macpherson. But now that he was here, he had no intention of retreating. "I'd like to purchase a piece of paper, an envelope and a stamp."

Macpherson stared at him. "You needed me to open the store for that? You know the mail won't even go out until Petey returns."

"Yeah, I know." Seen through Macpherson's eyes it did sound foolish, but Blue wanted to write Pa while he had the notion. After all, it wasn't like the notion came around often.

Macpherson shrugged. "Ah, well, seeing as you're here." He pulled out a sheet of paper and an envelope and went to the other end of the counter to get a stamp.

"Can I borrow a pencil?"

Macpherson handed him a stub so short Blue had to squeeze it between his thumb and forefinger. He wet the lead with the tip of his tongue and bent over the paper.

"Leave it on the counter when you're done," Macpherson said. "I'm going back to my supper."

"Thanks." Blue started the letter.

Dear Pa,
I'm okay. Sorry I haven't written in so long. I have
a job at the Eden Valley Ranch. You can send mail
to Edendale, Alberta. Work is slow at the ranch
at the moment so I am in town building pews for
the new church. I remember all you taught me

He looked up. Maybe not everything. Pa—and Ma before she died when Blue was twelve—had taught him to be a God-fearing man. He tapped the pencil on the counter a moment before he resumed.

about woodworking.
I trust you are well.
Fondest regards,
Your son, Blue

He folded the paper, put it in the envelope, glued it shut, wrote on the address and glued on the stamp.

"Thanks, Macpherson," he called.

"See yourself out," the man called.

As Blue returned to the church, he glanced toward the shack where Clara and the girls were. A faint glow came through the canvas. What did she do to entertain herself and her daughters?

From what Libby and Eleanor said, she must read to them from the Bible—the book of Exodus to be exact. He stepped inside the church and glanced about. The girls had stacked half a dozen pieces of wood next to the stove.

"So you don't get cold at night," Eleanor had said.

At the stack of wood next to the door, they'd arranged bark and scraps into what seemed to be a corral. He chuckled again. No doubt the groups of curled wood were animals.

He examined the pieces of oak that Clara had planed. She'd done a fine job.

He lay on his bedroll and picked up his book. Blue opened it to the page where he'd left off, but his gaze kept drifting around the room. Everywhere he looked he saw reminders of Clara and the girls.

If he wasn't careful he'd be forced to face his past and consider his future. He had no intention of doing so and focused his attention firmly on the book.

The next day Clara and the girls hurried over to the church as soon as they'd finished breakfast. Blue had come and gone without speaking more than a dozen words. Bonnie and Claude didn't seem surprised, so Clara decided it meant nothing.

"We have to get more snow for him," Eleanor said. "Maybe we didn't leave enough wood. I hope he didn't get cold in the night."

"I'm sure he could get wood from the pile if he needed to," Clara assured the girl.

"But it's our job," Eleanor insisted.

"Only when we're there. Other times he takes care of himself."

"Okay." The child didn't sound convinced.

Libby skipped from one patch of bare ground to another, avoiding the skiff of snow. "He needs us."

Clara laughed. "I doubt it, but it's nice to be able to help."

Later, as she planed a piece of wood, she realized how true her words were. It did feel good to help. She would have never thought she'd find so much pleasure in working with wood. Could God have given her this opportunity so she could learn the skill and perhaps, one day, use it to support herself and the girls? It was a fantastic dream, but for the first time maybe in forever, she felt as if the future offered something more than survival and running.

She sat back and watched Blue sawing through a piece of wood. She hadn't done that yet and hurried to his side. "Can I try using the saw?"

He stopped what he was doing and stared at her. "It's like playing a musical instrument—"

"Those who do it well make it look easy," she finished for him. "But most musicians have to learn by doing." She held out her hand for the saw.

"Very well. Wait while I find a spot you can manage." He cut a few more inches, turned the wood around. "There are a few things you need to know about saws." He talked about crosscut and ripsaws and which one was needed for the job. He showed her how to hold the tool, then handed it to her. "Put the blade next to the pencil mark and make a nice kerf."

"Kerf?"

"An opening in the wood so you can get started."

She tried to follow his instructions, but the blade skipped away from the wood.

He came to her side, placed his hand over hers on the saw, held her other hand in place on the wood and guided her through the motions.

She forced herself to concentrate on the task, to ignore the warmth of his body so close to her, the strength of his hand over her fingers. What would it be like to share life with a strong man? One who allowed her to do something useful?

He stepped back, and she jerked her thoughts from the slippery slope they'd started down. She meant to prove she did not need a man to take care of her.

Focusing on the task, she successfully completed the cut and, filled with pride, stepped back and grinned at him. "I enjoyed that."

He looked surprised. Did he think she meant his hand on hers? Or sharing the work with him? Who knew what the man thought? It certainly didn't matter to her, but lest he get the impression it did, she said, "Woodworking is pleasant."

"I agree." He turned to examine an uncut board.

"Can I plane this piece I just cut?" she asked, eager to be doing something.

"Go ahead. You seem to have the knack for it."

The work was soothing and required her concentration, allowing her no time to think.

Then, happy with the job she'd done, she sat back and watched Blue. He noticed her attention on him and reached for the planer and another board. "I'll work on this."

She observed for a few minutes as her thoughts drifted back to the prior evening. After the girls had fallen asleep, she had been restless as she sat at the table. Her only reading material was the Bible, but she longed for something more even though she couldn't say what it might be. Another book? Something to occupy her hands…some sort of needlework maybe? Someone to share a cup of tea with? She thought of returning to the Morton home and seeking Bonnie's company, but she didn't care to intrude on the couple's time together.

"Blue, what do you do to occupy yourself in the evenings?"

"Hmm. Nothing much."

"Surely you don't stare into the dark corners of the room with no thought on your mind."

"Nope. Sometimes I work on the pews. I sharpen the saws or the blade of the planer."

"You can't do that every evening."

He lifted his head from his work. "Last night I wrote a letter to my pa."

"Oh, that's nice. Where does he live? Is your mother alive?"

"He lives in Texas, and my mother passed away years ago."

She looked past him into the distance. "My mother died when I was a baby. My father raised me. Or rather, a succession of nannies did." She felt his gaze on her and dipped her head to watch his hand moving up and down the piece of wood.

For some reason she didn't want him to express sorrow over the loss of her mother. "It wasn't like I missed her. I don't even remember her." But she'd often wondered what her mother was like. Did she sit idly while Father decided when she would move? Had she secretly exerted her independence in little ways as Clara had learned to do as Rolland's wife?

She met Blue's gaze and saw only acknowledgment

of her words. "I did always wonder what my life would have been like if she lived. Would I have been raised differently? I like to think I would have."

"Different? How?"

She shrugged. She longed to tell him, but was it safe? "I can't help but think my mother would have seen me as someone of worth."

"Your father didn't?" Then understanding flashed through his eyes. "It was him that made you think you were only a pretty little object, wasn't it?"

"Maybe." She ducked her head.

"Guess you know better now."

Her head came up so quickly her neck protested. "Why do you say that?"

He shrugged. "Isn't it obvious? You have two girls you take care of, you are traveling on your own, you're learning woodworking. And I expect you've learned a good many other useful things, too."

She let his words sink in. "You're the first person who has acknowledged all that."

He shrugged again. "Seems fairly evident to me."

It was far from evident to her. At his words, a sense of satisfaction grew inside her. If she appeared so competent to Blue, perhaps she might eventually feel confident in herself.

He spoke again. "I read a lot. I always have a couple of books with me."

She realized Blue had returned to her former question as to what he did in the evenings.

"I've been reading the Bible. Is that one of the books you read?"

"No, ma'am." He said it without rancor, without any

emotion, as if he might have been talking about the color of snow.

"Why not? Don't you believe in God?"

"I kind of quit believing when my wife and children died."

She could not say if she would have had the same reaction to such a terrible event, but somehow the idea of not believing in God seemed even more terrible. "Tell me what happened."

"They perished in a fire."

She heard the tautness in his voice and ached for his pain. "How awful."

"The worst part was I saw the house burning and couldn't get there in time to do anything."

Horror darkened her heart. "That's dreadful. How old were the children?"

"Beau was four, Nancy five." His hands had grown idle. He stared unblinkingly at the wall before him.

She shuddered, and for the space of a minute or two couldn't pull a word to her mind. "I can't imagine what I'd do if anything happened to my girls."

"It's a man's job to protect his family."

She pushed slowly to her feet. "I don't need a man. I'm more than a pretty object."

He rose and faced her, deep lines gouged in his face. "I didn't mean it that way." Silence echoed in the church as she wondered what he meant and if he would explain. "Not all men expect or want a woman who is pretty but helpless," he finally said. He looked serious. "Some even teach a woman woodworking."

She smiled, both surprised and pleased at his comment. "Yes, some do."

He jerked away and picked up the saw.

She chose another piece of wood to plane.

Did he think a woman could be self-sufficient and yet benefit from the protection of a man? It certainly hadn't been her experience. In her life protection had only brought with it a form of domination. That was not something she wanted for herself or her children.

Then the real meaning of his words reached her brain. He didn't mean her or just any woman. He had been talking about his own loss and how he'd been unable to save his family.

She glanced at him, wishing she could undo the past few minutes or say something to acknowledge his pain, but he seemed absorbed in sawing a piece of wood.

After a moment of studying him, she turned away.

Anything she said now would draw attention to the fact that they each had their own problems and concerns.

Surely she could work at his side for a few days and keep their personal lives out of the picture. She realized with a shock that she'd told him more than she had meant to. Perhaps he'd done the same.

From now on, she'd be more cautious of her words lest he learn too much about her and put her future in jeopardy.

Chapter Six

Blue resisted the urge to slam his head into the wall. What had come over him to tell her how his children had died?

Yes, it had felt good to say the words even though they ripped a bloody trail through his heart. Maybe it had felt good because Clara didn't try to console him with empty words. Only an acknowledgment of his pain. Of course, she knew what loss was like. She'd lost her husband. She'd offered condolences for his loss, but he'd not said a thing about hers.

What could he say to make up for his oversight?

"Clara?"

Her head came up. Her eyes were wide with surprise and blue as the morning sky.

"You've known loss, too. I'm sorry."

Not a flicker of acknowledgment.

"Didn't you say your husband died? No, wait. It was Eleanor who said she didn't have a papa. I assumed…" He trailed to an end without finishing. Had he misunderstood?

"My husband is dead."

"I'm sorry," he said again. Shouldn't she express more emotion, or was she trying to bury the pain even as he did?

She nodded. "Thank you. It was a loss for all of us. But he was much older and sick even before I married him. It seemed like he had disappeared from our lives long before he passed."

"Then why did you marry him? Seems you could have had your pick of suitors." The words came out uncensored. As soon as he'd spoken them, he wished he could pull them back. Hadn't Ma always warned him to think before he spoke?

She gave a thin smile. "My father arranged the marriage. It suited him."

This time he didn't have to censor his words because none came to his mind. What she said didn't make sense. Did she marry a man she didn't love simply to please her father, or to avoid confronting him? Though he knew of many arranged marriages, hers seemed wrong.

"My father is very controlling."

"Appears so." He studied her, trying to piece together the things he knew of her. "It's hard to believe he lets you travel about the country on your own."

"Indeed." She returned her gaze to the piece of wood in her hands.

Indeed? That was it? And what did it matter to him?

They worked together the rest of the morning without speaking of anything but the task at hand.

When they returned after dinner, he could not contain his curiosity any longer. "Does your father know you are here?"

Clara had her back to him and kept it that way for

the space of two heartbeats. Then she slowly turned and faced him. "Why do you want to know?"

He'd asked himself the same question for the past two hours and had yet to come up with a satisfactory answer, so he simply shrugged.

She closed the distance between them until she was within reach and favored him with a scowl fit to curdle his dinner. "Do you think I need my father's permission? Just like you think I need a husband? Well, I don't. I can take care of myself and the girls, and I intend to." She turned away. "Now, are we going to work or spend the afternoon talking?"

The girls had been out filling his buckets with snow, and they raced indoors in time to see the look on their mother's face. They skidded to a stop.

"Mama?" Eleanor sounded uncertain. Maybe even afraid.

Blue answered the question. "Your mama's okay."

Libby marched up to him. "Did you hurt her?"

"I don't think so. Did I, Clara?"

Her shoulders slumped. "Of course not. I'm just letting you know where I stand."

Libby giggled. "Mama, you're standing in the middle of the floor. Mr. Blue can see that."

Clara turned, squatted and swept Libby into her arms. "What would I do without my sweet girls?" She signaled Eleanor to join them and hugged them both.

Blue's chest muscles eased so he could get in a decent breath. Then forgotten words came unbidden.

Every child is a flower in God's garden with the simple task of bringing beauty and joy to the world.

It was something Alice had often said as they had reveled in the joy of their children.

He turned away to hide the pain that surely enveloped his face even as it claimed every corner of his heart. That joy had been stolen from him, leaving him an empty shell of a man.

The girls left their mother's arms, and Libby caught his hand. "Mr. Blue, did you see how full we got your buckets?" She dragged him to the doorway, where they'd left the pails. Each one was packed hard with snow. "Didn't we do good?"

"You did indeed."

She looked up at him with blue expectant eyes.

What did she want?

"Did we earn a hug?" she asked.

His insides froze, then slowly melted with the warmth of her trust. He bent over and hugged her, then reached for Eleanor, who came readily to let him wrap his arm about her and pull her close.

Over the top of the girls' heads, Clara's gaze pinned him. She didn't need to say a word for him to hear her warning loud and clear. *Be careful with my children's affections.*

He had every intention of being careful. Not only with their affections but his own. That meant he must stop the talk and memories of his family. Must mind his own business when it came to questions about Clara's activities.

She could follow whatever course of action she chose.

So long as it doesn't put her or the girls in danger, a little voice insisted. But he couldn't imagine she would ever do that.

He extricated himself from the girls' gentle arms and turned to the piece of wood on the sawhorse.

He had no say in any of her choices, whether or not they were risky. And that's just the way he wanted it.

The rest of the afternoon he managed to keep his thoughts centered on the work before him. Measure, measure again, cut, plane. When he measured, Clara held the end of the tape. She insisted on doing her share of sawing, and he had to admit she did a fine job. And when it came to using the planer, he had to confess he couldn't do better himself.

He did admirably well at resisting thinking of anything but work.

"I'm hungry, Mama," Libby said hours into the afternoon.

He glanced up and saw the sun's rays slanted through the west windows. "Looks like it's supper time. Shall we go?"

The girls scrambled into their coats in record time. Clara had hers on and waited at the door. "Aren't you coming?"

"Just a minute." He went to his saddlebags. "Do you want to borrow one of my books?" He pulled out the one he wasn't currently reading.

"Really?" She hesitated even though her eyes lit with anticipation. "You're sure?"

"Very sure. I borrowed it from Eddie at the ranch. He has a whole library of books and allows me to help myself to them. He does the same for everyone."

"Then yes, I'd very much appreciate borrowing it."

He handed it to her, and she clutched it to her chest. He grinned. It felt good to have a little share in providing her with pleasure.

They crossed together to the Mortons' and sat across from each other at the table. He looked around at the others, finding it hard to believe that only three days ago all he wanted was to be alone with his thoughts. Now here he was, sharing the meal with two children and three other adults.

What would happen after Clara and the girls left? After he finished at the church? Would he be able to get back to the state of solitude he preferred?

Did he still want to be left alone?

The questions went round and round in his head even as he returned to the church and sat on his bedroll. How had he gotten into this position of having a woman and two sweet little girls in his life? It was the very last thing he wanted.

He opened his book and forced his attention to the words.

When they left, he would surely miss them.

And that was exactly why he didn't want to be involved in the first place.

The girls had fallen asleep. Finally. For some reason they wanted to giggle and whisper tonight. Several times she hushed them. Again she'd heard them mention Christmas and something special they anticipated. She didn't ask what it was because, in the depths of her heart, she feared they'd be disappointed.

Her shoulders sagged. All she wanted for Christmas, and prayed for, was a home where they'd be safe, a job so she could support them all and prove to anyone who cared to challenge her that she could take care of herself and the children. *God, you see my need. Please provide.* Now she must do as she counseled the girls— trust God to answer.

In His way?

She jerked her head up and stared at the stack of boxes next to the table. What if His way was different than what she wanted?

She shook her head. Trusting could be so hard at times. She needed to pray. *The Lord is my shepherd. He leadeth me beside still waters.*

The peace and calmness that came with still waters was all she needed. God knew that.

It was time to let the matter rest, so she reached for the book Blue had loaned her.

It was *The Virginians* by William Makepeace Thackeray.

She ran her fingers along the cover. Lifted the book and inhaled the scent of it. Father had a fine library back home, but Clara had been forbidden to choose any books from it. *Young women should not read such books. They're too stimulating. Too adventuresome.* The books Father deemed appropriate for her, apart from the Bible, were boring and dull.

She opened the pages and was soon engrossed in a story of war and adventure.

Some time later, she knew she must put off more reading until the next evening. She put a marker between the pages, turned out the lamp, crawled under her blanket on the bedroll and fell asleep with a contented smile.

The next morning, she couldn't wait to tell Blue how much she enjoyed the book.

He'd left before them after breakfast, and she hustled the girls across the frosty ground toward the church. The sky was a vivid blue today, and the sun promised warmth. Barely a breeze stirred. It might be winter, but she certainly couldn't complain about the weather.

Blue was sawing a board when she entered, and she waited impatiently for him to finish. He looked up. "Something wrong?"

"Not at all. I just wanted to say how much I'm enjoying the book and to thank you for lending it to me."

"You're welcome." He set aside the wood.

"Have you read it?"

"Not yet."

"Oh." She swallowed back disappointment.

"I'm glad you're enjoying it." He considered the pile of cut wood. "What do you think? Should we put together more pews today?"

"Sounds like a fine idea." She'd sooner discuss the story, but he didn't seem to be so inclined. She tried to convince herself it didn't matter.

He called the girls over to help hold the end pieces and by dinnertime they had four more pews put together.

They stood and admired their work.

"What did I tell you?" he asked.

"I don't remember."

"Didn't I say you'd look at the final product and know a real sense of pride?" He turned to study her face. "You do, don't you?"

She laughed. "More than you can ever imagine. Bear in mind it's the first time I've made anything of significance. Well, except for—" She nodded toward the girls and felt heat rush up her face at such a comment. But they were her greatest accomplishments, and she meant to make that clear.

He followed the direction of her gaze. She watched emotions chase across his face and tried to identify them. His smile seemed to indicate pleasure in her little girls. Then the smile faded, replaced with regret, then sorrow and pain.

She touched his arm. "Blue, I am so sorry for what you've lost. I know it must hurt like fury to see two healthy, growing children."

He shook his head. "It doesn't hurt. I have to confess I enjoy your girls. But I will never forget my own two children." His hand rested on hers.

She wondered if he realized he squeezed her fingers. He seemed so lost in his past. "No one would ever expect you to forget them. Why, that would be an insult to the beauty of their short lives." She turned to the girls. "Why don't you go outside and play in the sunshine?"

They needed no second invitation.

Clara led Blue to the nearest bench and pulled him down to sit beside her. "You can do your children no greater honor than to keep their memory alive. Tell me about them."

He leaned over his knees. "They were beautiful. To my chagrin, Nancy inherited my coloring. I confess it looked wonderful on her."

She studied him. His reddish hair didn't look bad on him, either, but she kept her thoughts to herself.

"Nancy was a little mother hen. Eleanor kind of reminds me of her. She always thought she should tell Beau what to do." He chuckled softly. "Beau only listened to her if it suited him. He was all boy. Clumsy, rowdy. Oh, how he liked to be tossed in the air." He sighed deeply and leaned back. "I miss them so much. I miss Alice, too."

"Of course you do. Your wife is a part of you. Your children are a piece of your very soul. You could only forget them if you ceased to exist."

"Maybe that's what I've been trying to do."

"Cease existing? But why? Surely you can still enjoy the rising sun, the song of a bird, the laugh of a child. Even the pleasures of food such as Bonnie serves."

"I guess." He sounded less than convinced.

She considered all he'd confessed. "I don't think I could walk through the valley of the shadow of death without the comfort of God's rod and staff."

"That's the psalm they read at the funeral service."

"The Twenty-Third Psalm."

He continued to face ahead. She wished she could see his eyes to know what he was thinking. She didn't have much time to wonder because he suddenly pushed to his feet. "Bonnie will be expecting us."

She called the girls to join them as they went across to enjoy another dinner.

When they returned to work, they did not resume their conversation. Feeling content with the moment, willing to momentarily forget the threat of her past and the worry about tomorrow, she simply settled into enjoying her part in making the church pews.

She hummed as she worked. The joy of the words overflowed her heart, and she softly sang aloud. "Praise God from whom all blessings flow. Praise Him, all creatures here below."

God had been good to her and her children. Providing them a safe place to wait for the stagecoach and a way to work so she could feed herself and the girls. The words of the doxology swelled in her throat. She wanted to raise her voice to the rafters.

"Mama?" Eleanor's voice drew her from her moment of worship.

"Yes, sweetheart? What is it?"

"Mr. Blue is a blessing, isn't he?" Eleanor gave Blue a shy smile, then turned to Clara with innocent expectation.

Clara darted a glance at Blue, who looked as stunned by the question as she was. How did one answer such a question? Certainly Blue had played a vital role in her present circumstances. He'd been there when she needed someone—provided by God's providential hand. But he also represented risk. He knew too much about her. If someone asked questions, he could answer them. And then her girls would be torn from her. A loss she couldn't let herself consider.

"Mama?"

She had to give an answer and went to her daughters. She knelt at their side. "Remember how we prayed that God would take care of us? I told you we could trust Him to provide. Well, I believe He sent Mr. Blue in answer to our prayer. So, yes, he's a blessing, and we should thank God for him."

Libby knelt and grabbed Clara's hand and squeezed her eyes shut.

"Libby, what are you doing?"

The child cracked one eye open. "You said we should thank God."

Here? Now? Right in front of Blue? Grateful she had her back to him and couldn't see his reaction, Clara closed her eyes. "Father God, You promised to always guide and direct us and provide our needs. Thank You for sending Mr. Blue for that purpose. Amen."

She thought that would be enough, but Libby said, "I want to pray, too." And she did. "Dear God, I know You are big and mighty and can do anything, but it's nice You gave us someone with arms to hug us and hold us. I like Mr. Blue's arms. Amen."

"My turn," Eleanor said. "Dear God, I don't know where we're going. Mama won't say. But maybe this is where. I'd sure like that. Amen. Oh, yes, don't forget what we asked for Christmas."

Clara remained where she was, stunned by what the girls had revealed. Asking God for Christmas gifts was bad enough. Hadn't she taught them to trust God for their needs? In their small minds, she reasoned, Christmas was a need. But asking God to let them stay here? And thanking Him for Blue's arms? What had she gotten them into?

She pushed to her feet, but she couldn't bring herself to look directly at Blue as she spoke. "I'm sure that was very awkward for you, but they're just innocent little girls. I've tried to shield them from the harsh realities of life."

"Like you say, they're innocent children." His voice was gravelly. Did that mean he was touched or hurt? She didn't think she cared for either.

"Shall we get to work?" he said.

She was only too happy to comply.

The awkwardness between them made her movements jerky. After a few failed attempts at trying to plane a piece of wood, she gave up and circled the room, imagining the place full of worshippers. She glanced out each window, went into the entryway that would eventually be a separate room and tried not to think how pleasant it would be to be part of a small congregation where everyone had had a hand in making the church possible.

Would there be a church at Fort Calgary? Surely

there would be some place of worship. After all, there were people there.

She returned to the sawhorses where Blue had placed a piece of wood and helped him measure and then measure again. Her mind wandered, and Blue grunted.

"We'll have to measure it again."

"Sorry." She placed the end of the tape where it needed to be, but Blue didn't pull his end taut.

She wouldn't lift her face to see what caused his delay.

"Clara, I don't know why you let what the girls said bother you. You and I both know you are only here until your plans—whatever they are—materialize."

She sighed softly. "But they prayed. How can I fail them?"

"Seems to me they prayed to God. Doesn't that make it His responsibility to answer as He sees fit? Not yours?"

She jerked her gaze to his. He considered her with steady gray eyes, silently challenging her.

"Why, Blue, I do believe you have given me a one-minute sermon." She grinned. "A very timely one, too."

He lifted one shoulder in a self-mocking gesture. "Just saying it how I see it."

He was right. God would have to answer the girls' prayers. But she'd remind them they weren't staying in Edendale and that Christmas this year would not be like their previous ones.

She did so later when they were in their little shack and the girls were ready for bed.

The girls just exchanged secretive looks when she mentioned Christmas, but when she reminded them they weren't staying here, they faced her with demanding eyes.

"But, Mama." Eleanor wasn't the one who usually challenged Clara. "How do you know this isn't where God wants us to be?"

"I just know."

"We have to cross the Red Sea yet," Libby said.

Clara shook her head. Her seven-year-old came up with some strange conceptions. "We won't cross the Red Sea."

"Oh. Then what? We gots to see God part the waters."

"We need God to provide a stagecoach and some fast horses," Clara corrected her child.

Both girls assumed stubborn looks.

"I don't want to leave." Eleanor scooted into her bedding and turned her back to Clara.

"You always knew we weren't staying here."

"Why not?" Libby demanded. "Isn't it a nice place?"

"It is." But it didn't feel far enough away from Father. Eight days of hard riding would bring him or some hireling of his from Fort Macleod. Eight days was not far enough. Ten days likely wasn't, either. Maybe she'd continue moving north.

But she didn't want to keep running. She wanted to make a home for herself and the girls. A safe home. She added her prayers to those of the girls. *God, lead us to a safe place, and, please, could You make it in time for Christmas so the girls won't be disappointed?* She dared not ask for anything more though she longed for Eleanor and Libby to have a memorable Christmas.

Chapter Seven

Blue wandered about the darkened church interior. The day had been an emotional quagmire.

He rubbed a spot in the middle of his chest. Little Miss Libby liked him holding her, did she? And Eleanor wanted to stay here.

They were just the silly wishes of innocent children, he reminded himself. The Westons would leave. Everyone knew it. Everyone expected it. And they would disappear from his memory as if they had never entered his life.

Unlike his own family whom he had expected to be permanent.

He rubbed his breastbone trying to ease the pain centered there. He'd told Clara about Alice and the children. Something he'd vowed he'd never bring up in his thoughts, let alone in conversation.

She'd questioned him. But he didn't have to answer her questions. So why had he? He couldn't say. Any more than he could say if he appreciated or resented having told her.

Yea, though I walk through the valley of the shadow

*of death I will fear no evil for Thou art with me. Thy
rod and staff, they comfort me.*

He hadn't given the words any thought since the funeral service when he'd bitterly dismissed them.

What did he fear? That was easy—the memories
and the pain.

Was God with him even though he didn't feel Him?
Sort of like Blue had been with Beau when he learned
to walk.

Fiercely independent, the boy would accept no help,
so Blue hovered at his back, holding to his shirt so he
wouldn't fall facedown on the rough ground.

Because Beau couldn't see Blue he thought he managed on his own.

Was it like that with God? Was God guiding Blue's
steps even when he didn't believe it?

Maybe someday he would be ready to believe again.
Someday.

In the meantime, he would finish up the pews and
get back to the ranch. He'd ask Eddie to let him be the
one to check the cows grazing on the lower pastures.
He'd get back to forgetting about his past.

Another week should see him done.

He lit the lamp, throwing a patch of light into the
room, sat on one of the pews and opened his book. But
he couldn't get his eyes to follow the line of print.

He pursed his lips. For the next week all he had to
do was concentrate on the work and avoid Clara and
the girls as much as possible—which might prove a bit
of a challenge since they spent their days helping him
and took meals at the same table.

But he'd had plenty of practice at pulling his thoughts

away from others and what they were doing. He knew he could do it again.

The next morning he managed to eat breakfast without looking directly at Clara, managed to respond to Libby's cheerfulness without thinking about her sweetness. He even managed to give Eleanor a reassuring smile when she looked at him with her face wreathed in worry. He did well throughout breakfast, then hurried to the church.

Soon Clara and the girls would join him; then he'd get to see if he was as good at keeping his thoughts under control as he thought he was.

"Good morning," Clara called, and the girls echoed her greeting, smiling at him so sweetly his resolve wavered.

"Morning." It entered his mind to warn them he meant to keep their activity focused entirely on the job at hand but the words never reached his mouth.

While Clara hung up her coat, the girls grabbed his buckets.

"We'll fill them to the top," Eleanor informed him as they went outside.

Clara took the planer and set to work on pieces they had cut yesterday.

He turned his back to her as he measured another piece of wood.

"Is the weather always so pleasant this time of year?" she asked, which brought a chuckle to his throat.

"Last winter we got an early snowfall that buried some of the cows up to their bellies. If Eddie wasn't so conscientious about bringing them down to lower pastures for the winter, he might have incurred heavy losses. Some of the other ranches weren't as fortunate."

Realizing he had turned to talk to her, and had said far more than a man who meant to shut himself off from others would, he clamped his mouth closed and turned back to the wood. He had only measured once, but it was enough this time. He sawed, making further conversation impossible.

Not that it deterred Clara. She waited until he was done. "I suppose as long as the snow holds off travel is possible."

"I suppose so. Though it depends where you mean to travel." He shifted enough that he could watch her.

She shrugged. "I'm just making conversation."

He knew it was more than that, but she said no more and bent over her work.

"I sure hope you know what you're doing."

She smiled at him. "I should. You're the one who taught me."

He wasn't talking about the woodworking and guessed she knew that as well as he. "I haven't taught you everything."

Their gazes fused. His perhaps a little challenging and a touch regretful. Hers full of resistance.

"I think we are more alike than you know," she said after some length.

"Alike? In what way?"

She lowered her eyes, freeing him to gather his thoughts. Yet he found it impossible to sort out the confusion that accompanied his conversations with her. Shouldn't he be in more control of his words and feelings when she was in the room? Shouldn't he be less ready to enter into conversation with her? Shouldn't he be able to remember that he meant to keep his memories locked away?

"I think we are both trying to outrun something." Her words were so soft he barely heard them.

He recalled something she had said. "In your case, not something but someone? Perhaps your father?"

She did not answer him.

"What did he do?" Had he tried to influence her decisions? He could see her taking objection to such.

She kept her head down and didn't say a thing.

The girls clattered in with buckets full of snow, their coats unbuttoned and their hats hanging down their back. Seemed the sun had grown warm as they worked.

"We filled them to the top, Mr. Blue," Eleanor said. "Aren't you glad we're here to help?"

"You are indeed a great help." Hopefully she wouldn't notice he hadn't truly answered her question. Because he couldn't bring himself to say he wasn't glad of their presence, nor could he allow himself to confess he was. Not even to himself. The boundaries of his life were threatened by a stampede of smiles and hugs and admiring glances from two little girls. Even as the barriers of his heart were threatened by their stubborn mother.

Oh, for the peace of a mountain cabin and the company of nothing but cows and horses and the occasional crow.

Libby stood before him, her head tipped up as she regarded him curiously. "Mr. Blue, is Blue really your name?"

He nodded. He'd surely heard that question before.

"Why did your mama and papa call you that?"

"Libby!" Clara sounded shocked at her little daughter. "You know better than to ask personal questions."

"No, I don't."

Blue laughed despite himself. "It's okay. She's not

the first to wonder." He dipped his head toward Libby. "See my hair? What color is it?"

Libby trailed her fingers through his hair, sending waves of crashing memories through him. Nancy had done the same as she'd said, "Papa, you and I are just the same." She'd meant their hair, but her comment had always made him laugh.

"Maybe not exactly." He and Alice had shared a look and a smile at Nancy's innocence.

Libby pondered a moment before she answered. "It's kind of reddish. Sort of sandy red. Right, El'nor?"

Eleanor nodded, her expression eager.

Blue straightened. "It's red, and I don't mind if you say so. Well, when I was born, my papa saw my red hair and said he didn't want a son called Red, so he would name me Blue."

Libby tipped her head. "Why didn't he call you Yellow? I like yellow. It's my favorite color."

"You never call a man yellow." He pretended to be shocked. Some men would take objection to even an innocent child using that term to describe them. Best she know that.

"Why not?"

"Because it means he's afraid."

"Scared?" she asked.

He nodded, and both girls giggled as they hurried away to the corner where they had bits of wood and shavings arranged in another play stage.

He shook his head. He remembered how little girls could get giggles over the silliest things.

Clara regarded him with eyes far too wide. "Blue, huh? And I thought it was a nickname." She ducked her head, but if he wasn't mistaken, her shoulders shook.

"Are you laughing at me?"

She shook her head and stifled her amusement. "Just at your poor father worrying about you being called Red."

He grinned. "Actually, he was more concerned I'd be called Pinkie."

She burst out in laughter. It echoed inside his heart, touching chords long silent, thrumming them to life.

He leaned back and let chuckles roll from his chest.

Their gazes caught and held. Slowly, their laughter ended, yet they continued to stare at each other. Her eyes darkened to dusky blue. Her look went beyond the surface and probed at his deepest thoughts and feelings, resurrecting yearnings he had buried when Alice and the children had died.

He reminded himself of that day. Of how he had vowed he would never again care that deeply for anyone.

Yet the reminder did not give him the strength to pull from her look.

It was Clara who broke away first. She stared at the planer in her hands, but she did not move it. Perhaps she was as stunned by the intense moment as he was.

Clara stared at her idle hands. For the life of her, she couldn't think what to do with them. Why had she let herself be pulled into his gaze? Why had she allowed it to go on and on as if she'd wanted to learn his deepest thoughts and feelings? Had she forgotten her goal—to be free of a man's control? She could trust no man.

Not that he was offering her anything but a temporary job.

Her thoughts righted, and she almost laughed as she

realized she had overreacted to an unguarded moment. Nothing more.

All she had to do was get through the next few days until the stagecoach came again. It meant working at the church in order to pay for her meals, but she'd be sure to permit no more unguarded moments.

A noisy conveyance rattled by. She rushed to the window with a street view, hoping against hope that Petey had returned with the stagecoach. But it was only a couple of men in a wagon who pulled up to Macpherson's store and went inside.

With a quiet sigh she turned away from the window. She felt Blue watching her. No doubt he was curious why she'd hurried to the window, who she thought would come to rescue her.

She clenched her teeth. She didn't need rescuing. All she needed was a way out of this town and to Fort Calgary.

For the rest of the day she asked no more questions. She managed to keep the girls occupied so they didn't come up with anything unexpected.

It proved exhausting, and by the time they returned to the Mortons' for supper, she could barely put one foot in front of the other. The girls seemed subdued, as well, and for that, she felt regret.

She hadn't meant to dampen their spirits.

Later, as she prepared the girls for bed, Eleanor turned to her. "Mama, why are you angry at Mr. Blue?"

"What makes you think I am?"

"You wouldn't talk to him all day, and when we wanted to, you shooed us away. Are you mad at us?" Eleanor's bottom lip quivered, and Libby's eyes filled with tears.

Clara's heart burned within her. She had inadvertently hurt her precious daughters. She sat between the girls on their bedding and pulled them to her sides. "I wasn't angry at you or at Mr. Blue. I was only concerned that both of you are acting like this is where we're going to stay. You know it's not."

"But why not?" Eleanor demanded.

"Because I have other plans."

"Can't you change your plans?" Libby begged, her eyes pleading. "All we want for Christmas is a—"

"Libby!" Eleanor's warning stopped her sister before she could complete her thought.

"What is it you want?" Clara asked. "Perhaps I can help you get it." Though her resources were limited, God's, she reminded herself, were not. He owned the cattle on a thousand hills. Nothing was too hard for Him.

"Can we stay here?" Eleanor's voice was tight with emotion.

"We could if I thought it was best for us, but I don't think it is." Clara's resolve strengthened as she thought of Father finding them. She could not let him catch her and take the girls.

"Who says?" Libby always had doubts.

Clara wasn't sure if that would serve her daughter well as she grew older or be her downfall. "Remember what I said when we started our journey? We would pray and trust God?"

Eleanor shifted so she could look in Clara's face. "What if what we pray is different than what you pray? Who does God answer?"

Clara smiled as she recalled what Blue had said.

"It's God's responsibility to answer our prayers as He sees fit."

Eleanor nodded, a smile flitting across her face as if she believed God would give her what she wanted.

Clara wished it could be so. "That doesn't mean we'll get what we ask for but what God thinks is best. We have to trust Him no matter what."

Eleanor sagged as if she'd been denied her fondest wish.

"Now, I know two little girls who need to get to sleep." She tucked them in and heard their prayers. Tonight they were rather restrained.

Clara picked up the book Blue had lent her and sat at the table to read.

The girls shuffled closer to each other and whispered quietly for a few minutes until she told them to go to sleep.

The story that had been so engrossing the evening before failed to hold her attention tonight, and she closed the book. Why did life have to be complicated? Why must her father be so controlling? Why the delay in her plans? She'd hoped to have started a new life by now. Instead, she was putting in time waiting.

Her own words accused her. She'd told the girls to trust God when things didn't go as they wished. Seems she would have to do so, as well.

God, it's hard to trust when the pathway ahead is invisible. May Thy rod and Thy staff comfort and guide me.

The next morning she crossed over for breakfast with renewed resolve.

"Should be a busy day today," Bonnie said.

Clara looked her way, saw the excitement in her face. "Why is that?"

"It's Saturday, and people will be coming to town. I'm making four times as many biscuits and lots of cookies. The bachelors love my baked goods. Of course, more and more of them are finding wives and that's good, too. I look forward to visiting them when I take batches of food to the store."

Tension caught Clara's neck in a vise. People would be coming to town? No doubt they would be curious and asking questions about the unfamiliar young mother and her children.

She recalled her prayer from last night and repeated it silently. Trusting, she admitted, was sometimes hard.

She waited for the girls to finish their breakfast, then hurried them over to the church. Perhaps people would not discover them there.

The girls rushed out to fill the buckets with snow.

Clara realized she'd have to keep them indoors the rest of the day so people coming to town wouldn't see them.

Blue seemed no more inclined to chat this morning than she was as they measured and cut and planed. Slowly, the pleasure of the work calmed her nerves.

Until a wagon rattled by. She sprang to the window to see a young couple make their way to the store.

A wagon came from the other direction and turned toward the store, as well.

"Looks like Macpherson is going to be busy today." Blue spoke from directly behind her.

She managed to control her startled reaction at his nearness as she watched several cowboys ride to the store.

"Slim, Buster and Eddie," Blue said. "Eden Valley cowboys and the boss. I expect Eddie will come by when he's done at Macpherson's and check on how things are progressing here."

They were coming here? She had to leave. She sidestepped around Blue. "I have something to do. Girls, come along."

Libby opened her mouth to protest, saw the look in Clara's eyes and merely obeyed her mother's command. She hurried into her coat and followed Clara and Eleanor from the church.

"What's wrong, Mama?" Eleanor said when they were away from the building. "Why are you so scared?"

"Too many people are learning our business."

"Are we going to run away again?" Eleanor's voice picked up Clara's concern.

"Maybe not today." *Unless the stagecoach shows up*, she silently added. She'd keep a watch for it. "But we'll stay out of the way for now."

She slipped into the little shack and stared at the four narrow walls. What was she to do in here all day? How was she to keep the girls entertained?

Somehow she must.

She didn't want to frighten them with her worries that among those coming into town could be a man looking for her. A man sent by her father to take the girls from her.

Chapter Eight

Blue stood with his head against the window frame. He'd craned his neck to watch Clara and the girls as they hurried toward the shack. As soon as she'd heard Eddie and the cowboys might stop by the church, she had called the girls and bolted. It was obvious she was afraid someone might recognize her. But who did she fear so much? She'd said her father was controlling, but surely that wasn't reason enough to fear him.

He might never know who she was afraid of, because she'd steadfastly refused to provide him with so much as a clue.

What would she say if he offered to protect her and the girls? Likely she'd laugh.

His heart grew cold and brittle.

And well she should. He'd failed to protect his own family and would never again take on such responsibility. Would never open his heart to the pain it could bring.

But someone needed to take her home and look after her and the girls.

He pushed away from the window. Time to get back

to work, or Eddie would think he wasted time. He returned to the sawhorse.

A few minutes later the door opened, and he straightened, waiting to see who had come calling. It wouldn't be Clara. She would have come through the back door closer to the Mortons' shack. He told himself he wasn't disappointed. After all, he knew better than to let his heart go in that direction.

It was Eddie who entered, taking his hat from his head. "How's the work going?"

"Fair to middling."

Eddie looked at the pews Blue and Clara had put together. "A fine job."

"Thanks."

Eddie circled the room, examining the wood still to be cut and the pieces waiting to be assembled and glancing out the windows.

Blue wondered what his boss really wanted. "How's your wife?"

"Linette is getting impatient for the baby to be born, but other than that she is doing fine."

Perhaps there were problems among some of the newlyweds or the new wives. Hadn't Alice said that adding a woman to any group changed the way people acted? At Eden Valley Ranch there had been three new brides just the past few months.

"And the others?" he asked. "Roper, Cassie and the children? Jayne and Seth, Brand and Sybil? Mercy and Abel and the twins?"

"Everyone is doing fine. There's a lot of visiting back and forth. Seems one or another of the ladies is always at the house or the children are going from one house to the other."

It was the main reason he had chosen to spend some time at the church. Where he'd be alone. It hadn't quite turned out that way. Funny how things had worked out. He knew he should regret it, but when he saw how Clara had run away frightened a few minutes ago he was glad he could offer her a few days of safety.

"Macpherson says you have someone here with you."

Of course Macpherson knew. What did Blue expect?

Eddie gave Blue a quizzical look. Clearly, he wanted the details.

"A young woman and her two girls." He explained how he had found her unconscious down by the river, with no place to go and no one to take her in. "She insisted she must do something to pay for her keep, so I've been teaching her woodworking. Turns out she's pretty good."

"Good. Good." Eddie plunked down on one of the pews. "Miss Prudence Foot came looking for me as soon as I reached town to complain that you and a young woman were in the church without adequate chaperoning. She's very offended at such disregard for the sanctity of the church. Her words. Not mine."

Blue leaned back on his heels and studied the man who was his boss and known to be fair in his dealings. Too bad Miss Prudence couldn't be fair, as well. It surprised him that a man like Rufus who ran the livery barn without judging man or beast should have such a judgmental sister.

Eddie waited for him to explain the activities at the church. "Her daughters are always here. They sleep in Bonnie and Claude's little shack. There need be no concern about our conduct. Besides, you know me. I'm not interested in becoming involved with a woman." *Es-*

pecially one with children, he added silently. Though he realized he felt less and less sure of his conviction.

Only because it bothered him to see her so fearful, he told himself. Someone ought to take care of her.

"Why don't I take her out to the ranch? Linette would be happy to have her."

Blue nodded. "I thought of that, but she refuses to leave town. Says she's waiting for someone."

"She's expecting someone to come for her?"

"It would seem so."

Eddie sighed. "Can she be persuaded to wait at the ranch?"

"I doubt it. She's rather stubborn."

Eddie laughed. "I remember trying to convince Linette to go back to England. It was a waste of breath."

Blue nodded. He figured it would be a similar waste to try and change Clara's mind.

"Well." Eddie planted his hands on his knees. "I trust you to act wisely in the matter." He pushed to his feet. "Tomorrow is Sunday. Why not bring her and the girls out to the ranch for church?" He looked around the building. "Soon we'll have a proper building to meet in, but I have to admit I'll miss gathering in the cookhouse with Cookie and Bertie leading the service."

Eddie wasted no more time. He went out to meet up with the Eden Valley cowboys. "I'll leave you to your work," he told Blue. Then they rode away.

Blue returned to his saw, and the echoing silence mocked him. How had he gone from dwelling in his own thoughts and enjoying complete solitude to thinking the place was too quiet?

Clara and the girls were how.

And he would pay a stiff price for letting them worm their way into his life.

Maybe if he took them to the ranch, Clara would see that it was a far better place than here to wait for… whoever she waited for. He'd ask her when he went for supper.

As soon as it was a reasonable time to show up for supper, he left the church and made his way to the Mortons' house. He stepped inside and looked about. Clara and the girls weren't there yet. Was he that early?

Bonnie noticed his surprise. "Clara has been busy all day. She washed clothes over at the shack. I said she could do it here, but she insisted she could manage, though goodness knows how she did with only a small pan to work in. Then she bathed the girls and washed their hair. She said their hair is still wet, and she didn't want to take them out in the cold, so she took food over there to eat." Bonnie came up for air. "Sit."

He did. How was he to ask Clara to go to the ranch if she didn't come for supper?

He had no choice but to go to the shack. Never mind what Miss Foot would say. He wouldn't go inside, so if Miss Foot watched, she would see that.

Bonnie rattled on about all the people who had come to town. Claude added a comment or two, but Blue just listened.

Finally, the meal ended. Blue thanked Bonnie and Claude and hurried from the house. He crossed to the shack. From outside the door he heard murmured voices from inside, but he couldn't make out what was said.

He stepped forward and knocked.

Instant silence greeted him.

He wanted to slap his forehead. Knowing how she feared someone, he should have called out a warning.

"It's me. Blue. I need to ask you something."

"Wait a minute."

He heard sounds from inside, like something being shoved across the floor and shuffling. Had she pushed boxes against the door to stop someone from entering uninvited? The thought made his nerves twitch.

He leaned against the door frame and waited.

When she opened the door, her cheeks were pink as if from exertion. "Yes?"

He glanced past her. The girls stood by the stove dressed in white nightgowns, their hair hanging down their backs. The homey scene touched a lonesome spot in his heart.

He shifted his gaze, not welcoming the reminder of what he had lost and buried two years ago.

"Yes?" she said again.

"Everything okay here?" That wasn't what he'd come to ask, but it was what he wanted to know.

"Yes, fine." She backed up as if preparing to close the door. "Thank you." The words were uncertain. Spoken, no doubt, out of politeness when she really would rather have told him to leave her alone.

"Wait. I wanted to ask you something."

She glanced over her shoulder, then stepped outside and closed the door.

He swallowed a protest. Did she think he meant to say or do something that would hurt the girls? Why, he'd do all he could to keep them safe if she'd let him. He quickly amended his thought. He might if he hadn't promised himself he would never again care deeply enough about anyone to risk having his heart broken. He meant to keep that promise.

He cleared his throat and his thoughts. "Tomorrow is Sunday. Everyone at the ranch gathers for church at the cookhouse. It's a simple, informal gathering, but it's good." Seemed a poor way of describing it. "Refreshing." Still not what he meant. "Encouraging." Now satisfied, he plunged onward. "I wondered if you wanted to go. I could rent a wagon and take you and the girls."

Her eyes brightened. She opened her mouth as if she meant to accept his invitation. Then hardness overtook her face.

"I'm sorry. I can't. I have some things I need to tend to. But thank you." She hurried inside and closed the door, leaving him staring at it.

How odd. He was certain she liked the idea, then had refused it anyway.

Didn't she realize she'd be safer on the ranch than here in town? What he wouldn't give to know who she feared. Then he'd find that person and warn them to stop making life miserable for Clara and the girls.

Or what?

He didn't answer his question because he didn't have the answer. What could he do to protect them without involving his heart?

Clara stood with her back against the door as she sorted out her feelings. Her heart had leaped at his invite. Oh, to go to church, sing with others, have her faith renewed and strengthened.

To accompany Blue on the half-hour ride to the ranch for the service... Well, wouldn't it be great to feel safe for just a little while? Her nerves had twitched with fear all afternoon. There were too many people coming and going to the store. How was she to know if one of them looked for her?

Despite the hunger of her soul, she couldn't go with Blue. What if Petey came, and she missed her ride? She dared not risk that. Today had made one thing clear: she would never feel safe in Edendale.

Besides, she had no business looking to Blue to make her feel safe. She had to prove she could take care of herself. Not only to prevent her father from taking the girls from her but for her own peace of mind. Otherwise, Father's doubts about her ability would always have a stronghold on her thoughts.

"Mama?" Eleanor sounded worried. "Is something wrong? What did Mr. Blue want?"

She wouldn't tell the children about the invitation to church. Instead, she thought about another service—the Christmas service in their new home in Fort Calgary. Wouldn't it be wonderful if they could make it in time for Christmas? "Just to make sure we were okay seeing as we didn't go over for supper."

"Oh. What did you tell him?"

"I said we were fine."

"Oh." Eleanor didn't sound convinced. Libby, she noticed, looked equally doubtful.

"We are, my girls. Hasn't God always taken care of us?" She'd have to trust Him completely tomorrow when Blue went to the ranch. She'd be alone.

Of course she would be, and she could handle it. Wasn't that the whole point of striking out on her own? She hadn't forgotten her goal. She would not be afraid. *The Lord is my shepherd.* But she admitted she would miss his company.

"Now let's get your hair dried so you can go to bed." She sat on a chair before the stove, pulled Libby to her lap and brushed her fair hair to speed its drying.

"Tomorrow is Sunday, isn't it?" Eleanor's voice filled with concern.

"Yes."

"Are we going to have church in the church?"

"It isn't really open yet." Eleanor's question gave her an idea. "We could have our own service there, though. Wouldn't that be fun?" She injected as much excitement into her voice as she could manage. Just the three of them wouldn't give her the same satisfaction, but she'd make it fun for their sake.

"I guess," Eleanor said.

"Will Mr. Blue be there?" Libby asked.

"I think he has other plans."

Libby bounced from her lap to face her. "Like what?"

"Libby, he can come and go without our permission." Sometimes her daughter's strong emotions frightened her. She wished she could have prevented Libby from growing so attached to Blue. "He has a life that doesn't include us."

Libby's bottom lip came out. Her eyes flashed denial and then filled with tears.

Clara pulled her back on her lap. "Libby, you knew that all along." Clara reached for Eleanor and pulled her to her other knee. She held them close. "We all knew that."

Libby sobbed softly, and Eleanor clung to Clara. Clara rocked them and hummed. "Soon we'll find a place where we can settle down and have a home again."

The girls quieted.

"For Christmas, right?" Libby demanded.

"I hope and pray so." Clara could promise them no more.

"I wish it could be here," Eleanor whispered.

Clara nodded. "I know you do, but it can't." Today had reinforced that fact in her mind. Every time someone rode into town, she would fear it was someone looking for her. Fort Calgary was farther north, less settled. Surely it would be less inhabited. If she understood correctly, the man she hoped to work for lived on a farm. Perhaps, God willing, it was far enough from the fort she could remain unnoticed.

She finally got the girls' hair dried and tucked them into bed. They didn't whisper or giggle. In fact, they seemed subdued, convincing her she needed to get them settled in a new home as soon as possible.

Sunday dawned bright and clear. She'd told Bonnie not to expect them over for meals, insisting the woman deserved time off from cooking for them. Instead, she had brought over food from the evening meal.

They ate together at the tiny table. As they cleaned up afterward, the beat of horse hooves grew close. She peeked outside. Blue sat astride his horse. He pulled the animal to a halt and met her gaze, then touched the brim of his hat and continued on his way.

She stared after him. How long would he be gone? Likely all day, for he had no reason to hurry back. She sighed. Why should it matter to her? Her plans did not include him. Yet the hours suddenly stretched ahead of her—a long, lonely day.

The girls called for her attention, and she returned to them. "I'll braid your hair, and then we'll go over to the church."

Eleanor stood quietly as Clara did her hair but Libby twisted and turned. "Will Blue be there?"

"No. I told you that last night."

"Well, maybe you're wrong."

"I saw him ride out of town a few minutes ago."

"Oh?" She grew quiet a moment. "Where was he going?"

"Libby, I'm sure I don't know. Perhaps out to the ranch."

Eleanor watched Clara finish Libby's hair. "Maybe we should wait for him."

"I don't think that's necessary." She fixed her hair, handed the girls their coats, put on her own and picked up her Bible. "Let's go to church."

The girls followed without arguing. When they entered, the church was still warm. Blue's bedroll was stashed neatly in one corner. The tools had been cleaned and put away, the wood neatly stacked, the floor swept clean. Plenty of evidence of Blue's presence. Everything but the man himself.

Not that she missed him. She was only used to seeing him here. She pulled her thoughts back to her plan and indicated the girls should sit in the front pew. She sat between them and opened her Bible.

"You have to stand in front," Libby said. "Or it isn't church. It's just our mama reading to us."

Clara nodded and stood before them. "I'm going to read from Exodus chapter fourteen."

"Don't we need to sing first?" Eleanor asked.

"What song would you like to sing?"

Eleanor beamed as she answered. "'A Thousand Tongues.' It makes me smile."

Clara cleared her throat and sang the words, "O for a thousand tongues to sing my great Redeemer's praise."

Eleanor knew most of the words, and her voice rang clear and certain.

Libby's voice was equally clear, though the words were a bit muffled.

Clara's heart swelled at the joy of their united voices.

"Let us pray," she said when they finished. She smiled as the girls folded their hands and bowed their heads. She had much to thank God for—life, health, peace and, most of all, God's love and protection.

Then she read from her Bible, the words catching in her throat as she read how Pharaoh thought the Israelites were entangled in the land, shut in by the wilderness.

It echoed her own thoughts. She felt entangled and lost, but God was in charge. She would trust His guidance.

She continued on until the fourteenth verse, when she had to stop. The words had hit her with such assurance she couldn't speak.

"Mama?" Eleanor's brow wrinkled with worry. "What's wrong?"

"Girls, listen carefully to this verse. 'The Lord shall fight for you and ye shall hold your peace.' Isn't that a wonderful promise that God will take care of us?"

They nodded obediently.

She reached the part where Moses held out his rod, and the waters of the Red Sea parted.

Libby's eyes grew wide with amazement. "That was exciting."

Clara nodded. "God can do anything. Nothing is too hard for him. He is our guide and protector." The words of a hymn came to her mind. "We'll sing 'My Shepherd Will Supply My Need.'"

"In pastures fresh He makes me feed, beside the living stream." The final words calmed her soul. "No more a stranger, nor a guest, but like a child at home."

She dismissed the girls, then sat on the pew and meditated on the words. *A home. Safety. Belonging. Acceptance.* The words circled through her thoughts.

Would she ever know such things? Would God provide them? She couldn't ask for a better Christmas present for them all than that.

She silently poured out her longing to her God and Savior, asking that He would give her the desires of her heart.

Realizing the girls waited at the door for her, she rose. They left the church to return to the shack.

They removed their coats and sat staring at one another.

"Girls, why don't we play a game?"

They nodded, eager for some amusement.

"I'm going to Grandmother's house, and I'm taking a satchel."

They went round and round, adding things to take with them and having to remember everything that had gone before.

Eleanor was every good at it, but Libby kept forgetting items. When her turn came next she said, "Will we have to go back to Grandfather's?"

Clara recoiled. "I thought you understood that we are going to make our own life."

"Yes, but I heard—"

"Shush," Eleanor said.

Obviously the pair had a secret. "What did you hear?" Clara asked.

Libby gave Eleanor a defiant look and answered. "Mary said Grandfather would never let us go. She said he would find us and make us go back even if you didn't want to."

Clara swallowed her swelling fear. Her father would not hesitate to do as he said. What could she do? Nothing except keep running until she felt safe and then build a life that proved she would provide for the girls.

She needed to leave Edendale while she could.

The girls waited for her answer. "Who are you going to believe? Me or Mary?"

Libby giggled. "You."

"There you go."

She fed the girls from their dwindling leftovers. Her inability to provide for them mocked her. She looked about. If Father saw where she lived, he'd have no trouble convincing everyone she'd failed.

It was stuffy inside. The walls closed in on her.

"Girls, let's go outside and enjoy the sunshine." She hurried them out the door and lifted her face to the warmth of the sun.

"Can we go down to the river?" Eleanor asked.

Clara granted permission, and they followed the path through the trees and down the bank to the water.

She looked at the place where she'd fainted. Where Blue had found her and carried her to the church.

As the girls played along the water's edge, she brushed off a fallen log and sat down.

Here she was. Back where she started. It wasn't an encouraging thought.

Like the children of Israel, she felt entangled in the land. Up against the wilderness.

God had guided the Israelites through.

What trials must she face before she reached safety?

Chapter Nine

Blue had resolutely ridden away from town but not toward the ranch. He didn't have any desire to go out there and face the questions and curious glances from those who would have heard about a woman and two children keeping him company at the church.

However, the horse needed exercise, and he needed to be alone. He'd galloped for several miles, the rushing air sifting past his ears. He slowed the pace and looked about. Two years ago when he came out to Alberta, he could ride mile after mile without seeing anyone, but now there was a house to his right, smoke coming from a chimney to his left and likely more of the same up ahead.

It was getting harder and harder for a man to be alone.

Edendale, too, was growing. More businesses. More people.

His insides tightened. Too many people coming and going. He pulled the horse to a halt. People coming and going and no one there to look out for Clara and the girls. What was he thinking leaving them in town alone? Someone could have approached from the other direction and he'd never know.

He reined around and urged the horse to a gallop. His heart thudded in time to the hoofbeats.

He skidded to a halt before the church and left the horse at the hitching rail, then jogged over to the little shack. This time he remembered to call out first.

"Clara, it's Blue."

His announcement was met with dead silence that grated up his spine and jabbed into the base of his head. "Clara? Girls?"

No answer. Perhaps they were having a Sunday afternoon nap. He jiggled the door and gave them enough time to waken but still nothing.

He glanced around, saw nothing to alarm him and no one watching. He pushed open the door. It took less than a second to see the place was empty. His heart banged into his ribs hard enough to make him flinch.

They were gone.

He clattered back outside and looked around. He could detect no tracks. Had Bonnie or Claude seen anything?

A sharp noise caught his attention. Like a child yelling in play. Was it them?

He stilled his ragged breathing and listened. *Yes. Down by the river.* He jogged down the path and saw the girls and Clara. His breath whooshed out. They were safe.

For a moment, he didn't move. How had he let himself care so much? He shook his head. It was only concern about their safety. Nothing more. Almost convinced, he made his way down to the river.

"Hello, Mr. Blue," Eleanor called.

Libby grinned from ear to ear. "Hello, Mr. Blue."

"Hello, you two." Only then did he allow himself to look in Clara's direction.

"Hello, Blue." She smiled, and his heart threatened to melt. He sucked in air and stopped the notion.

"I thought you'd be at the ranch longer."

"I was only out riding." He went to her, and they sauntered along the rocky shore.

"It's good to be outside. The girls are really enjoying it."

He could think of nothing more to say.

"I thought you intended to go to church at the ranch." She sounded concerned. "Would you go if you were there?"

"I go when I'm at the ranch." She already knew he didn't have much faith left, so he felt no need to explain further.

"I hope you don't mind, but I took the girls over to the church and we had a little service by ourselves."

"I don't mind." In fact, if he'd known, he might have joined them.

Clara stopped and tipped her head back to study him.

He forced himself not to blink before her intensity and knew she'd tell him soon enough what was on her mind.

"I read Exodus chapter fourteen and was very encouraged."

"How's that?" If anyone else had said the same thing, he would have closed his mind to what they had to say. Yet he wanted to know exactly what had provided encouragement for Clara.

She told him about the children of Israel being up against the Red Sea. "The sea or the desert. It looked hopeless, but God led them there so He could show His power and they would know He was God. I feel like I am between the desert and the sea, but I know God has brought me here to show me the way through. Isn't that wonderful?"

He nodded, glad she had found such courage through reading the Bible.

"Do you ever feel against the sea or lost in a desert?"

Her gaze demanded honesty, and he couldn't stop himself from giving it. "I've been in the desert since my family perished. A hot, dry, burning desert." He tried to contain the way his voice crackled with emotion. He failed.

Her hand came to his arm, and she rubbed gently, soothingly. "Blue, did you ever think that God could bring you out of the desert into a land flowing with milk and honey?"

He shook his head. "I figured to live in the desert the rest of my life."

"Oh, I hope not. God says He will fight for us that we may go forward. Maybe it's time for you to go forward."

Forward? His heartbeat thudded in his ears. Did he want to move on? How could he? "How can I leave the past behind?"

"Maybe you don't. Maybe you take it with you and make it part of your future."

He rocked his head back and forth. How was it remotely possible? "I can't forget the past, and I don't see how I can take it into the future. Seems I'm stuck."

"I wish I could help. After all, you've been so kind to us. I'll pray you find a way to come unstuck."

A shriek rent the air, and they spun toward the sound.

Eleanor stood on the bank screaming her lungs out. She pointed, and Blue saw what upset her.

Libby had fallen into the river. She floated away, weighed down by her wet clothes.

His whole body tensed. Ice filled his veins. He shook away the sluggishness and rushed past Clara. "I'll get her. You stay with Eleanor." *Please don't try and get Libby yourself. I don't need to try and pluck both of you from the waters.*

The rocks bit into the soles of his boots and caught at his toes, slowing his progress. His legs pumped but seemed incapable of forward movement. *Move. Move. Move.* He ordered his limbs to rush onward and ran downstream until he was even with Libby. His heart thundering in his ears, he plowed into the river. Shock seared through him as icy-cold water soaked his legs and filled his boots. Libby had been in the water several minutes. Her blood would be ice by now.

The water impeded his movement.

He forged on, his muscles strengthened by the remembrance of running to save Nancy and Beau and Alice. He'd arrived too late that time.

He would not fail this time.

Libby was almost within reach. If she would lift her arm, he could catch her.

"Libby, give me your hand."

She turned her head slowly. The cold had already numbed her. She drifted on, out of reach.

He dived for her, the cold water penetrating his clothes. His brain begged to be free of this torture, but he did not listen.

He caught the tail of Libby's coat as it floated behind her.

Send For
2 FREE BOOKS
Today!

I accept your offer!

Please send me two free novels and two mystery gifts (gifts worth about $10). I understand that these books are completely free—even the shipping and handling will be paid—and I am under no obligation to purchase anything, ever, as explained on the back of this card.

102/302 IDL GHP3

Please Print

FIRST NAME

LAST NAME

ADDRESS

APT.#   CITY

STATE/PROV.   ZIP/POSTAL CODE

Visit us online at
www.ReaderService.com

◄ Detach card and mail today. No stamp needed. ◄   © 2015 HARLEQUIN ENTERPRISES LIMITED. ® and ™ are trademarks owned and/or used by the trademark owner and/or its licensee. Printed in the U.S.A.

READER SERVICE—**Here's how it works:**

Accepting your 2 free Love Inspired® Historical books and 2 free gifts (gifts valued at approximately $10.00) places you under no obligation to buy anything. You may keep the books and gifts and return the shipping statement marked "cancel." If you do not cancel, about a month later we'll send you 4 additional books and bill you just $4.99 each in the U.S. or $5.49 each in Canada. That is a savings of at least 17% off the cover price. It's quite a bargain! Shipping and handling is just 50¢ per book in the U.S. and 75¢ per book in Canada.* You may cancel at any time, but if you choose to continue, every month we'll send you 4 more books, which you may either purchase at the discount price or return to us and cancel your subscription. *Terms and prices subject to change without notice. Prices do not include applicable taxes. Sales tax applicable in N.Y. Canadian residents will be charged applicable taxes. Offer not valid in Quebec. Books received may not be as shown. All orders subject to approval. Credit or debit balances in a customer's account(s) may be offset by any other outstanding balance owed by or to the customer. Please allow 4 to 6 weeks for delivery. Offer available while quantities last.

▼ If offer card is missing write to: Reader Service, P.O. Box 1867, Buffalo, NY 14240-1867 or visit www.ReaderService.com ▼

BUSINESS REPLY MAIL

FIRST-CLASS MAIL   PERMIT NO. 717   BUFFALO, NY

POSTAGE WILL BE PAID BY ADDRESSEE

READER SERVICE

PO BOX 1867

BUFFALO NY 14240-9952

NO POSTAGE
NECESSARY
IF MAILED
IN THE
UNITED STATES

"Don't let it come off," he yelled, hoping to get through to her numbed brain.

He planted his feet and pulled her to him. The coat hung from her elbows, but it held, enabling him to catch her. It saved her.

He crushed the child to his chest as his heart thundered in his ears. She was like holding a block of ice. If she didn't get warm soon—

He would not think of the consequences and rushed out of the water and up the bank.

Clara and Eleanor raced toward him.

"Is she—" Clara's voice caught.

"She's cold. I need to get her to the shack and get her warm." No need for both of them to think the worst.

Clara made it to the door first and threw it open. "Bring her in."

He carried Libby toward the stove. Clara was already adding wood to the coals and stirring up the flames. He snagged a chair and sat down, Libby on his lap. He worked off Libby's dripping coat.

Her eyes were big, her skin bluish.

Clara grabbed a blanket and held it toward the stove to warm it.

Libby sat in her wet dress. If this were his child, he'd have no worry about removing it. "She needs to get her wet things off."

Clara handed him the warmed blanket, and they switched places.

He should leave them to their privacy, but he couldn't go until he was certain Libby was okay. He held the blanket to the stove as Clara removed the wet dress and petticoat.

With the blanket before him to shield the child, he

waited for Clara to remove the last of her wet things; then she wrapped Libby tightly in the warm blanket he handed her.

Clara rubbed Libby hard. "Thank you." A sob caught in her throat. "Thank you."

His teeth chattered.

Clara brought her gaze to him. "You're cold and wet."

"I'll go change." He rushed from the shack and over to the church. He quickly shed his wet clothes and put on dry things. He'd been able to save her. He fell to his knees. *Why, God? Why could I save someone else's child and not my own?*

But there was no answer. Only regret and sorrow. Also satisfaction that Libby had not drowned.

But she had been frightfully cold. Was she really okay?

It took him several minutes to pull his wet boots on again, and then he trotted back to the shack.

He paused outside the door. "It's Blue. Can I come in?"

"Come ahead," Clara called. She glanced up as he entered. "Where's your coat? You must be cold. Come and sit by the fire."

He obeyed without thinking and lifted the corner of the blanket to peek at Libby swaddled in her mother's arms. "Is she okay?"

Her blue eyes were wide and watchful. "You saved me." Her voice filled with awe.

He chuckled. "I guess that answers my question. Mind telling me how you fell in the river?"

Clara caught Libby's chin. "I'd like to hear, too."

Libby sat up and clutched the blanket around her.

Seeing Eleanor watching with such longing, Blue lifted her to his lap. She snuggled close.

"I was trying to be Moses." Libby seemed disappointed.

"I told her she couldn't make the waters part." Eleanor's voice was muffled against Blue's shirtfront. "But she wouldn't listen. She never listens to me."

Blue laughed. "Sort of reminds me of someone." He'd tried to make Clara see she couldn't keep running, that she needed to let people help her, but she stubbornly insisted she had to do it her way. He waited for her to understand who he meant and grinned when her eyes flashed a protest.

"I'm certain I don't know who you mean."

He lifted his eyebrows, just as certain she did.

She ducked her head and looked directly into Libby's eyes. "I'm grateful you're safe, but please don't do anything so foolish again. There might not be anyone around to pull you out."

"It was awfully cold."

Clara held her close again and wrapped her tightly. She brought her gaze to Blue. "Are you sure you're warmed?"

He nodded. Maybe the cold had affected his brain because he couldn't seem to extricate himself from this situation. More like he couldn't think why he should. It felt good to be sitting by a warm stove holding a little girl with a woman and another child at his side.

"I once—" He broke off. Did he mean to tell the girls about his children? He got to his feet and deposited Eleanor on the chair. "I best be going." And he rushed back to the church with even more haste than he had left it.

He could not let himself be drawn into another family.

"Mama, why did Mr. Blue leave so suddenly?" Eleanor asked.

"Maybe he was cold. After all, he got all wet in the river." Though he hadn't seemed cold at first, she realized. And what had he been about to say? *I once—* Once what? Once had a family? Once had a home and children?

A groan tore through her insides. It must hurt him deeply to have been able to save Libby but not his own children.

What could she do to make it up to him? Likely he'd say he only wanted to be left alone for he'd confessed he was stuck in the desert of his life. The desert had to be a lonely, unhappy place. If she could get him to see he could leave such desolation, she would feel she'd paid her debt of gratitude.

How was she to do that? She considered her options, which were few. Would he join them for supper?

She slipped her hand under Libby's blanket. "You feel warm now."

Libby nodded.

"Then it's time you got dressed."

She helped her daughter into dry clothes and hung the wet things to dry. "You two stay here. I'm going to ask Bonnie if she can give us supper." She had no money and could offer no services in exchange for the food, but this time she had something more important to consider than her pride.

She went next door and knocked. When Bonnie answered, she explained how Libby had fallen in the river but was okay. "I don't want to bring her out so soon after her soaking. Would you mind—" It was harder to ask than she imagined. "Could I—"

"That poor child. I'm grateful she's okay. You must certainly keep her good and warm. It would be dreadful if she took a chill. Why don't I send over enough food for your meal?"

"Thank you. You're a generous woman."

"Nonsense. In this country we help each other. We never know when we might be the one in need of assistance. Wait right there, and I'll dish up enough for you."

Bonnie ladled thick, savory-smelling stew into a smaller pot. Clara was grateful to see how generous she was. Bonnie cut half a dozen thick slices of bread and wrapped them in a towel. She tucked dishes and silverware into a sack. "Can you manage everything?"

Clara held the items easily. "Thank you ever so much. I will be sure to pass the kindness on every chance I get." And she'd start by sharing the food with Blue, showing her gratitude by letting him remember what it felt like to be part of a family circle.

Bonnie smiled. "That's the way to do it."

Carrying the pot of food carefully, she made her way to the shack. "Girls, I am going to invite Mr. Blue to have supper with us to thank him for rescuing Libby."

The girls grinned.

"Eleanor, would you go ask him?" He'd have a harder time saying no to her than to Clara.

Libby headed for the door. "I want to go, too."

"You can't. Your coat is wet."

"I could borrow yours."

Clara laughed despite herself. "Not this time." Blue's

coat was wet. What would he wear? Perhaps this wasn't a good idea. But Eleanor was already gone.

Maybe he would refuse.

Why was she having second thoughts? She stiffened her backbone. She wasn't. The man was lonely, lost in a desert, and she owed it to him to help him find his way out.

Eleanor returned as Libby and Clara were setting the table.

She was alone, and Clara could not deny her disappointment. "Isn't he coming?"

"He said he'd be along in a minute. Said he had to take care of his horse."

"Did he seem glad of the invitation?"

Eleanor shrugged. "Of course he was."

Clara didn't know if Blue had expressed pleasure or Eleanor had assumed it. She decided not to pursue the discussion.

They moved the trunk closer to the table for the girls to sit on so Clara and Blue could sit on the two chairs.

Clara looked about. All her washing had dried and was put away. All that still hung were Libby's wet things.

Clara's heart missed a beat. She could have lost her daughter. She owed Blue a huge debt. She had to repay him before Petey returned with the stagecoach.

A knock sounded at the door. "It's Blue," he called.

The girls rushed to let him in.

He stood at the door, twisting his hat in his hands. "Eleanor said I should come."

"I wanted to show my gratitude." She indicated the table with the food set out.

"That's not necessary."

The girls dragged him forward and held the chair for him.

He sat down but looked ready to flee at any moment.

"Blue, relax—we aren't going to bite."

The girls giggled.

He nodded, but his gaze went to the door.

She sat on her chair and the girls perched on the trunk. Then she realized someone would have to say grace. She glanced at the girls. They looked at Blue as if expecting him to do the honors.

She hoped he wouldn't disappoint them. "Blue, would you ask the blessing?"

His gaze darted from the door to her face, then to the girls. He dropped his hat to the floor beside his chair, scrubbed his palms along his thighs and nodded.

"Thank you, God, for food and friends. Amen."

The girls looked ready to giggle at his short prayer, but Clara quelled them with a look. "Now let's eat." She pushed the pot of stew toward Blue, and he ladled out two scoops. Then she assisted the girls with their food. Everyone began to eat. Except Blue, who stared at his plate.

Clara put her fork down. "Blue, what's the matter?"

"Nothing." He picked up his fork.

"Maybe he doesn't like eating with us," Libby said.

Clara waited for him to answer.

"Of course I like eating with you. I'm especially happy to see that Libby's appetite hasn't been affected by her fall in the river. And it's good to see Eleanor's excellent table manners. Yours, too, Libby."

The girls beamed at his praise.

There was so much Clara wanted to say to him, but

now, with the girls listening to every word, was not the time or place.

"Mama taught us good table manners," Eleanor said.

"But Grandfather said we had to eat in the kitchen." Libby sighed. "He said children should be seen and not heard."

"I'm sure Mr. Blue doesn't want to hear about Grandfather." Clara hoped they wouldn't say any more.

Eleanor turned her fork over and over. "He said little girls were useless. Education shouldn't be wasted on them."

Clara forced herself to swallow the food in her mouth. She met Blue's questioning gaze boldly, not wanting him to guess at any more details about her father.

His eyes darkened, and then he turned to the girls. "I've always thought little girls were very useful. You help at the church. You help your mother. Why, I think you could do most anything you set your minds to. Just like your mama."

The girls glowed under his praise, and so did she. Whether or not he believed it, it felt good to hear the words. "Thank you," she murmured.

"Except make the waters part," Libby said, her voice full of disgust.

Clara and Blue looked at each other and laughed.

The atmosphere grew considerably lighter after that. The girls asked Blue where he had gone earlier, and he told them of his ride.

"I saw a herd of antelope while I was riding."

The girls leaned forward. "Antelope?"

"Yup. Did you know they can run faster than a horse?"

The two girls got wide-eyed. "Can we see them?"

"You pay attention and you might." He went on to talk about other wildlife he'd seen in the area. "Even wolves and bears up in the mountains."

"Was you scared?" Libby asked.

Eleanor sprang to his defense. "Of course he wasn't. Mr. Blue isn't scared of anything. Are you?"

"Bears and wolves aren't animals a man should stop being afraid of."

"Oh." Eleanor sounded disappointed.

"A person just has to be cautious and not let their fear control them." He looked at Clara, a challenge in his eyes.

Did he think her fears controlled her? Well, to a certain extent they did. But sometimes fear was a good thing.

"I think fear should drive us to action," she said. "Not drive us into retreat."

The look he gave her was filled with denial.

She hadn't meant to be so challenging. Would her words make him draw back? She soon had her answer.

He pushed from the table. "Thank you for sharing your supper with me. Now I must go."

She watched him stride away, her heart heavy with regret.

How was she going to undo her words?

Chapter Ten

At the church, Blue worked his wet boots off again and propped them by the stove to dry. He changed his socks and picked up his book. With a groan, he dropped it to the nearby pew. He wouldn't be able to read with his mind full of turmoil.

What was he thinking to challenge Clara about her fears? Who was he to say she shouldn't let them control her?

He strode to the windows facing town and stared at the empty streets. Miss Prudence Foot lived next to the livery barn with her brother. He glanced from her house to the little shack where Clara and the girls stayed. Could the woman see it from her place? He shrugged. What difference did it make? He'd only been at the shack a short while and had left well before dark.

He crossed to the other side of the church and looked out the windows. The street led away from town, away from the ranch. *Away.* Maybe it was time to ride away.

He turned to face the interior of the building. He couldn't leave. He had to make the pews. Besides, someone had to make sure Clara and the girls were safe. The irony of not wanting to care and yet being so concerned about their well-being was not lost on him. Nor did he try to reconcile the two. He'd been able to save Libby. It didn't make up for losing his own children, but it was something. Just as making sure Clara and the girls were safe allowed him to do something that helped ease the pain of not being able to save his own family.

Tomorrow he would apologize for his rash words and make things right between them. Then he could find the peace of mind he sought.

The next morning he hurried over for breakfast, anxious to assure himself they were all okay. Libby bounced about so excitedly her mother had to scold her.

"Her soaking doesn't appear to have harmed her," Blue said.

Clara shook her head. "Certainly hasn't slowed her down."

Bonnie and Claude expressed their concern over Libby's fall into the river.

"Mr. Blue saved me." Libby gave him such an adoring look that he almost choked on his food. He was growing far too familiar with the adoration of two little girls even though he'd tried to resist it from the beginning.

"And we're all grateful," Clara said. "But perhaps, Libby, you could stop chattering and finish your breakfast so people can get on with their day."

Libby nodded and concentrated on her plate of food, but she wriggled about as if she were about to explode.

Blue was already done and pushed away from the table, thanked Bonnie and Claude for the meal and hurried to the church. As he waited for Clara and the girls to join him, he rehearsed what he wanted to say.

The girls clattered in first and dived for the buckets. Just as quickly they raced outside to fill them with snow.

Clara waited for them to dart by her before she stepped inside. She heaved a huge sigh of relief. "I hope Libby will settle down once she gets busy on her chores around here."

He chuckled. "She's full of vinegar today."

"You could say that."

They looked at one another. Their expressions grew serious.

"Blue, I want—"

He spoke at the same time. "I need to apologize. I didn't mean—"

She stopped. "You go first."

"Okay." He was afraid if he didn't get the words out right away, he wouldn't be able to. "I didn't mean to offend you last night by talking about your fears."

"Wait a minute. You think I was offended?"

He nodded.

She spoke. "I was afraid *I* had offended *you* and meant to apologize."

He thought back to what she'd said. *Fear should drive us to action. Not drive us into retreat.* "You think I retreat?"

"Don't you?"

"I wouldn't call it that so much as…well, maybe…" He could think of no other way to describe it.

"Wandering in the desert?" she supplied.

He shrugged. "Something like that."

"Isn't it time to get out of the desert?"

Why was she so insistent? It wasn't as though she had any understanding of what he needed. Or wanted. But then, it seemed he didn't, either. "I don't know."

"You don't know if it's time? Or you don't know how to do it?"

He didn't much care for the way this conversation was going. It made him feel exposed. But wait. He wasn't the one running away. "What about your running?" he shot back. "Who are you afraid of?"

Her eyes darkened and filled with fear and caution as if she'd seen the person she feared. "I—" She shook her head. "It's safer if you don't know. If you forget you ever met us."

"Safer for who? And how do you expect me to do that? I've been trying to forget for two years. Forgetting is not easy."

"Then what are you going to do?"

He scrubbed at the back of his neck. "I don't know." All he knew was that forgetting her would not be any easier than forgetting Alice and his children. "What do you suggest I do?"

The look in her eyes begged for something, though he couldn't say what. Her look went on and on. Probing, searching, uncovering, revealing, and he was powerless to stop it. It seemed as if the light of the sun and moon and a sky full of stars burst through the barriers of his heart. He knew he should be concerned, but he wasn't. Knew he should close his heart, but he couldn't.

He'd deal with the aftermath of her searching look later.

"I don't know." Her words were an honest cry.

"Nor do I. It seems we're both locked in a past we don't like and facing a future we can't control."

Light flared through her eyes as if she'd been stricken by a revelation. "Of course we can't. Why do we think we can? I choose to trust God. You should, too. It's so much easier than kicking and fighting against circumstances."

"What makes you think I want it easier?"

Her smile was sweet, almost overriding his lingering resistance. "I think you want what we all want. Assurance we will find the strength to face the trials and challenges of the future. A reason to go on. Trust in God gives us that."

"I wish it was that easy." He envied her the serenity and peace that filled her eyes.

"Maybe part of the problem is it's so easy. We long to earn that which God offers freely—His love and care. But it's already paid for in full."

He nodded. "I know all that."

"But you still don't believe?"

"I can't remember how." How did he believe without putting aside the memory of Alice and his children? And to do so would be to waste their lives.

She took his hand and placed her palm to his; with the fingers of her other hand, she stroked the back of his hand. It was a hypnotic caress that eased his worries and freed his thoughts.

"I will pray you find the way back to your faith."

The girls thudded into the room, banging the buckets against the door frame as they tried to get through together.

Clara released his hand. He stepped back, barely able to pull his thoughts into some semblance of order. Clara grabbed the end of the tape measure, and they soon settled into the comfortable rhythm of the work.

But something had changed. There was a sense of understanding between them that he wondered at. How could two people, both intent on going their separate ways, share anything more than the work they did together?

He was at a loss to explain it except to acknowledge there was a sense of having walked the same path for a few hours.

He watched the girls playing their pretend game by the pile of wood. He'd grown to care for them.

He studied Clara bent over a piece of wood, deep in concentration as she ran the planer over it. He'd grown to care for her, too.

Caring cost.

Caring hurt.

But the reminders came a little too late.

Clara wondered if she'd said too much. Her words had come from a heart that almost burst with sorrow for him. He was so lost. Several times throughout the day, she stole glances at him when he wasn't looking her way. He seemed thoughtful but not upset.

She could only hope and pray her words would help him move forward in his life.

Three times she sprang to the window when she heard a rider or a wagon in the street. Was it the stagecoach? But it never was. At the same time, it didn't appear to be anyone looking for a woman and children. At least, she assumed so when the rider left the store with a bundle of supplies.

How long before Petey returned? "How long, oh, God, how long?"

Blue chuckled. "Are you complaining against God?"

She turned with a sheepish grin. "You weren't supposed to hear me."

"Then you shouldn't say it out loud." He trailed his finger over her chin.

Likely he meant it to be teasing, but his touch danced through her like pretty little butterflies alighting on every nerve ending.

Without conscious thought, she turned her face against his finger.

And then the touch ended, and he stood before her, his hands jammed into his pockets, his eyes dark as dusk.

Reaching inside to some secret store of strength, she smiled, hoping her lips did not tremble and give away her reaction. "I'll try to remember in the future to keep my thoughts silent."

"Don't bother for my sake." Was his voice husky, or was she only imagining it?

He turned suddenly and returned to the sawhorse, where he set to work. She likewise returned to her task.

That afternoon, they put together four more pews. The girls insisted they line them up as they would for a church service.

"It looks nice," Eleanor said. "When are you going to have a real church here?"

Blue leaned back on his heels. "Well, let's see. Once we're through making the pews, these all have to be finished to preserve the wood. Then the walls at the back have to be done. And I suppose we need a pulpit. Oh, wait." He seemed rather surprised at whatever he'd thought. "I suppose we need a preacher, too."

Libby looked him up and down with a great deal of interest.

Clara held her breath, wondering what the child had in her head.

"Why couldn't you be the preacher?" Libby asked him. "You're a nice man, and you saved my life."

He stared at her; then he blinked and opened his mouth, but merely shut it again. "Libby, that's a very kind thought, but it takes more than that to be a preacher."

"What?"

"Well, I suppose you have to go to school and learn lots about the Bible. You have to have lots and lots of faith in God, and it has to be your job."

"Oh." Libby's shoulders sagged.

Eleanor stood before Blue and commanded his attention. "I wish you could be the preacher. Then I'd want to go to church every day."

Clara felt sorry for him. Her girls could be very direct and very opinionated. And, no, despite Blue's insinuations, they didn't take after their mother. More like their grandfather. She only hoped and prayed she could direct their strong beliefs into a more charitable attitude than her father's went. Most of all, she would teach them to believe in their strength.

Blue again looked as if he had no idea how to respond to Eleanor. Then a slow, teasing smile brightened his face. "Every day? Really? I think you'd get plenty tired of that especially if I dragged the service on for three or four hours."

Eleanor looked shocked. "Would you do that?"

Blue knelt to her eye level. He smiled gently and cupped his hand over the back of her head. "No, Miss Big Eyes. Because I'm not a preacher."

Libby went to her sister's side. "He's a cowboy, not a preacher. Right, Mr. Blue?"

He cupped his other hand over the back of Libby's head. "That's right, little one."

Libby grinned, pleased at her observation and likely just as pleased at Blue's attention.

Clara hurried to a window that gave her a view of town. She'd heard no wagon or horse, but she needed to get away from the scene of Blue with her daughters. It hurt too much to think of all they missed. They'd never had a father who showed interest in them, let alone affection. Her own father had treated them with about the same regard he gave to the dog that lived with the gardener. Blue alone had shown them affection and it was only temporary.

Sometimes it was hard to trust that God knew best, but like she'd said to Blue, anything other than trust didn't make sense. So she'd take these days—however long they'd last—as a gift. God's way of teaching her girls that not all men saw them as useless.

That evening, as she tucked the girls into bed, she again reminded them they weren't staying there.

"But why not?" Libby demanded.

"Does Grandfather know we're here?" Eleanor asked, her face wrinkled with worry.

Clara considered how to respond. She didn't want to make the girls afraid of their grandfather, but perhaps they shouldn't trust him wholeheartedly, either.

"Will he steal us from you?" Libby's lips quivered, and her eyes glistened with tears.

Clara contained her shock and surprise and answered calmly. "Why would you think such a thing?"

"Mary said her father heard Grandfather saying that. Isn't that why we left without saying goodbye?"

It shocked her clear to the core that they'd known, or

at least suspected, all the time that her fear was more than Father forcing them to go back. "Girls, I intend to keep you with me. That's why we can't stay here."

Libby nodded.

Eleanor did not. "Then where are we going?"

"I think it's best if no one knows. Not even you."

Eleanor persisted. "I heard you talking to the stagecoach man."

Clara had tried to be discreet but perhaps hadn't succeeded as well as she hoped. "Whatever you heard, pretend you didn't."

Eleanor flopped back on the bedding. "I suppose we will run forever."

"Of course not."

"If we can't stay here, I don't care where we go." Eleanor turned her back to Clara.

"I don't know why you don't like Mr. Blue." Libby's look accused Clara of having something wrong with her. Then she, too, turned away from Clara.

Clara sighed. What was the point in explaining to them that she liked Blue just fine? He had many admirable qualities. A quiet strength, a tenderness with the girls that made her eyes sting, a depth of emotion that she longed to explore further.

Liking him or not wasn't the problem. So what was? The answers were clear.

First, the only way she was safe here was with Blue as her protector. She didn't want a protector. What was the point in trading one man's control for another, even if, in the trade, she found a man who didn't use his control unkindly?

There was an even bigger reason she couldn't stay. Blue wasn't prepared to step into the future.

The next morning, she again reminded the girls to keep in mind they would only be there a few more days.

Eleanor and Libby nodded but refused to meet her eyes.

She told herself she must do what was best for all of them.

As she joined Blue in the church to work, she settled her mind into the measuring, cutting and many details of the work.

There was little need to talk as they knew what each needed to do next and neither of them seemed inclined to make conversation. The girls played quietly in one corner.

She let the pleasure of holding and shaping the wood calm her.

"Mama?"

She looked up to find Eleanor and Libby standing at her elbows.

The expectant looks in their eyes made her wary. "Yes?"

"We want you and Mr. Blue to come to our tea party." Eleanor reached for Clara's hand and Libby for Blue's.

"We're busy." Her protest fell on deaf ears, and Clara reluctantly allowed herself to be propelled across the floor. She didn't look at Blue to see his reaction.

When they reached the corner, she saw that the girls had fashioned vessels from bits of bark and leaves.

"You sit there and be the father." Libby showed Blue the spot she meant.

The father! What were the girls up to?

"Mama, you sit here and be the mother." Eleanor drew her to a place across from Blue. Clara sat on the floor, her skirt tucked about her legs.

Her daughters sat on either side of her.

"This is nice," Libby said.

Clara raised her gaze to Blue, intending to apologize, but he met her look, his eyes full of surprise, regret, hope and despair. Her words stalled on her tongue. Was he remembering his own children? Was he finding this situation difficult? But perhaps a little enjoyable, too? She should play along until he indicated what he thought.

"Where did you get all the fine dishes?" she asked.

"We made them." Eleanor sounded pleased with their efforts.

"Mama, you pour the tea." Libby handed Clara a piece of wood that faintly resembled a teapot.

Feeling somewhat foolish, she offered tea to Blue.

"Thank you." His voice grated as if he was as uncertain about this party as she.

"We made cookies and cake." The girls passed around trays made of bark with tiny morsels of moss and other found objects.

A long slow ache crept up Clara's veins. At her father's house the girls had a beautiful china tea set. She'd purchased it for their Christmas gift last year, but they'd left it behind. She'd known they couldn't take much in the way of belongings on their trip.

"We should talk about things," Eleanor said.

Clara contained her thoughts. "What would you like to talk about?"

"Family things."

Clara sent Blue a regretful look, silently apologizing for the awkward position the girls had put them in.

He shrugged, and then a teasing smile caught his lips. He turned to Eleanor. "Tell us about your family."

She ducked her head. "It's a pretend family with a mama and a papa and where children sit at the table with them. Like yesterday."

Blue caught her chin and turned Eleanor's face toward him. "That sounds like a very nice family."

Clara held her breath as Eleanor's eyes widened. Libby leaned forward, clinging to his words. Clara, too, dreamed of such a life. But how could she start over? It didn't work that way. The girls sighed in unison, then turned back to the tea party.

"Mama, you're the mother. You ask the father how his day was." Eleanor waited expectantly.

Clara's throat closed off. This pretend game offered too much while reality denied it. She pasted a smile on her face and turned to Blue. After drawing a tight breath, she asked, "How was your day?"

Blue's eyes were dark.

She shook her head. "Never mind. Girls, Blue and I have work to do."

She started to get to her feet, but Eleanor caught her hand.

"Mama, don't you like our tea party? Did we make too much mess?" Her voice carried a wail. "Aren't we good girls?"

Libby hung her head. "We're not good girls."

Clara sat down again and reached for them, but they both shrugged away from her hand. "You are the best girls in the whole world. I'm sorry if I made you think otherwise."

They continued to stare at the floor.

"It's why we can't stay," Libby whispered.

"Of course it's not." Hadn't she explained why they must leave and that it had nothing to do with the children? Her heart threatened to crack wide-open and spill sorrow and disappointment all through her.

She wanted to trust God, but it proved hard when her girls were hurting. *Oh, God, please help them understand. Help them not to take it personal. Send Petey here soon so we can reach our destination and the girls can feel settled.*

Perhaps with winter deepening, her father would not bother them. Travel would be difficult, sometimes impossible.

All she needed was a few months in which to establish a home and prove she could care for them on her own.

A wagon rattled by, and she rushed to the window. Perhaps even now God had sent the stagecoach. But it was only another farm wagon with two men aboard.

She turned back to her children. They scooped up the party things and carried them away without looking at Clara.

Blue shook his head.

Whether to indicate regret over the tea party or over the way she had ended it so abruptly, she couldn't say.

"I'm sorry," she murmured, though she couldn't have said for what and hoped he wouldn't ask her.

"It was all pretend."

Did he mean the party? The girls' wishes? Or something else entirely? "What is?" She hadn't meant to ask the question, but the words had spilled out. In truth, she wanted to know the answer.

He held her gaze, a dark emptiness in his eyes. "Family."

"No, it's not. Surely someone, somewhere, has real family. What about the people at the ranch?"

He stared past her. "I suppose." He paused a beat in consideration. "Though it seems most of them have had to deal with something difficult in their lives."

"Really?" For some reason, she'd thought they were without problems.

"Eddie's wife, Linette, came out to Alberta expecting a marriage of convenience. She meant to get away from a marriage her father had arranged but which she found impossible. And Cassie, the woman who started the business the Mortons now run, had lost a husband and two babies. She wanted to be independent. Instead, she and Roper rescued four children and are now their parents."

He didn't meet her eyes as he continued. "Grace—well, Ward found her in an awful situation. Eddie's sister, Jayne, came out to escape the memory of seeing her fiancé shot dead before her eyes. And then there's Brand. He came from an outlaw family. And Abel was a widower with two little children to raise." He shook his head as if to clear his thoughts. "I never realized before that they all came through hard times to their present families."

"And they're all happy?"

"Far as I can tell."

His words fell like warm drops of rain on her heart. Their gazes finally met. Did he see the same offer of a future full of hope and fulfillment she did?

Was it possible that at the end of this journey she might find a place of belonging?

But the thought brought no peace to her heart. Instead, it ached. Finding that place of belonging meant leaving behind the temporary pleasure she had found right here.

Chapter Eleven

Throughout the day Blue managed to let measuring and cutting fill his thoughts. Or at least he tried. But every time the girls came into sight, his heart twisted. They longed for family. Even though they'd known it and lost it, they still wanted to have it again, believing it would mean love and joy for the rest of their lives. He shook his head. Children had such faith in the impossible.

Clara, too, kept invading his thoughts. No matter how he tried, he could not forget what he'd said to her. How all the new families at the ranch had come together despite hard times in their past.

Somehow they'd found a way to move into the future.

He slid his gaze to where the girls had laid out their tea party and told him he was the father. Did they wish he could be their papa? He swallowed a large lump in his throat and forced his thoughts to go elsewhere.

The girls had made their tea set out of wood scraps. He knew they had no books. Now he realized they had no toys, either.

Nancy had had a doll she'd loved to rags.

Beau's favorite toy had been a little wheelbarrow

Blue had built for him. He smiled as he remembered Beau trying to persuade their pet cat it wanted a ride.

Clara watched him. "Something pleases you."

He started to deny it, then decided against it. "I was thinking of my children playing."

She squeezed his arm. "It's nice to see you enjoying memories of them."

Her touch made him lean a bit closer. Had he said what he did in the hopes she would reach out to him? Was he getting as bad as the girls, wanting something beyond the realm of possibility? Allowing himself to pretend?

He didn't believe in make-believe and eased away. "I remember lots of good things about them." He picked up a board and returned to work before she would ask him to share his memories. Maybe he would one of these days. If she stayed around long enough. He realized that sometime over the past few days he'd been able to think of his children and smile. And it felt good.

No doubt having two children playing underfoot had made it possible.

He'd like to do something for Eleanor and Libby. All afternoon, he thought of what he could do. He considered making them something out of wood. Perhaps a doll cradle, but they had no doll to put in it.

Then he recalled something and knew what he would do.

He waited until supper time. "You go ahead. Tell Bonnie I'll be there shortly." He watched until they stepped inside the Morton home; then he turned his feet up the street and went directly to Macpherson's store. Bright red and silver balls, a little toy farm wagon, an embroidered ladies' hankie and half a dozen fancy cards with a winter scene and Christmas trees formed part of the window display. All reminders of the season he had resolutely ignored for two years.

Macpherson was thankfully alone inside the store.

"I'll take that." Blue pointed at the display behind the glass counter.

Macpherson stared at Blue. "That?"

"Yes, that. How much is it?"

Macpherson named a sum, and Blue dug the correct amount of money out of his purse.

When the man saw that Blue was serious, he pulled out the box and wrapped it in brown store paper and tied it firmly. "I never thought I'd see the day that Blue Lyons bought himself a—"

"Let it go, Macpherson. And best if you keep this to yourself."

"Oh, for sure. You can count on it."

Whether he could or not, Blue didn't know. He took the package and returned to the church. Now to wait until tomorrow when he could give it to the girls.

The next morning, he was awake early. Too early to go for breakfast. He stared at the package on the pew. What was he thinking to buy them a gift? Would Clara refuse to let the girls have it? Would she want to pay for it? He chuckled. Likely she'd try to do both. But he kind of figured she wouldn't be able to resist her daughters.

He spun away and stared out the window at the pink dawn. Surely breakfast would be ready by now.

He shrugged into his coat and trotted over, slowing his steps when he drew abreast of the shack.

Libby's voice reached him. "Mama, my coat's all twisted."

"Let me see."

He imagined Clara fussing over her younger daughter while Eleanor stood by, watching and worrying.

Someone ought to take care of all three of them... protect Clara from whomever she ran from, take over Eleanor's worries, keep a check on Libby's impetuousness.

He curled his hands into fists and denied that he imagined himself taking on that role. Seems he'd picked up on pretend play from the little girls.

Clara's voice snapped him from his thoughts. "There you go. Now put it on."

Blue hastened onward lest he be found lurking outside their door. He was seated at the table when they reached the Morton place.

Libby dropped her coat on the floor, picked it up at her mother's reminder, then skidded to her place. She waited only for Claude to ask the blessing before she started to chatter about a dream she'd had that seemed to involve a cat, a dog and a horse who all fell into a river.

Clara shook her head. "Libby, would you eat your breakfast?"

Blue had eaten steadily while the child talked and had already finished. Seeing no call to linger, he thanked Bonnie and Claude and headed for the door.

"We'll be right there," Libby said and began to spoon the food into her mouth at a furious rate.

Clara touched Libby's hand to signal her to slow down.

Eleanor finished and pushed her plate away. "Can I go with Mr. Blue?"

Blue jerked to a halt. Wouldn't it ruin the surprise?

Clara shook her head. "You can wait for us."

He rushed away. By the time he reached the church,

his heart pounded in a fast tempo. Perhaps as much from nervousness as activity. He didn't intend to change his mind about the gift, though he had a dozen arguments as to why he shouldn't have done it.

The girls clattered through the door and grabbed the buckets. Eleanor noticed the package and skidded to a halt. She didn't voice her question, but her eyes sought his and asked it.

Libby wasn't as constrained. "What's that?"

"Lib," her mother scolded. "I don't believe it's any of your concern."

"Oh." She hung her head, and Eleanor's shoulders slumped.

"This time it is," Blue said. He grinned as the two little girls stared at him, their eyes filled with interest. "It's something for the both of you. Why don't you see what it is?"

Their mouths went round with surprise.

Libby was the first to regain her power of speech. "Is it a Christmas present?"

It proved the perfect occasion. "An early one."

Libby turned to Eleanor as if seeking her approval. *How strange.* Libby normally rushed into things without any forethought.

Eleanor's gaze darted from Libby to Blue and back. She looked puzzled for a moment; then her expression cleared. "It's not Christmas yet." The words were meant for Libby. "So there's still time."

"Time for what?" Clara asked, but the girls clamped their lips tight and shook their heads.

Whatever their secret, they weren't about to share it. But Blue began to think his little surprise was going to fall flat. "Don't either of you want to see what's in the parcel?"

"I do!" Libby hurried to the pew with Eleanor right beside her. They lifted the package, wonder and curiosity in their faces. Then they carefully untied the string and folded back the paper to reveal a doll with a porcelain head and muslin body. The green satin dress looked like something a special girl would wear.

"Oh!" That was all Eleanor said.

Libby squealed. "A dolly." She turned to Blue. "You bought us a dolly?"

He nodded.

Libby ran to him and hugged him about his waist. "Thank you."

A lump lodged in the back of his throat.

Eleanor simply stood at the pew staring at the doll. "She's beautiful," she whispered. "Thank you."

The lump swelled to impossible size. He'd had plenty of special times with Nancy and Beau. The good memories tangled with the pain of loss. Then an overwhelming volume of sweet, happy thoughts filled him until he thought he'd burst.

He took Libby's hand and drew her back to Eleanor's side. He sat on the pew and pulled a girl onto each knee. "I want to tell you something."

Clara fought a mixture of emotions. Why had he bought the girls such an expensive gift? She could never afford to pay him back. But how could she deny her daughters this pleasure, especially when she had nothing else to offer them? It would have to serve as their Christmas present even though it was obvious the pair had something else in mind.

Her insides twisted with regret that she would likely fail in providing whatever it was.

Still, it was just too extravagant. She couldn't allow it. Just as she was about to open her mouth and refuse the gift, Blue pulled the girls to his knees and started to talk.

"I once had two children who would be much your age."

Every protest died on Clara's lips, and she held her breath, waiting for him to continue. Was this an answer to her prayer that he would leave the desert and move forward?

"You did?" Libby sounded surprised and a little curious.

"Yes, a girl named Nancy and a boy named Beau."

"What happened to them?" Eleanor asked, her voice cautious as if fearing it was something bad.

Clara knew it was and wondered how Blue would explain it.

"There was a fire." His voice broke, and he couldn't go on.

Eleanor wrapped one arm about his neck and pressed her head to his. "And they died?"

He nodded.

From where she stood, rooted to the floor, Clara saw his mouth twist. Her heart went out to him. Oh, the pain of such a loss. It was unimaginable.

Libby's eyes grew wide. "Did Nancy have a doll like ours?"

Blue smiled. "She had a very nice doll her mama made her. She loved it so much she almost wore it out."

Libby looked pleased. "I guess she was happy."

"How do you know?" Blue asked.

"'Cause her mama loved her 'nough to make a special dolly and 'cause she had you for a papa."

Blue sucked in air and squeezed his eyes shut tight. When he opened them, they met hers over the girls' head. His eyes darkened with soul-deep sorrow.

Oh, Blue. She rushed to his side and sat next to Libby on the pew. She draped her arm about his neck, over Eleanor's cradling arm and pressed her head to his shoulder.

"I 'spect Beau was happy, too," Libby said.

Blue nodded.

Eleanor patted Blue's neck. "But you miss them lots—don't you?"

When she felt a shudder ripple down Blue's arm, Clara pressed her hand to his to still it.

"That's very sad." Eleanor kissed his cheek.

Beneath her palm, Clara felt Blue's arm jolt.

"We'd be your little girls if Mama would let us," Eleanor said, and Libby nodded agreement.

The statement rocked Clara clear to her core. She'd done her best to protect her daughters against this kind of hopeless wishing, against the pain that would come. She'd tried and failed. She must have a long talk with them this evening and make them understand how impossible their wishes were.

"Girls, take the doll and go play with her. Mind you don't get her dirty."

"We won't," they chorused in unison and eased off Blue's knee. Together they carried the box containing the doll to their favorite corner and carefully lifted the lid and removed her.

For a moment Clara enjoyed observing their pleasure and how they cooperated. Then she pulled her thoughts back to Blue and tried to think what to say. So many things ran through her head but only one of them formed into a reasonable thought.

"Blue, I wish you hadn't done that." She no longer had her arm about his neck and their arms barely touched, but nevertheless she felt him jolt.

"How can I move forward unless I tell people about my children?"

"True, but that's not what I meant."

"You mean the doll? Are you going to let your stubborn pride get in the way of someone else giving your girls a tiny bit of enjoyment?"

His head came around slowly, and his gaze rested on her, but she kept her attention on the girls. His words made her feel small and uncharitable.

She shrugged helplessly and lifted her eyes to his. She saw the barely contained emotion there. "I've made you angry."

"Yes. It seems wrong to let pride so influence one's choices that the children pay."

"I—" What could she say? How could she explain? "You need to understand something." But dare she tell him? She examined her choices. It wasn't as if he didn't know she was running from someone. Or that she could hope to remain anonymous and invisible. How many questions would her father have to ask for anyone to realize she was the woman he sought even though she'd disguised her name?

It wasn't that she didn't trust Blue to keep her secret. Seemed he had lots of practice in keeping secrets.

She rose and went to one of the windows that gave her a view of town. But what would he do if he knew?

Would he try and persuade her to stay and let him take care of her?

The idea was so tempting. But the girls weren't his. Would Father still take them away? Could he? He'd surely think he had the right, and how would she prevent it? And wouldn't the law stand behind him? It wasn't a risk she was willing to take.

A rider approached from the far side of town, and she watched him with detached interest. However, when he didn't rein in at the livery barn, and then passed Macpherson's store without stopping, all the while carefully looking from side to side, her nerves began to twitch.

The rider drew closer to the church. His hat was pulled low so she couldn't see his eyes, and his mouth drew down in a harsh, threatening line. He looked directly at the window.

She jerked away and pressed to the wall, her hands balled to her chest as if she could still the pounding of her heart.

He was a man looking for someone. Had her father sent him?

"Clara?" Blue gave her a curious look.

She held up a hand to signal him to be quiet and strained to hear the passing hoofbeats. Did they pause in front of the church?

She mentally measured the distance to where the girls played. Could she grab them and dash out the back door before the rider opened the street door?

She took a step on faltering legs, then heard the horse walk by. Clara edged toward the windows on the other side, careful to stay out of sight.

Her lungs emptied with a whoosh when she saw horse and rider leaving town.

Her faltering legs turned to pudding, and she crumpled to the floor.

Blue squatted at her side. "Clara, what's wrong?"

She grabbed one of his hands and hung on, finding strength. "That man."

He nodded. "The one that rode through town just now? Do you know him?"

She rocked her head back and forth. "I don't think so, but he might be looking for me."

He sat beside her, his back pressed to the wall, his shoulder against hers a source of encouragement, his hand still gripped in hers. She had no intention of letting go until her insides stopped quaking.

"Why would he be looking for you?"

She checked on the girls. They played contentedly with the doll and were out of earshot. "My father might have hired him." She forced herself to take three slow breaths.

Blue waited silently, not moving, not rushing her, making no demands.

His patience steadied her. "I told you my father is controlling. That's not the worst. He thinks I am incapable of taking care of myself, let alone the girls." She told him how she'd been raised. How she'd gone home after her husband's death. How she had discovered the girls were learning the same helplessness she'd learned.

Blue chuckled at little at that. "You're about as helpless as a grizzly bear. In fact, you make me think of something Alice used to say. 'Sooner come between a mother bear and her cubs than a mother and her children.' You are as fierce as any bear."

"Thanks. I think. But Father doesn't see it that way. When I said I wanted to be in my own home, he bluntly refused and said if I tried to make my own way, he'd take the girls from me."

"So you ran?"

She nodded, misery flooding her eyes. "But I know he won't leave it at that. He'll find me." She closed her eyes and thought of all the places they'd been and how obvious they were. "A woman traveling with two girls isn't hard to notice. He might have hired someone to find me for him."

"It appears that rider had something else on his mind. He rode right through without even stopping."

Clara nodded. "I wish it made me feel better, but it doesn't. I know it's only a matter of time until Father or a hireling finds me." She bolted to her feet and crossed the room from one side to the other, checking the windows.

Blue waited until she stopped flying about, then came to her side.

"So what do you plan to do?"

She faced him. "I trust you'll not repeat a word of this to anyone."

He held her gaze without his expression changing.

She nodded, satisfied, though she'd known he wouldn't even without asking. She shifted her attention, saw Eleanor watching her and smiled as reassuringly as she could.

Eleanor seemed satisfied and turned back to playing with the doll.

"Let's go to the entryway." She went to the little room separated from the sanctuary part of the church by a half-constructed wall. The girls wouldn't be able to see them or hear what she had to say.

Blue followed, leaned against the wall and waited.

She paced in the tiny space, twisting her hands as her mind went round and round with what-ifs and if-onlys.

He caught her hands and pulled her to a halt facing him. His gentle smile calmed her.

"My plan is to go to Fort Calgary, where I hope there is a job waiting for me on a farm out of town." She told him of writing in answer to a notice about a man needing someone to care for his children. She omitted the worry that her letter might still be en route. "I thought I'd be there by now, but Petey said he had to go to Fort Macleod. As soon as he comes back, he said he'd make the trip."

Blue rubbed the backs of her hands with his thumbs. "What makes you think you'll be safe there?"

She lowered her head, unwilling to admit she had no assurances.

"Seems to me," Blue added, "if your father is that determined, he'll find you."

"I'm hoping winter will prevent him from traveling, and then perhaps by spring he'll reconsider. By then, I hope I'll have proof I can manage on my own."

"And if he doesn't accept it?"

She brought her fierce gaze to him. "I hope and pray I can stay one step ahead of him."

He smiled. His eyes filled with compassion. "Clara, are you going to run forever?"

"I will never let Father take the girls from me." Tears clogged her throat.

He pulled her to him, and she buried her face against his broad, strong chest.

He patted her back gently. It calmed her fractured nerves, and she released a heart-easing sigh and sank deeper into his embrace. Oh, if only she could find this safety in her entire life, not just in a moment of crisis.

"You deserve better. You and the girls."

His voice rumbled beneath her ears. "Better would be nice, but Father is a stubborn, prideful man."

His chuckle bounced his chest, and she smiled.

He said, "I'd say it was a strong family trait."

She felt a faint desire to argue, but it quickly faded. Instead, she smiled against his shirtfront. "The only thing I've ever been stubborn about is keeping my girls."

"Then perhaps you need to accept help."

She reluctantly pushed away from his arms. "But don't you see? The only way I can hope to convince my father I am responsible enough to take care of the girls is to prove I can manage on my own."

His hands rested on her arms, enticing her to return to his embrace. But she stepped back.

Like she'd said, she had to prove she was strong and capable, and that meant not leaning on any man. Physically or emotionally.

She put the distance of two more feet between them. Far enough that she could resist the temptation of his arms. "You've been very kind to us, and I'm afraid I'll never be able to repay you."

He made a protesting noise, but she continued. "Perhaps one day you will be able to move forward into a new life. That would please me."

Unable to remain in the small space and resist all he offered, she returned to the larger room and went to the girls. "Have you named your doll?"

"Mary," they said in unison.

"Good choice. Now you have a friend again."

She spent the rest of the morning trying to work without looking at Blue, without giving him a chance to say anything more about her decision. If once or twice she caught herself watching him when he was otherwise occupied, she excused it as regret over having drawn him into her problems.

It was time to rebuild the walls around her life— walls she'd never meant to break down in the first place.

Chapter Twelve

Blue's brain filled with a hundred thoughts. He tried to sort them into some kind of order. Certainly he was pleased that the girls had welcomed the doll and Clara had allowed them to keep it. But the feeling paled in comparison to his worry about their safety. There must be something he could do.

He pressed his hand to his cheek; then he realized it was the same spot Eleanor had kissed when she offered to be his girl. A smile tugged at his mouth and warmed his eyes. He'd like two little girls. He'd like to be able to take care of them and their mama. Their stubborn, proud mama.

His smile faltered. His chest tightened.

Could Clara's father take the children? Blue wasn't sure what the law would say, but it seemed those in authority often measured a person's worth by the size of their purse, which left Clara with little defense.

He should take them to the ranch. They'd be safe there.

"Clara, can we talk?" Surely he could persuade her.

He'd tell her of the others who'd been threatened and how they'd found safety at the Eden Valley Ranch.

"Do you need me to help measure?"

"No, I have a suggestion."

She shook her head.

"You don't need to run," he whispered hoarsely.

She ducked her head and ran her finger up and down the piece of wood she worked on. "You don't know my father, so how can you say that? You know what it's like to lose your children. Do you think I'm willing to risk losing mine?"

Of course he didn't, but he felt as if he was about to lose two children and a woman and live his pain all over again. Only this time he'd wonder if they were safe and if he couldn't have done more.

"Leave it be," she said.

He knew by the stubborn set of her mouth that she wouldn't entertain any more discussion on the matter.

Swallowing a bitter taste in the back of his mouth, he turned to the work at hand.

How long would she run? To where? Who would make sure they were safe?

He would. He'd go with them. Oh, she'd protest, but she couldn't stop him. Anyone who could pay for passage could ride the stagecoach. The matter settled in his mind, he relaxed.

If he thought his decision would make her relax, too, he would have voiced it. But he knew he was wiser to keep the information to himself, so they spent the rest of the day in strained silence, speaking only when it was essential.

The girls, thankfully, were too occupied with their doll to notice.

At the meal Bonnie and Claude might have wondered at the tension between Blue and Clara, except the girls chattered nonstop about their doll.

After supper, he trudged across to the church. Restless, unable to concentrate on his book, he wandered about the building. His steps stalled at the main door. He and Clara had stood there as she confessed her plan. He stared at the spot where he'd held her in his arms. She'd fit so neatly, her head tucked under his chin, her arms around his waist.

He realized he pressed one palm to his chest as if he were holding her there, and he pulled his hand away. She didn't belong with him, wouldn't stay in Edendale. Nevertheless, he wasn't about to let her venture out into the wild north on her own.

The thud of a passing horse stole his attention, and he hurried to the window. It was the same rider who had passed earlier. Blue recognized the same harsh set of his mouth, the same guarded watching as if he was looking for someone.

Blue drew back even though he was certain the man couldn't see into the darkened building. Good thing he hadn't lit the lantern yet, or the man's attention would be drawn in this direction. He might be curious enough, interested enough, to investigate further.

The man rode on by, and Blue crossed to the other side to watch him make his way into town. He stopped at Macpherson's and dismounted. The man walked with purpose toward the store, glancing right and left before he entered.

Would he ask Macpherson about a woman and two girls? Like Clara said, the trio drew attention wherever they went and not solely because they traveled alone.

The man reappeared carrying a small bundle and rode out of town.

Blue's brow knitted. Why would a man ride through town one way in the morning and back the other way in the evening?

If anyone knew the answer, Macpherson would.

Blue donned his coat and left by way of the main door. He strode casually to the store as if he had nothing in particular in mind.

Macpherson was about to lock up when Blue reached the store. "You need another doll? 'Cause I'm plumb out."

"Just want some candy."

Macpherson opened the door for Blue to enter. "You're a constant surprise, Blue Lyons."

"Thanks."

Macpherson hadn't meant it as a compliment and chuckled.

Blue went to the candy display to choose his favorites. "Didn't I see someone leaving just before I got here?"

"You did."

"Don't think I recognized him."

"Neither did I, though I've seen plenty like him." Macpherson leaned against the counter as Blue slowly picked out a licorice stick and then a cinnamon one.

"How's that?" Blue asked in an almost bored voice as if making reluctant conversation while inside he burned with a need to know everything about the stranger.

"Hard. The sort of man who offers no information and lets it be known he wouldn't welcome questions."

Blue nodded. He'd met plenty of the same.

Macpherson quirked an eyebrow. "Sort of like you used to be."

Used to be? Had he changed? Perhaps he had. Whether it was for the good or the bad, he couldn't say.

"The stranger was just passing by, then?"

"He didn't say, and I didn't ask. You about done?"

Blue paid for the candy and left. As he stepped from the store, he searched left and right. Seemed the man had passed through, indeed. He wasn't a threat to Clara and the girls.

Exhaling the breath he didn't know he held, he returned to the church.

That same sense of relief lingered over the next two days. Still, as he worked beside her, he constantly considered what options he could present to her. Going to the ranch still seemed ideal. Following her came in second. He wanted Clara to never have to run in fear again, but he could think of no way to ensure that.

Midafternoon of the second day, Clara passed a window and ground to a halt. Her face blanched. "Blue."

At the quiet desperation in her voice, he hurried to her side.

"It's him."

The same rider who had sent her into a panic a few days ago rode down the street, his hat hiding most of his face yet giving Blue a good view of the hard set of his mouth.

The muscles along Blue's spine tightened, and he drew Clara away from the window.

"Who is he, and what does he want?" she whispered, clinging to his arm.

"I don't know." But he intended to find out. He watched the man saunter by and again leave town by the other direction. Blue knew the trails that led from town. One would take the rider to the Eden Valley Ranch. One would take him to the northwest toward a number of other ranches, including the big OK Ranch and several smaller ones. If the rider angled toward the south, he would enter a reservation. If any of them had been the rider's destination, he would have continued in that direction earlier in the week.

"He doesn't seem to be interested in people in town." He hoped the words would give Clara some reassurance.

She shuddered, and he wrapped an arm around her shoulders and held her to his side.

"If only you'd let me help," he whispered.

"Seems to me I am and have been for the better part of two weeks. What I should have done was find a way to continue my journey."

They both knew there was no way to get to Fort Calgary unless someone took her. Something he wasn't about to do. He pressed his cheek to her head and held her until she relaxed. Still, neither of them seemed inclined to end the moment.

He breathed in the lemony scent of her soap, the aroma of wood and smoke. His arms must have tightened for she turned to look into his face, her eyes full of contentment.

"I suppose I am worrying about nothing," she said with a sigh. "He's likely just some wandering cowboy."

Blue didn't believe it and suspected she didn't, either.

He didn't want to alarm Clara, so he said nothing of his plans and waited until after supper to ride west, following the direction the rider had taken. At the fork of the trails, he paused. Should he go north, south or west? He chose north and rode on for another twenty minutes or so in the growing dusk, always watching for any sign of the man he sought.

He caught the glow of a campfire by the river and turned aside from the trail. "Hello?" he called and waited for acknowledgment. He didn't think this was the sort of man he wanted to ride in on without announcing his presence.

A man emerged from the shadows. The stranger he sought. He still wore his hat, pulled low over his eyes, his mouth drawn into an unfriendly frown.

Blue rode in even though the man had not offered an invitation. He dismounted. "Coffee sure smells good."

The man handed him a tin cup and filled it from the pot.

Blue hunkered down. "You a stranger hereabouts?"

The man sat nearby, his legs crossed, both hands cradling his cup. "Yeah."

"Got a destination in mind?"

"Maybe."

"Bad time of year to be looking for work on one of the ranches."

"Guess so."

"'Course a man could run a trapline."

"I suppose."

The man sure wasn't about to share any personal information, and Blue wasn't used to making conversation. He had run out of questions he could ask without the man taking offense.

Blue downed the rest of his coffee and handed the cup back. "Thanks. I best be getting on my way."

"Safe travels."

Blue added, "I work at the Eden Valley Ranch to

the west." Let the man think that was his destination. Though he might wonder why Blue had come this way.

"Oh, yeah?"

"Good place."

The only acknowledgment was a grunt.

Blue knew he'd get nothing more and swung into his saddle and rode away. He'd learned nothing, and that left him edgy. Could be the man was a loner, or he could be looking for someone and not wanting to reveal his intention.

It was dark by the time he returned to the church. The glow of a lamp came through the canvas of the shack. At least Clara and her daughters were close by where he could keep a watch on them and make sure they were safe.

He fell into a troubled sleep filled with dreams of a dark, forbidding stranger who chased Clara and the girls. Blue tried to catch them to rescue them, but every time he got within reach, a fire flared up blocking his way.

Smoke filled his senses.

He jerked awake, feeling sweat beaded on his brow. It was only a dream, he told himself.

But the smell of smoke lingered. He breathed deeply to clear his mind of the thought, but the smell only grew more real.

His heart slammed into his chest. It was real. He leaped to his feet, pulled on his trousers and boots and snagged his coat as he rushed outside.

He saw no flames. But the smell intensified. He turned his head back and forth, sniffing to pinpoint a direction. It seemed to come from the Mortons' house, and he raced toward the yard.

He passed the shack and slowed his feet. Still no flames, which provided a flicker of relief. But the smell of smoke grew stronger. He squinted into the darkness and saw a faint glow. He hurried over to the ash pile and saw that the wind had fanned some of the embers into life.

He found a shovel nearby and smacked the coals till they were out. To be safe he pumped a bucket of water and dowsed the ash pile. Exhausted by the effort but even more by the fright rushing through his veins, he leaned over the shovel handle.

The Mortons' door opened, and Claude stepped out, holding a lantern high. "Blue? Is that you? What's going on?" Behind the man, Blue saw Bonnie hovering in the doorway.

"Coals were smoldering. The smell woke me up."

Claude held the lantern up to look at the pile. "Looks like it's out now."

"Yeah."

The door of the shack opened, and Clara slipped out, wrapped in her coat. Her blond hair hung loose in waves that caught the glow of Claude's lamp.

"What's wrong?" she asked.

Blue explained again.

Clara's eyes widened. "What if—" She choked off the question.

Blue wanted to assure her they'd never been in danger. Not really. Claude had wisely put the ash pile a good distance from any building. But if the wind had grown stronger, if some stray leaves had fallen on the coals and then blown to the canvas roof of the shack…

He shuddered as the memory of flames filled his thoughts. He tried to stop the vision, the agony, but his throat tightened and a groan ripped from his gut. He tried to keep it from escaping but couldn't.

Clara came to his side and pressed her hand to his arm.

He concentrated on her touch, finding escape from his fear.

"We're all safe, thanks to you," she murmured.

"Yes, Blue. Thanks for catching this." Claude clamped a hand to Blue's shoulder. "I'll be more careful with the ashes in the future."

For a moment, no one moved. Then Claude dropped his hand. "Seems everything is okay now. We should all return to our beds." He held the lantern high to light the way for Clara.

She patted Blue's arm, then hurried to the shack.

Blue waited until she closed the door. He handed Claude the shovel and trekked back to the church. He leaned against the door and waited for his ragged breathing to return to normal.

One thing was certain. Clara and the girls were not safe in that shack. Not only did the dark stranger pose a threat, but now Blue would never feel the shack provided any protection from fire.

He shuddered.

If anything happened to them… He bent over his knees as pain ground through him.

After a moment, he forced himself to straighten. His mind was made up. She couldn't stay there.

Now all he had to do was convince Clara.

Clara huddled under her covers and tried to dismiss the fear that had gripped her when she'd heard the noise outside. Her first thought was that the man had come.

She'd felt trapped in the shack. Her only defense was a broom, and she had clutched it and stood in the dark, poised to defend herself and the girls.

Then she'd heard Blue and Claude talking and hurried outside to see what was going on. It had been coals glowing in the ash pile. It seemed so insignificant in light of the threat she'd imagined that she had let out a sigh of relief. Then she'd realized how the thought of a fire had frightened Blue. She wanted to say there had never been any danger. The embers would burn themselves out. But she knew all he would think was how his family had perished in a fire.

She longed to be able to offer more comfort than a brush of her hand on his arm and vowed she would do so the next morning.

He joined them for breakfast and was quieter than usual. Libby had to ask him a question twice before he answered.

Clara hoped she could relieve his mind. She'd explain how she kept a bucket of water nearby and how she positioned herself and the girls so they could escape quickly.

She took the girls to the church once they'd finished breakfast and waited until they went outside to get snow before she approached Blue.

There was a tightness about his mouth she hadn't seen for many days. She faced him, her hands on his arms. "About last night—"

"You can't stay there."

She blinked at his harsh words, then took a calming breath. He was naturally overly concerned about fires. "Blue, we were never in danger."

He gripped her shoulder. "How can you say that? Do

you know how little it would take to start that shack on fire? And how quickly it would burn?"

"That's why we sleep close to the door." She refused to let his words frighten her.

"And that man! I followed him last evening and spoke to him. He's hiding something. And why does he hang about town? He's looking for someone."

It was a fear she couldn't deny. She shivered. "What do you suggest I do?"

"Let me take you to the ranch."

She considered the offer. It would be nice to feel safe. But if that man was searching for her, how hard would it be to go to the ranch? Not nearly hard enough.

"My best chance is still to head north," she said. Even to her ears it sounded less and less like a reasonable option. But it was still the only way she could think of that would prove herself capable of keeping her girls. She repeated her belief. "Unless I can prove I can do this on my own, I will never be able to defend myself against my father."

Blue went to a window and stared out. He jammed his hands in the front pockets of his trousers, then turned to face her. "At least let me take you to the ranch tonight. We can stay overnight and attend church tomorrow."

"What if Petey comes while I'm gone?"

"He won't leave on a Sunday. He'll spend the day visiting with Rufus. They're old friends."

"You're sure?"

As if sensing her weakening, he added, "I'll ask Rufus to tell Petey so he'll wait. The man isn't about to turn down paying customers."

It would be nice to feel safe for a few hours and to

attend a real worship service. "You're sure we won't be an imposition?"

He chuckled. "The boss's wife always welcomes travelers. She'd love to see you and the girls."

Clara hovered between the need to prove she could manage on her own and the desire to attend church. Then she made up her mind. Surely it didn't make her look weak to spend a Sunday worshiping. In fact, it might prove what a good parent she was—making sure the girls got their religious instruction. "Fine. I'd love to go to church with you."

He blinked as if surprised at her agreement. "Really?"

She laughed, although she felt somewhat annoyed. "Why did you ask if you expected me to refuse?"

"Because I'm worried. I don't want to see anything happen to you or the girls."

Her annoyance fled, replaced with gratitude for his concern. "Blue, you're a good man."

She watched, surprised, as he turned pink beneath his tan. She chuckled. "Not used to hearing compliments?"

He merely shrugged. "Shall we leave after dinner?"

She considered. She would have preferred to wait and make sure Petey didn't arrive with the stagecoach, but Blue seemed convinced the stagecoach driver would want to spend a day with his friend. "So long as you can assure me the stagecoach won't leave without me."

"I can do that."

The girls returned, their cheeks rosy from playing in the snow. They set the buckets down and hung their coats on the hooks by the door, then withdrew to their favorite corner to play with their doll.

Blue and Clara turned their attention to the work left to do, though Clara's thoughts drifted away several times. Blue seemed to truly care about her safety and that of the girls. Like she'd said, he was a good man. *He should really remarry. He has so much to offer. He—*

Not knowing where those thoughts came from, she slammed the door on them right quick.

If Blue Lyons chose to marry or otherwise, it was none of her concern. She had her own issues to worry about. There was no room in her life for wondering if Blue would ever consider taking another wife.

So why couldn't she stop wondering what it would be like to be married to a man who treated her like an equal and yet showed tenderness and concern?

Chapter Thirteen

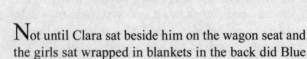

Not until Clara sat beside him on the wagon seat and the girls sat wrapped in blankets in the back did Blue really believe she had agreed to go to the ranch.

As they journeyed along the road, she looked about with interest and asked questions. Did he know the name of that mountain or that one? How far back into the hills did the ranch go? How long had Eddie been ranching here?

All too soon they approached their destination. She sat forward when she saw the big house. "That's a ranch house?" She seemed impressed.

He laughed. "Eddie's father wanted a replica of the estate back in England. From what I hear, he wasn't too pleased when Eddie married Linette and she said she meant to use the extra rooms to provide home and shelter for those in need of it."

"Yet Eddie let her do so?"

He laughed again. "I don't know if he would even try and stop her. Linette is very strong natured."

She shifted her attention to the rest of the buildings,

laid out like a little town. "There's a lot of cabins and barns."

"The cabins and house are for married cowboys and their wives." For some reason it no longer annoyed him to think of how many of the crew had married.

They reached the house, and Linette stepped out. "Blue, nice of you to bring me company. You must be Mrs. Weston. My husband told me you were helping at the church."

Blue helped Clara down and introduced the women. He signaled the two curious girls forward and introduced them, as well.

"Do come in and have tea. You, too, Blue."

He would normally go down to the cookhouse and beg a cinnamon roll off Cookie, but he allowed himself to be shepherded inside with Clara and the girls.

Linette, heavy with child, led them through the house to the big kitchen. She expected to have the baby before Christmas, which was three weeks away. For the first time in two years, he looked forward to the day. He'd spend it with Clara and the girls wherever they went.

Eddie threw open the back door and stepped inside. "Company. How nice." After Blue introduced them, he asked, "Are you done with the pews?"

"Not yet, but Clara wanted to attend church here tomorrow."

Clara's look warned him not to tell the whole truth.

He acknowledged her with a quirk of his eyebrows, silently promising he wouldn't say any more about her reasons and fears than she herself was willing to tell.

Five-year-old Grady raced into the room and skidded to a halt at the sight of two girls.

Linette introduced their adopted son. "Grady, take the girls and show them your toys."

Libby was already on her feet, ready to join him, but Eleanor hung back.

"It's okay, little one," Blue reassured her. "Grady has a fine collection of carved animals to play with."

She nodded and joined the other two. They retreated to a corner of the room where Grady showed them a basket of his toys.

As she served tea, Linette tried to draw Clara out, but Clara grew quiet, not talking about her father or her plans. Did Linette think the woman was shy or secretive? Before Blue could determine which, she turned the conversation to ranch news.

Clara perked up as Linette told her the history of each couple on the ranch and those who had moved on. Her eyes flashed with what he took as surprise. "Blue told me some of this, but it's truly amazing at how these women overcame obstacles."

Eddie chuckled. "If you stay around, you'll soon learn that the women here are strong and perhaps a little stubborn." He gave Linette a teasing look.

"Sometimes women have to be," she said.

Blue contemplated Linette's words along with Clara's plan to escape her father. Could she be persuaded to change her mind and find safety here?

Eddie pushed from the table. "I need to get down to the barn. Blue, feel free to take the day off. Maybe Clara would like to see the rest of the ranch."

Blue turned to Clara. "Would you?" He'd like a chance to talk to her about the role of women on the ranch.

She turned to the girls.

"They're welcome to stay here and play," Linette said.

"Very well, then." She spoke to the girls, who seemed content to stay behind.

Blue escorted her outside and down the hill. He pointed out the cookhouse. "Cookie makes the best cinnamon rolls. You'll get a chance to taste them tomorrow. Her husband, Bertie, leads the Sunday service."

They continued on their way. He pointed to the cabin where Eddie's sister, Jayne, and her husband, Seth, lived. "Jayne's friend, Sybil, lives in that cabin with her husband, Brand." He pointed to a new cabin beyond the first. They continued on their way. He pointed out the house where Cassie and Roper and their four children lived.

"Cassie's the one who started Bonnie and Claude's business, isn't she?" Clara stared at the house a moment, a thoughtful look on her face.

"That's right." Was she seeing how these women faced challenges and dangers and refused to budge? He led her over the bridge, past the wintering pens and up the hill. Would she see how safe and protected these women were? How valued? No one would dare suggest to Linette that she couldn't do anything she put her mind to. The same went for the others.

They reached the top of the hill, and a cold breeze caused them to draw back into the shelter of the trees.

Maybe Clara would decide to stay.

And if she did, was he prepared to open his life, his heart to more pain?

It hardly seemed worth it.

And yet, hadn't Clara and the girls already claimed a large portion of his heart?

That didn't matter. His concern was to persuade her

to stay on the ranch where she would be surrounded by people willing to protect her and the girls. Where he could make certain she was safe.

As his thoughts whirled, he continued to tell her about the others. "Seth and Brand and their wives are only spending the winter in the cabins. They have plans to start their own ranches come spring."

"Do you have similar desires?"

"I don't think about it much."

She stood before him, her blue eyes searching his thoughts. "Don't you want a place of your own? I can't imagine anything better."

Her piercing gaze made it difficult to think clearly. But one question surfaced. "Did you not have such a place when you were married?"

She shrugged. "It was always Rolland's, and he made certain I understood that. He was much older than I and grew feeble, which allowed me some measure of freedom. I gave it up all too readily when he passed. Not that I had much choice. Father is executor of the monies Rolland left." Her expression grew troubled.

Wanting to comfort her, he pulled her to his chest. "They were both sorely mistaken about your abilities, weren't they?"

"What do you mean?" She looked up at him, her eyes begging for reassurance.

"They don't know how strong you are, do they?"

"I am?"

He studied her flawless skin. It reminded him of the porcelain face on the doll he'd bought the girls. Her eyes were so blue he felt as if he'd stepped into a summer day. His gaze lingered on her mouth. Then he realized she waited for his answer.

"You can make a fine church pew. You can find your way across the country while taking care of two children. I'd say that was evidence enough." He'd said it before but she needed to hear it again.

Her eyes darkened, revealing how hungry she was for such acknowledgment.

The smile on his lips carried a gentleness he'd grown unfamiliar with. "Clara, you are strong and sweet, independent, gentle, stubborn and loving."

She held his gaze as the moment ticked by, full of expectation and hope and things he'd forgotten to believe in.

There was only one thing to do in response. He lowered his head and claimed her lips.

She was everything he'd imagined. Strong and at the same time yielding. Her arms came around his waist, and she pressed her hands to his back, letting him know she wanted this kiss as much as he did.

His heart filled with such sweetness he stifled a groan and lifted his mouth from hers. He pressed her head to the hollow of his shoulder and held her tightly. She snuggled close and sighed, the sound of contentment.

He looked out at the snow-dusted landscape. Did this mean she would stay? He would ask, but he didn't want to spoil the richness of the moment. He'd bring up the matter later.

For now, he wanted to enjoy the feel of Clara in his arms.

Clara rested in Blue's embrace, safe and cherished. She couldn't say what the kiss had meant on Blue's behalf. Goodness, she couldn't even say what it meant on her behalf. Or why she'd even allowed it. Perhaps because of the hope and acceptance she felt at Eden Valley Ranch. From what she'd heard of the women who lived here, they were allowed to be strong and independent. They had all found a marriage where they were valued and their strengths acknowledged.

Was such possible for Clara?

Perhaps, if she could believe her father would not take her children away. She had to deal with that fear. But for now, she simply wanted to forget her troubles and enjoy the encouragement Blue had given.

"It's getting cold," Blue said. "We need to get back."

She made a tiny sound of protest, then realized how weak it made her sound and straightened. She didn't mind that he kept his arm around her shoulders.

It remained there as they made their leisurely way down the hill. Not until they reached the pens did he drop his arm to his side.

That unfamiliar sound of protest again came to her lips.

He walked her up the hill to the big house. "I'll leave you here."

"Where are you going?"

"I'll eat at the cookhouse, then join the other cowboys in the bunkhouse."

She reached for his hand, feeling a sense of abandonment. "But I don't know Linette and Eddie."

He smiled. "You know them well enough. You'll be fine. I'll see you at church tomorrow."

She clung to his hand. Where was the strength he said she had? She was acting like a weakling.

"Of course, I'll be fine." She forced herself to drop his hand. "Enjoy visiting with your friends." She reached for the doorknob then hesitated. It was harder to say goodbye than it should be. "Thank you for the tour of the ranch."

"Thank you for the kiss," he murmured.

Heat raced up her neck and stung her cheeks. Yet she was pleased to know he'd enjoyed it, too.

"Until tomorrow, then." Her hand lingered on the knob without turning it. What was she waiting for?

"Until tomorrow." He trailed his knuckles along her jawline.

That's what she was waiting for, though she hadn't known it.

A touch to convince her she hadn't imagined the tender moment between them.

She stepped inside, hung her coat inside the door and followed the sounds of the children back to the kitchen.

Linette smiled at her entrance. "What do you think of our ranch?"

"It's very nice." Though it wasn't the ranch she thought of. It was the way Blue had kissed her and held her and called her strong.

She held back a sigh. Was she strong enough to do what she must?

Linette pressed her hand to the small of her back. "This little one is getting heavy."

"Why don't you sit and tell me what to do?"

"You wouldn't mind?"

"Not at all." She checked the potatoes and sliced bread at Linette's request. "When is your baby due?"

"Soon, before Christmas, I hope, but I don't mind confessing I'd be happy for it to come any day. Clara—you don't mind if I call you that?"

Clara shook her head.

"Did you have a doctor when your girls were born?"

She nodded. "We lived in Toronto, and my husband insisted on the finest doctor in the city."

"We have no doctor." Linette gave a brave smile. "This is my first, so I'm not sure what to expect."

Clara's gaze went to Grady. "Your first?"

"We adopted Grady. I met his mother on the ship over. She died before we reached shore." Her eyes lit lovingly on her son before she turned back to Clara. "What's it like?"

Clara knew she meant delivering a baby. As they sat across from each other at the table, she told Linette what to expect. "And then they put the baby in your arms, and you fall instantly in love, amazed that you are responsible for creating this perfect little life." Warmth filled her heart as she watched Eleanor and Libby playing. Nothing mattered but these two children. Not her own wishes, not her desire for a real family. Nothing but keeping them safe and with her.

Eddie returned a few minutes later, and Clara called the girls to help set the table.

After the meal, she insisted Linette sit while she cleaned the kitchen. "Is there anything else?"

"Oh, you've done plenty already, and I appreciate it."

Clara laughed. "I recognize an evasive answer when I hear it. What else do you need done?"

"I always prepare a big meal for Sunday dinner. If the vegetables were prepared and something for dessert…" She trailed off. "It's unfair of me to even suggest it to a guest."

Clara waved away her protests. "Then think of me as a friend."

"I'd love to."

Clara, with direction from Linette, prepared vegetables and a baked pudding.

The girls and Grady played happily enough, but Clara caught a whining tone in Libby's voice. "The girls are getting tired." As was Linette. "They won't go to bed in an unfamiliar place unless I'm with them."

"I'll show you to your room." Linette led her down the hall.

Eddie was in the library working at a big desk. He glanced up as Linette paused at the door. "Going to bed? I'll be up in a bit. Good night."

They climbed the wide staircase, and Linette showed Clara to a nice room with a bed wide enough for the three of them to sleep together.

As soon as the door closed, Eleanor turned to Clara. "A bed just like we used to have."

Libby's bottom lip came out. "I'd sleep on the floor forever if it meant we could stay with Blue."

Clara helped them prepare for bed. "Libby, we've talked about this many times. We can't stay."

"Why not?" Libby clearly did not like Clara's decision.

Clara was tired of this oft-repeated argument. "Because I said so."

She heard the girls' prayers and tucked them into bed. She crawled in the far side and turned out the lamp.

The women here were strong and independent to a degree that made her ache. If only she could find the same. Could she if she stayed here? Maybe not on the ranch but in the area where the women seemed to have what she wanted. And maybe with someone who saw her strengths.

Like Blue.

Her heart twisted with regret that it wasn't possible.

Chapter Fourteen

Blue rose early Sunday morning. He put on his best duds, which in truth were nothing special. Only a white shirt with blue stripes, a newish pair of black pants and a black string tie.

The other cowboys watched out of the corner of their eyes. The youngest, Buster, was openly curious. "You courtin' that woman?"

Blue took his time about brushing his hair into place before he answered. "What makes you think that?"

Buster shrugged. "Ain't never seen you fuss so much about getting ready."

"You just weren't paying attention."

Buster nodded, understanding the conversation was closed, and grabbed his hat and left the bunkhouse.

Blue watched him depart, hoping he hadn't offended the young man. But he was glad to see him go because with Buster gone Blue could head over to the cookhouse without looking too eager. The morning had seemed awfully long so far.

He grabbed his hat, placed it carefully on his head and left.

No one came down the hill. Either they hadn't left the big house or they were already inside. He picked up his pace in case it was the latter.

He hadn't seen Clara since shortly after he'd kissed her, and all night he'd thought of that kiss. He'd tried to convince himself it was only a gesture of comfort. But he'd failed entirely. Something between them had shifted. He didn't know what it meant nor how to proceed from here.

What did he want?

What did she want?

He could answer, in part, for himself. He wanted her to stay on the ranch where he believed she and the girls would be safe.

And where he could see her on a regular basis? He wouldn't answer the question except to remind himself again that caring for someone carried the risk of being hurt. He stepped into the cookhouse. No one from the big house was there yet. And no, he wasn't disappointed. They'd be along in time.

Cookie barreled down on him, enfolded him in her motherly arms and whacked his back hard enough to make most men stumble. But he'd learned to be ready for her greeting. "Where were you last week?" she asked. "We missed you." She'd already seen him and greeted him at breakfast, but that didn't stop her from repeating herself. She didn't wait for him to answer as Seth and Jayne entered, and she turned her attention to them.

"Howdy, Blue." Seth held out a hand, and the two shook.

A steady stream of people started to file in. Finally,

Eddie and Linette entered with Grady and the girls behind them. Clara brought up the rear.

Blue hoped he managed to keep his smile narrow,
revealing none of the gladness that tingled along his
nerves.

Her gaze skimmed the group until she found him.
She acknowledged his presence with a small smile, but
the brightness of her eyes said she was as happy to see
him as he was to see her. Was she remembering yesterday's kiss? Wondering what it meant? Where they
went from here?

He went to her side. "Good morning."

She took in his outfit, and her eyes smiled approval.
"Good morning."

"Company." Cookie bore down on them.

Blue grabbed Clara's arms, prepared to hold her
against Cookie's onslaught.

"I'm Cookie. And you're Clara Weston." She hugged
Clara and patted her back.

Then Cookie turned to the girls.

Eleanor shrank back, but Libby stepped forward and
gave her name.

Cookie cupped Libby's face between her palms.
"What a sweet face."

Libby glowed under the praise, then moved aside as
Cookie waited for Eleanor to step forward.

"And what's your name, sweet thing?"

"Eleanor. And how do you know I'm sweet?"

Clara looked about to scold her daughter for such a
bold question, but Cookie's laugh made talk impossible.

"Why, all I have to do is look at your face, see the
gentleness in your eyes and I know." She pulled both

girls to her and hugged them. Surprisingly gently, Blue noted.

"So nice to have you all here." She hurried away to bear-hug the latest cowboys to enter.

Blue took Clara and the girls around and introduced them to the crowd, wondering how many of them she'd remember. Then he led them to a space on one of the benches. The place was crowded, forcing them to sit in a tight spot. He pulled the girls to his knees and smiled down at Clara pressed to his side.

At her trusting smile, his heart filled with hope. He would not allow himself to say what he hoped for.

Bertie and Cookie went to the front, and Cookie led them in a hymn. Never before had the familiar tune and words meant more as Clara sang to his left with a clear bell-like voice, and Eleanor sang on his right knee. She knew every word.

Libby did her best to sing along, too.

For the first time in two years, Blue felt the meaning of the hymn in the depths of his heart. *Savior, like a shepherd lead us, much we need Thy tend'rest care; in Thy pleasant pastures feed us, for our use Thy folds prepare.*

Then Bertie stood before them. "I know you're all cowboys or wives of cowboys." His gaze rested on Clara. "And if you don't fit either category, I expect you've seen enough of cowboys to understand what I'm about to say." He swept his eyes over the entire gathering. "I know you all don't often give sheep much thought. Maybe you even think of them as stupid creatures. But God often refers to His people as sheep." He read the Twenty-Third Psalm. "'He restoreth my soul.' There was a time I was a poor lost sheep. Life seemed so empty and meaningless. But God found me. More than that, He restored my soul. He prepared a feast of good things. He promised me goodness and mercy all the days of my life."

The words burrowed into Blue's mind. Could he be restored? Able to face life again? More than that, embrace it? Could he feel secure enough to share his life with others?

He leaned a little to the left, and Clara responded by pressing into his arm. He hugged the girls closer, and they snuggled against his chest.

Maybe, just maybe, he could open his heart a little.

The service ended. Cookie brought out tea, coffee and hot chocolate and passed around her cinnamon rolls.

She waited as Clara bit into one.

Clara sighed. "These are the best I've ever tasted."

Cookie grinned, and many of the others chuckled.

Blue looked about, wondering if there was some acceptable way to get Clara to himself so they could talk. And, yes, maybe kiss again, at least once or maybe twice. But before he could devise a way of extracting them from this crowd, Linette rose awkwardly, her large belly making movement difficult.

"You're all invited up the hill for dinner. It will be ready in a couple of hours."

Sybil, Cassie, Mercy and Jayne jumped to their feet. "We'll help you."

"I will, too," Clara said and took the girls to follow the general departure.

Blue sat back, hoping his disappointment wasn't obvious.

"I'll be right along," Eddie said. "We menfolk will watch the children."

Blue remained seated as the husbands prepared to leave.

"You, too, Blue," Eddie said.

Blue normally didn't join those going for dinner, but this time he would endure the talk of so many people so he could be close to Clara and her daughters. With a great deal more eagerness than he'd known in a long, long time, he joined the trek up the hill.

Eddie led the men into the front room, where they settled in for a visit with the children playing nearby.

Seth leaned forward over his knees. "How long is this fair weather going to last? I don't mind saying I expect a snowstorm any day."

A snowstorm? Would that keep Clara here, or would she leave and be caught in one? Another reason she must stay. Or he must go with her.

The men considered the weather and talked of the cattle.

When a lull came, Blue spoke. "Has anyone seen a stranger around?"

Abel, who had married pretty little Mercy and lived a few miles away, nodded. "Big man. Dark hat. Would that be who you mean?"

"Might be." Blue would have described him in a similar fashion.

"I saw him riding the trail toward the upper pastures."

Eddie turned to Blue. "Are you worried about him for some reason?"

"He rides in and out of town as if looking for someone but never talks to anyone or asks after any person."

"Huh." Eddie shrugged. "Lots of mountain men around here who have little to do with others."

"That's so, but this man strikes me as a bit different." Blue would not speak a word of Clara's reason for being concerned. "Just thought I'd mention it."

Eddie nodded. "Never hurts to keep our eyes open. We know that from other times."

The men nodded agreement. Too often a stranger on the trail meant danger to someone they cared about. A villain had followed Eddie's sister, Jayne, all the way from England and had kidnapped her. Good thing Seth had taught her how to use a gun. She was able to injure the man and escape.

Then there was Brand's family—an outlaw gang that had caused all manner of trouble. There'd been others, too—rustlers, petty thieves, troublemakers.

The best thing for Clara and the girls would be to stay on the ranch, where they were surrounded by people willing to protect them. He'd convince her of the fact first chance he got.

It would mean returning to town alone. Finishing up the pews by himself.

He shrugged off a sense of melancholy. It had always been his plan to be alone. Why should he feel sad about it now?

The women announced the meal was ready, and they all gathered around the table. Blue sat with Libby between him and Clara. Eleanor sat on Clara's other side.

He wondered what he'd say in the midst of more than two dozen people, but he needn't have worried. There was a continual hum of talk around him.

Clara laughed and commented when spoken to directly, but she, too, had little to add to the conversations that included more about the weather and Christmas plans.

Was she overwhelmed? Or simply being cautious about revealing too much about herself? He could have told her that these people would protect her from her father or any dark stranger.

By the time dessert was served, he was more than ready to find a quiet spot to share with Clara.

When the meal was over, she got to her feet. "Girls, help clean up."

Blue reluctantly followed the men back to the other room. As they talked, all he could do was count the minutes until Clara entered the room. It seemed an eternity before the women joined them.

He rose and said to Clara, "It's time to go back to town."

"Oh, but we haven't had a good visit yet," Linette protested. "Clara has been telling me about the girls as babies. I'm very interested. I know what." She looked pleased with herself. "Clara, why don't you and the girls stay here? I'd appreciate your company and your wisdom."

Blue held his breath as he waited for Clara's answer.

"I couldn't," she said. "But thank you."

Linette gave a disappointed smile. "If you change your mind, you're always welcome."

Blue rose. "Clara, do you mind leaving the girls here for a moment so you and I can take a little walk?"

Every adult eye turned to him. He felt their surprise. But it didn't matter. He had to talk to Clara.

Clara donned her coat and accompanied Blue outdoors. Did he want to again walk up the hill to the little grove of trees where they'd kissed? She wouldn't object if he did.

She smiled with anticipation as he led her past the buildings, across the little bridge and by the pens. Pigs oinked in one pen. Cattle lounged in another.

They climbed the hill. She was content to think of what waited for them at the top. Not just some trees and a nice view, but memories of their kiss and anticipation of another.

They reached the top, and he leaned against a tree and drew her close.

"Did you enjoy your day at the ranch?" He smiled down at her, causing her heart to flutter against her ribs.

She nodded and smiled, her gaze riveted to his.

"It's a good place to live," he said.

"I see that. I never imagined women could be treated like equals, and yet they are here."

"It's the kind of place where you belong."

"The kind of place I can only dream of."

He drifted his fingers through the hair above her ear, sending little pulses of pleasure along her nerves. Making it difficult to think straight.

"You don't have to dream any longer. You can stay here."

His words reached her ears, but it took seconds longer for her brain to accept them. "What?"

He repeated the words. "You can stay here." And he smiled as if it was the best news ever. "You'd be safe."

She drew back, forcing him to drop his arms to his sides.

He scrubbed his lips together before he spoke. "You yourself acknowledged how the woman here are accepted as equals, didn't you?"

"I did. But you mistake my admiration for capitulation. I am not staying here. I am going back to town."

"Plans can change." His voice had deepened. Did it mean frustration that she wouldn't heed his wishes or… did he really care? But how could he care and still ask her to give up her plans?

"I have to do what I have to do whether or not you understand."

He straightened and took two steps away to look out at the rolling hills. "I certainly don't understand."

She lifted a hand, wanting to pull him back. Wanting him to appreciate her reasons. But when he turned to her, his face was gouged with disapproval, and she lowered her hand to her side.

"What are you trying to prove?" The words were gravelly as if he forced them from a tight throat.

She drew herself up as tall as she could and pushed her chin out. "That I can manage on my own. How else can I prove to my father that I'm capable?"

His eyes narrowed, and the look he gave her made her wrap her arms about herself. "I thought you wanted to keep the girls. Now you say it's to prove yourself to your father."

She lifted her hands in defeat. "They're the same thing. Why are you twisting what I say?"

His eyebrows went up. "Are they?" He shook his head. "I don't think so. Are you doing what's best for them or fighting a battle between you and your father?"

"Blue, what's the matter with you? Why can't you see one is the same as the other?"

He shook his head hard. "No, it isn't. You are being ridiculously stubborn."

"And you think you must protect me." She leaned

closer. "I am not your wife. My girls are not your daughters. I'll look after them." She turned and stormed down the hill, not caring if he followed or not. She called over her shoulder, "And I will go back to town whether you take me or I get someone else to."

She paused before she reached the pens and turned around to confront him, but he remained where she'd left him. At the look of anguish on his face and the way his hands curled into fists at his sides, she forgot what she meant to say.

The words she spoken to him had been cruel. *Oh, Blue.* She marched back to his side. "Blue, I'm sorry. I didn't mean to hurt you. Can you forgive me?" She pressed her hand to his arm, but he shied away.

"There's nothing to forgive." There was a shrug in his voice.

Regret burned through her veins and seared every corner of her heart. How could they have gone from a tender kiss yesterday to this hard, unforgiving place today?

"I'll take you back to town." His words couldn't convey withdrawal any clearer.

"Thank you." If only she could take back the hurt she'd caused. But words, once spoken, were impossible to unspeak.

Chapter Fifteen

Blue brought the wagon to the house, lifted the girls to the back, helped Clara to the seat, said goodbye and thanked Eddie and Linette, but every action, every word seemed to come from a cold, distant spot.

Linette gave him a questioning look as she patted his arm. "Nice of you to come. I'm looking forward to next time you bring Clara and the girls."

There'd be no next time, but he didn't bother to tell her that. Instead, he perched beside Clara, careful not to touch her, and headed for town.

He should never have let himself grow fond of her and the girls. He'd warned himself against it numerous times. He should likely thank Clara for reminding him of the need to keep to himself. From now on, he'd keep it firmly in mind.

For the most part, the trip to town was taken in silence.

Twice Clara turned to him. "Blue, I—"

Both times, he'd held up his hand to stop her. "Enough has been said."

She'd glanced back at the girls and thankfully decided not to pursue the subject.

When they reached the church, he turned the wagon past it and pulled up at the Mortons'. He lifted the girls down, then helped Clara to the ground. Recognizing how fragile his determination was, he avoided meeting her eyes. She tried to catch his hand, but he pulled away.

He climbed back to the wagon seat. "Tell Bonnie I won't be back for supper."

Clara reached for him. "Blue, please."

He drove away. Told himself he didn't hear Libby demanding to know why he was leaving.

They'd soon enough forget they'd ever met him.

He returned the wagon to the livery barn and tromped back to the church to saddle his horse. He swung to the back of the animal, keeping his gaze away from the shack. He couldn't help hearing a thin sound coming from that direction. Was Clara explaining to the girls why he'd left so suddenly? He imagined Libby and Eleanor might protest.

He urged the horse to the street. Where was he going? What was he going to do?

Part of him wanted to ride west and disappear into the mountains. He could find a trapper's shack and spend the winter hunting for food.

But he couldn't leave as long as that man was hanging about. Perhaps he was already gone.

One way to find out.

He rode out of town to the west, then turned on the north fork. He rode slowly. Anyone observing him would think he was a man with no purpose, no destination, but he was alert to any sign of the mysterious stranger.

After a bit, he glimpsed a horse in the shelter of some trees, almost hidden from view. Same place where he'd seen the man a couple of nights ago. Same horse. He needed no further proof the man was still around.

Blue rode on awhile longer, then turned aside and dismounted. He hunkered down on the bank overlooking the river.

What was he going to do?

He snorted. Was it only this morning he had listened to the words "He restoreth my soul" and thought it was time to start over?

How could a few words have given him so much hope but for such a short time?

His thoughts came back again and again to the same thing. He'd accused Clara of fighting the wrong battle— one to prove something to her father when she should be fighting for the girls and her own freedom.

Was he guilty of the same mistake? Fighting the wrong battle?

For two years, he'd fought for aloneness and forgetfulness.

It no longer seemed a worthwhile battle.

But what was?

He snorted again, making his horse jerk his head up.

The answer was as plain as the nose on his face. One he'd already committed to.

He'd go back to Edendale and take care of Clara and the girls.

If they wouldn't stay at the ranch where he'd feel reasonably certain they were safe, he'd make sure they got on the stagecoach and he'd go with them.

Clara was relieved when it was time to tuck the girls into bed. They'd been full of questions about why Blue had left so suddenly. Questions she couldn't answer satisfactorily. Finally, they gave up on that topic and turned to recounting every detail of the visit to the ranch.

"They have cats in the barn. Grady said we could see them if we stayed long enough." Libby gave Clara an accusing look. "Why didn't we? His mama asked us to."

"It was very generous of her."

Eleanor sighed deeply. "It was fun there. We slept in a real bed and had lots of other children to play with. Did you see Mr. Gardiner's library?"

"I did."

"Grady said there are lots of books, and anyone is allowed to borrow them. All those books." Her voice drifted away in dreamy wonder.

"I'm grateful you girls had a good time. Now go to sleep." She left them and retired to the table to read.

But the words blurred before her eyes. Where had Blue gone? Shortly after they'd returned to town she'd been out getting water when she heard a horse and her heart had kicked against her ribs. Was it that man who hung about? She'd spun around to locate the source of the sound. She saw Blue riding away from town. Her heart had calmed momentarily. Then twisted with regret.

Hours later, she still had not noticed him return. If he'd ridden back from the far side of the church, she might not have heard him. Without going closer to the church, she couldn't see if the horse was back or if a lantern was lit inside of the building.

Had she offended him so much he'd left for good without so much as a goodbye?

She regretted her hasty words spoken out of a deep longing to have exactly what staying at the ranch offered.

The women had everything she wanted—recognition of their worth, a home, a family and a man to love them.

She stifled the groan that came to her lips lest the girls hear her. *Savior, like a shepherd lead us, much we need Thy tend'rest care.*

The words of the hymn they'd sung at church came to her, carrying with them thoughts of how she and Blue had sat with their arms pressed together, the girls contentedly on his knees. At that point, she still reveled in the memory of his kiss. She still hoped it meant something besides a desire to take care of her.

He didn't understand how she had to prove she could manage on her own. How could he? As a man he could do what he wanted, go where he wanted and no one questioned his sanity or ability. Certainly no one would threaten to take his children.

But even a man couldn't prevent disasters like the fire that claimed his family.

The thought accosted her. She pressed her fingers to her forehead. His concern about her safety was understandable given his loss. But they were separated by a wide rift of different needs based on different backgrounds.

Accepting she would not be able to read tonight, she turned out the lamp and crawled into her bedroll. She couldn't guess what the morrow would bring. Whether Blue would be at the church or gone. Whether the stagecoach would come and she could head north. Or if she must linger on, unable to find work to support herself and the girls.

She thought of the few coins she had left—enough to pay for the trip north. She couldn't use them. God would have to provide another way.

Eventually she fell into a troubled sleep, waking often to listen for Blue to return.

The next morning she hurried the girls over to the Mortons', hoping and praying Blue would be at breakfast.

He wasn't.

"I wonder what's keeping him," Bonnie asked and after a few minutes announced they would go ahead without him. "Perhaps he went to see Macpherson and got invited to have breakfast there."

Clara shushed the girls' questions, hoping they wouldn't say anything more about Blue's behavior. But her bones ached with disappointment and guilt. If he'd disappeared into the mountains to the west, she had no one but herself to blame.

With no assurance that Blue would be at the church, she insisted she and the girls would help do the dishes.

Once they were done, she faced a quandary.

Did she go over to the church? What would she do if he wasn't there?

The world seemed without purpose.

Nonsense. She had a very firm purpose. Get to Fort Calgary and the position that awaited her.

She led the girls across the yard and over the short distance to the church. Frost made the grass crunchy. Snow still clung to the trees and against the north side of buildings even though it hadn't snowed since they'd arrived. She prayed it would not until they reached Fort Calgary.

At her destination, she paused. If Blue was there, would he allow her to work with him? Or ask her to leave? She gave a soundless snort. If he did, she'd refuse.

But if he wasn't there, what would she do?

* * *

Blue stood by the sawhorses, his gaze on the door. Would Clara come? He smiled, knowing she would if only to prove herself to him.

The door creaked open, and the girls entered with much less gusto than normal. Libby cast him a look full of curiosity. Eleanor's expression conveyed disappointment.

Little one, you're no more disappointed by my behavior than I am.

The pair scooped up the buckets and darted back outside.

At least they didn't seem angry or afraid. That was something. He'd talk to them as soon as he made things right with their mother.

Clara stepped into the building and closed the door, clinging to the wall on one side.

Did she think she might want to escape quickly in order to avoid his anger or his demanding questions? He needed to make her understand she had nothing to fear.

He'd thought about what to say. Now was the time.

"Clara, I didn't mean to question your concern for your girls. As you said, you must do what you must do." She alone could choose to change the course of her decisions.

She nodded, her expression guarded, not allowing him to guess what was going on inside her head. "Do you forgive me for what I said?" she murmured.

He closed the distance between them. She looked up at his approach, allowing him to see the hunger in her eyes. If only he could undo the events of yesterday afternoon. He nodded. "I forgive you. We both said things we shouldn't have."

"Thank you." She dipped her head.

He could only stare at the warm hat she wore. He wanted to catch her chin and tip her face toward him.

"I was afraid you'd be angry." Slowly, her head came up again. "In fact, I wasn't sure I should come over."

His tension eased as her blue eyes met his. She was being cautious. He understood that and wasn't sure how to proceed. "I'm glad you came. What persuaded you to?"

Clara's gaze darted away and then back, filled with discomfiture. "If I say, you'll accuse me of being needlessly stubborn."

"Will I?" A smile began in the depths of his heart. "Were the girls the only reason?"

Her mouth twitched with a teasing grin. "Maybe not." She grew serious. "But they must always be the most important reason."

"I'd never suggest otherwise."

The girls could be heard giggling outside.

"Are you opposed to me talking to them?" he asked her.

"Not in the least. In fact…" She turned away, but not before he glimpsed a look of confusion.

"In fact what, Clara?"

Why was she reluctant to tell him what she meant to say?

He reached for her, relieved when she didn't resist. "What's wrong?"

"They've never had someone—" she spoke in a strangled voice "—treat them like you do. You listen to them and talk to them and encourage them." She shook her head, her eyes damp.

Moved by the threat of her tears, he pulled her close. "It's because I care about them."

Her fingers burrowed into the fabric of his shirt. "I know."

Just as he cared for her. He didn't know how to say it without making her grow defensive. So he settled for tipping her head back and smiling. "Clara." Was that hoarse voice his?

The look of anticipation in her eyes touched a tender spot inside him. His gaze drifted to her sweet, smiling, kissable mouth.

"Clara." Her name came out as a sigh as he lowered his head, intent on capturing her lips.

The door rattled. Libby laughed and banged a bucket against the frame.

Blue sprang back. He wondered if he looked as regretful as Clara did at having their kiss prevented by two curious little girls. She indeed looked disappointed over being denied that kiss. He tucked the thought into his heart.

He stepped aside as the girls shuffled past with their buckets of snow. He'd offer to help them but understood their need to do it for themselves.

The truth of his thoughts made him blink. It was the same with Clara. She needed to prove she could take care of herself and the girls. For her sake as much as for her father's. And he could do little but wait patiently for her to see the truth of how strong she was.

Chapter Sixteen

Clara stood, content to watch, as Blue sat on a pew and took the girls to his knees.

When she'd realized he was in the church, her relief had been so great she'd grabbed the wall to steady herself. To have his forgiveness made the room brighter, and she knew it wasn't because of the morning sun.

She scrubbed her lips together. Forgiveness had mended the rift between them. She cradled her arms about herself to contain the disappointment in the pit of her stomach. Funny that a missed kiss could matter so much. She'd never been one for kissing. Rolland's kisses had been perfunctory at best, and as he grew weaker and less interested in her and the girls, they'd stopped altogether. In some ways, she'd felt like a widow years before he died.

She brought her attention back to the scene before her.

"I'm sorry I was abrupt last night," Blue explained to the girls.

Libby tipped her head to one side. "You didn't come for supper."

"Or breakfast," Eleanor added.

"I went for a ride."

"We wondered where you were." Libby studied him hard.

She thought poor Blue would be squirming inside before Libby's demanding look, but he smiled gently then dipped his head and touched his forehead to Libby's. "I should have told you."

Clara wanted to interrupt, to remind the children he didn't need to inform them of his whereabouts. The girls had no such claim on him, any more than she did.

Eleanor caught his chin and brought him about to face her. "We thought you left. Everyone leaves." Sorrow dripped from each word.

"Or we leave," Libby pointed out.

Eleanor shrugged. "Doesn't matter who goes."

"Remember the sermon yesterday?" Blue said.

Two little heads nodded.

"Then you know that Jesus is your good shepherd who leads you to still waters and green pastures."

Libby made a protesting noise. "Too bad God doesn't lead us to a nice home. I wanted to stay at the ranch, but Mama said no." She scowled at Clara.

"Sometimes we have to do things that are hard." Blue pressed their heads to his chest and gave Clara a look of such regret she had to blink back tears.

He cared for the girls. Did he care for her? What would it mean if he did?

Did she care for him? Perhaps more than was wise.

Before she could examine that admission, Eleanor and Libby scrambled from Blue's lap and went to the corner to play. He rose and turned her attention to work.

The pews would soon be finished. A mixture of regret and satisfaction tugged at her thoughts.

As she worked, she started talking. "Rolland was everything my father approved of—successful, well established." The words crowded to her mouth as if they'd been waiting for release.

"Older and sickly?" he added.

"He was twenty-five years older than me. I don't think Father knew his health was failing at the time we married."

Blue carefully marked the dimensions on the piece of wood then straightened to consider her. "Would it have made a difference?"

"I don't know." It didn't seem Father would be concerned for Clara's sake. But he might have seen it as failure on his part.

Blue still held the tape and pulled it through his fingers in a distracted manner. "Clara, he was everything your father wanted, but what did you want?"

She twined her fingers together as she considered her answer. She knew what she wanted, but would he misunderstand? He waited patiently, giving her all the time she needed to sort out her thoughts. This unhurried way about him was one of the things she admired and appreciated.

"What I wanted and still want is what Linette and Jayne and the other women at the ranch have."

He dropped the tape measure to the piece of wood and leaned back, his gaze probing hers, seeking truth. "What is that?"

"Freedom to be who they are capable of being."

He nodded. "It's what you are trying to discover,

and I believe you will. In fact, I believe you are very close to it."

She blinked at his response. He didn't try to reason her out of what she wanted. Didn't even offer to take care of her so she wouldn't need to do it herself. Yet she knew he'd help her as much as she'd let him. He was a man who would—

She managed to stop her thought before it finished. Before she could admit he was the kind of man who might honor her abilities like Eddie and Seth and the other husbands she'd seen at the Eden Valley Ranch.

But had he not suggested she stay at the ranch where others could help look after her? Was she longing for something out of her reach, even believing she'd found it where it didn't exist? Blue confused her. Made her think one thing and want another. How did he do that? Why did she allow it? She had so many questions about this man. Perhaps if they were answered, she'd better understand her own response and be able to control it.

"What was your wife like?"

He looked past her, into his memories it seemed. A gentle smile curved his lips. "You would have liked Alice. She wasn't afraid of challenges. We packed all our belongings in a wagon and left Texas for Wyoming when she was already expecting Nancy. I suggested we wait until after the baby was born." He chuckled softly. "She got all huffy and said she would deliver this baby in our new home, and she did."

Amusement tickled Clara's insides. "You poor man. How do you manage to get involved with stubborn women?" She hoped he wouldn't be offended that she had innocently aligned herself with his wife.

He quirked an eyebrow and sought her gaze. "Just fortunate I guess." He looked pleased with himself.

Clara ducked her head, afraid of the answering pleasure in her heart and uncertain how he'd interpret what he saw in her eyes.

To avoid further talk of his wife, she changed the topic to her children. "Eleanor was a quiet baby. She'd regard me with big solemn eyes as she nursed. I often felt overwhelmed at the trust she had in me."

"And Libby?"

Clara laughed. "She always had definite ideas of what she wanted even as a tiny baby. She did not like to wait to be fed. The nanny thought I spoiled her by feeding her when she wanted it."

"I hadn't thought about it, but of course you had a nurse for them."

"I did, but I let the nanny take care of the laundry and as they grew older, some of the meals. Mostly I insisted on taking care of the girls myself. I loved seeing every little milestone, having them turn to me when they wanted something." She let those sweet memories fill her thoughts. "Rolland assumed the nanny did all the work, and I never disabused him of the idea."

He chuckled. "Seems you always found a way to do what you thought best."

She nodded. "I tried."

"Many women would envy you a nanny and whatever other servants you had, but I have to agree with you. I can't imagine letting someone else raise my kids."

His words were like honey to her soul. When was the last time anyone had approved of her decisions? Had there ever been a time? Father didn't think her capable of making a decision on her own. Never had. She knew

Rolland would have disapproved of her choice in regard to the nanny, which was why she never told him. The nanny went along with her decision, but almost every day she made it clear she didn't approve. But since it meant less work for her, she protested quietly.

"You're the only one who has ever agreed with my choice about anything. Except for one maid who spoke to me just before I married Rolland. She said to remember who I was and what I was capable of. It was she who gave me my Bible. I wish I knew where she went. I'd thank her for it. It's been my comfort and strength for all these years."

They had both forgotten about the work before them and moved to a window though neither of them looked through it. He leaned on one side of the frame and she leaned on the other as they faced each other.

He studied her. "Do you find it a little odd that your challenges and disappointments have drawn you closer to God and mine have pushed me away?"

She touched his arm, knowing it was pain that drove the wedge between him and his faith. "I did not face anything like you did."

He nodded, and seemed to cling to her gaze as if seeking more from her.

She wished she'd had time to think about her answer, but instead she let it come from her heart. "Blue, perhaps you are just a lost sheep and our good shepherd is seeking you to bring you back to the fold."

He drew in a slow breath. "Yesterday when Bertie spoke of that story, I couldn't help wonder something along those lines. 'He restoreth my soul.' Maybe it's time for that."

She rubbed his arm. "God never leaves us even when it feels like He's turned His face away."

He nodded. "I know." He patted her hand. "I just want to say how much I admire you for insisting on taking care of your girls when you could have done otherwise and no one would think it unusual."

"Didn't your wife take care of your children?"

"Most of the time. I liked to help her. I especially liked to put them to bed at night. Beau wouldn't settle if I didn't rub his back. He insisted no one else knew how to do it right."

Clara grinned. "He sounds a little like Libby."

He turned toward the girls playing happily with their doll. Not once had they argued about sharing it. Clara was proud of them.

She watched Blue, picturing him helping with his babies, rubbing a little boy's back. Her throat tightened. "I'd say your wife and children were fortunate to have you as a husband and father."

He turned back to her, and their gazes caught and held. The moment filled with a sweet, fearful acknowledgment of the tender feelings between them.

Her attention drifted to his mouth. If not for the girls' presence, she would be sorely tempted to ease over and hope he'd kiss her.

She forced herself to look elsewhere, anywhere but at his tempting lips and his alluring eyes.

She dare not let herself forget Fort Calgary and get comfortable in Edendale.

A shudder crossed her shoulder and clamped about her spine.

Now was not the time to let weak emotions control her.

* * *

Blue couldn't help but notice her sudden withdrawal, the way she avoided meeting his eyes even when he tipped his head in an attempt to recapture her attention.

Perhaps she'd said more than she meant to—telling him he was a good husband and father. But he cherished the words. They reached into his heart and mended the broken places.

"You know, I've never spoken of my children to anyone but you since they perished. People around here don't even know about them."

She jerked her attention back to him. "I'm sorry."

She'd misunderstood, thought he accused her. It was quite the opposite. "I'm not. It's good to think of the wonderful times I had with them. You once said I had to take the past with me into the future. At the time I wondered how on earth that was even possible, but I think I'm beginning to understand." The words came slowly as his thoughts took shape. "Memories of Alice and the children have become a part of my heart. Maybe they've even caused it to grow stronger."

"Making you ready to love again?" She lowered her head as if she'd said more than she'd meant to.

He wasn't sure he was ready for what she asked. The notion of starting over had only become an option he could entertain. Loving again seemed too new to contemplate. He realized Clara waited for him to say something. "At least making me ready to move on." He shifted his gaze to the girls and shook his head. *Love? Not yet.*

He straightened. "Best get to work."

They both rushed back to the sawhorse. Seemed she was as anxious to get back to normal as he was. It didn't take long for him to realize he no longer knew what normal was. His thoughts drifted repeatedly to the pleasure he'd once known of coming home to a wife and two children eager for his return.

He'd told himself he'd never have such joy again. Didn't even want it.

Seemed his heart had not listened.

By supper time, the last of the pew pieces had been cut. He could perhaps prolong the assembly and clean up for two days. Then there was the shellacking. He smiled to himself. That could reasonably take several days.

His thoughts slammed to a halt. He was dreaming up ways to delay her leaving, but all it would take for the dream to crumble was the arrival of the stagecoach. Instead of building a home, he'd be following her to Fort Calgary.

Well, Fort Calgary was as good a place to build a home as any. For how long?

He answered his own question. Until Clara's father found them, or Clara thought he might, she'd always be looking over her shoulder, fearful of her father's threat.

All Blue could hope to do was go where she went, do his best to keep them safe.

He should have warned Eddie he might be leaving. Instead, he'd have to send a message.

He and Clara finished for the day and went to the Mortons' for supper.

He made the meal last as long as possible, even throwing out a conversation starter now and then.

"Linette must be going to have that baby soon." The comment was good enough for twenty minutes of talk.

Clara had finished and was helping Libby clean her plate.

He racked his brain for another topic. "There's getting to be quite a crowd at the cookhouse on Sundays."

That grabbed Bonnie's attention. "Any news on a preacher?"

The girls sat up taller.

Suspecting the reason for their sudden interest, he silently groaned.

"Mr. Blue could be the preacher," Libby said.

"Just ask him not to talk for three or four hours," Eleanor added.

Bonnie and Claude looked at each other, their eyes wide, and then Claude chuckled despite the warning look from his wife.

"Have you discussed this with him?" Claude asked the children.

They hunched forward, their heads down. "He said no," Libby said.

Bonnie squeezed Eleanor's hand. "I guess that's your answer. We'll simply have to keep looking for someone."

Blue didn't know whether to hide his face or chuckle along with Claude. He glanced at Clara. When she rolled her eyes, he laughed. "I doubt I could talk for an hour, let alone three or four."

Eleanor's head came up. "You're going to change your mind?"

"Nope. 'Fraid not."

The ladies rose to do dishes. Mealtime was over. But he didn't want to spend the evening alone. Didn't want to say good-night. He could hardly visit Clara in the shack. It wasn't appropriate, and Prudence Foot would probably take note.

Bonnie turned to speak to Claude. "This afternoon I saw a small herd of deer go by toward the river."

"Can we go see if they're down there?" Libby asked. Eleanor's expression was equally eager.

"I don't think so," Clara said. "Remember what happened last time we were at the river."

"But, Mama, I won't go near the water this time." Libby clasped her hands together and silently begged.

Blue managed to keep a wide grin from claiming his mouth. *Thank you, Bonnie, for giving me an excuse.* "I'll take you down if you like and if your mama gives permission." He knew if she did, she would accompany them.

Clara kept her gaze on the girls as she nodded. "That would be nice."

He wished she would look at him so he could gauge her response. Was she glad of the excuse or merely agreeing for the sake of the girls?

Either way, he only cared that he could delay saying good-night, though the approaching darkness would make it a short outing.

The girls quickly slipped on their coats. Blue and Clara grabbed their own, hurrying to keep pace with the eager children.

Blue caught them before they got out the door. "You'll have to be very quiet if you want to see any deer."

Nodding, their eyes bright, they tiptoed out and down the path toward the river. Clara stayed at his side. He tried not to think how good and right this felt...a family outing.

When they'd gone a few moments a flicker of movement in the trees caught his eyes. He planted his hands on the girls' shoulders to stop them and pointed to the left. "See them in the trees?" There were three deer in the shadows.

Libby squinted and shook her head.

Eleanor caught her breath, and a look of wonder came over her face. "I see them," she whispered, her eyes round with awe.

The animals' heads came up, and they pranced away, disappearing in the trees.

"I saw them. I saw them." Libby jumped up and down. "Can we go closer?"

"They'll be gone now." The deer's keen senses had picked up the human intruders.

"Maybe not. Can we go see? Please?" She turned her blue eyes on him as she begged.

He wondered how anyone refused her requests. "It's up to your mother." He glanced back at Clara.

"Is there any danger?"

He quirked an eyebrow. "Do you think I'd be okay with the idea if there was?"

She lifted her hands in the air and grinned. "What was I thinking? Go have a closer look."

Laughing, he led the way down the bank. The girls continued moving quietly as they scrambled down to the river.

He held out a hand to assist Clara, half expecting she would say she could manage on her own. But she took his hand. He smiled inside when she made no attempt to pull away once she reached the rocky shore. Nor did she resist when he pulled her closer, tucking her hand around his arm.

She didn't look at him, but he saw the smile curving her lips and his grin came from a spot deep inside his heart that had been locked and silent for two years. It felt good to again feel alive inside.

"Be careful," Clara called to the girls, who ran ahead. "Stay away from the water."

"Yes, Mama," they chorused.

Clara and Blue followed at a more leisurely pace. He, for one, was not anxious for this evening to pass. He allowed himself to think she shared the feeling.

They reached the spot across the river from where he'd seen the deer, and they drew to a halt.

The girls peered into the shadows.

Eleanor released a heavy sigh. "Aw, they're gone."

"'Fraid so," Blue said.

She turned her worried gaze to him. "Were they scared of us?"

"I expect so."

"But we weren't going to hurt them."

"How could they know that? And if they stayed to find out, and you did mean to harm them, it would be too late for them to escape."

Eleanor turned her serious consideration to her mother. "That's like Mama."

Clara pulled back. "What do you mean?"

Eleanor answered her mother's question. "You keep saying we have to leave, but like the deer, you don't stay to see if it's okay or not."

Clara stared at Eleanor, who gave a shrug and went to join her sister watching the trees, hoping to again see the deer.

Clara shook her head. "Sometimes she says the strangest things."

"She's just a child." But the similarities struck him. If the deer hung about, they would likely be shot. If she stayed, Clara feared her father would find her and take away her children.

"I do understand your need for caution," he said.

At some point she'd slipped her hand away, and he reached for it and brought her back to his side. "Just remember you aren't alone."

She nodded and allowed him to guide her farther along the rocky shore of the river. The girls ran ahead.

He rested his hand over her fingers where they lay on his arm. If only he could lock time to this place and this feeling, hold it forever in his heart.

Instead, he must be like the deer, too, running from the threat of danger in order to be with this woman and these children he'd grown to care about.

Of course, there was another choice. He could go back to being alone, pushing away the past, refusing to face the future.

His heart crowded against his ribs. He could not remain a prisoner of his past.

But would he ever find the life he wanted with Clara and her children? The wisest thing might be to leave them to their plans and seek a way to fulfill his.

Chapter Seventeen

Clara could think of many reasons she should end this evening. Not the least of which was her reluctance to do so. Blue had kept her on a wild wagon ride of emotions all day. From worry if he'd gone to concern that he was angry at her, to the pleasant feelings she got when he spoke about his family, to the warmth she felt at his touch—it all pulled her dangerously away from her resolve to go to Fort Calgary.

Deer ran to stay safe. She must do the same.

But there was no need for running tonight, so she kept her hand on Blue's arm and allowed herself to feel sheltered, protected and cared for. Emotions that she normally denied herself. Not that she'd allow her wayward heart to divert her from what she must do. She would simply enjoy the moment.

They continued walking along the edge of the river until they came to a narrow trail leading upward to the bank. The girls scampered up, and Blue and Clara followed. The sunset filled the sky with reds and pinks, purples and oranges. The snowcapped mountains blushed with color.

She gasped. "How beautiful."

They stood side by side, admiring the display.

"I wish life could always be like this." She couldn't say exactly what she meant. Beautiful as the sunset? Peaceful as the walk along the river? A moment shared with someone she'd grown to care for?

All of that, she realized.

He planted his hands on her shoulders, sending warmth and longing clear through her. Slowly, he turned her around to look back from where they'd come. "What do you see? Describe the scene."

She studied the view for a moment. "A winter scene. A partially frozen river, edged with ice. It's all black and white. A little bleak." It filled her with a sense of loneliness and despair.

He turned her back to the sunset. "Now what do you see?"

She smiled. "A burst of colors. The mountains are majestic. Looking this direction makes me happy inside. Hopeful even. As if God is smiling at me."

He chuckled. "I like that thought." He turned her so they faced each other. He looked into her eyes, searching, examining.

She let him take his time. Wondered what he sought and if he'd find it.

He drew in a slow breath. "Clara, we're standing in the same spot. It's the same time of day. So what's the difference between the bleak on one side and the hopeful on the other?"

She got the feeling he searched for the answer as much as asked her for it. "Why, I suppose the direction I look makes the difference."

At the way his eyes darkened with—dare she believe?—hope and understanding, she laid her hands on his chest.

He caught her fingers between his and held them there. "We can control which direction we look, can't we?" He grew thoughtful. "Life is a lot like that."

She didn't say anything as she considered his words. It was easy to see how this truth applied to his life. For him, it was simply choosing which direction he looked—to the past or to the future.

Perhaps a future shared with someone?

Sourness stung the back of her throat. Life was not as simple for her. Her choices were dictated by others—mostly her father.

"I want to be able to choose."

"Then choose. Stop letting your father control you. Decide what you want and do it."

Oh, how she wished she could. An ache the size of the sky overhead seized her heart. "My choices must always be secondary to the needs of the girls."

He opened his mouth as if to say something, then closed it without uttering a word. He dipped his head until their foreheads touched.

She took comfort in the gesture. The thought of going on, leaving him behind, made her knees weak.

The sound of her daughters playing gave her the strength to pull away. Reluctantly, she slipped her hands from his.

He reached out and cupped his hand over the back of her neck and pulled her close again.

She could not find the energy to resist even though she knew she should. Every minute spent with him like this would make leaving so much more difficult.

He leaned closer, feathered his lips across hers and straightened again before she could respond.

A protesting sigh escaped her. She was surprised at how much she regretted not being able to kiss him back.

"I think it might be time for both of us to move forward, led by our good shepherd."

His words roused her from her reverie and brought her back to their talk. Though she knew he didn't mean them so, she pretended to interpret them literally. "Yes, it's time to put the girls to bed."

His half grin informed her he knew she was purposely making it about the girls.

She called Eleanor and Libby, and they retraced their steps in the growing dusk. With the disappearance of the sun, the temperature had fallen appreciably, and they hurried despite her reluctance to end the evening.

They passed the Morton home. Through the window they saw Claude and Bonnie sitting at the table, the lamp between them.

They reached the shack, and the girls hurried inside. Clara would like to linger outside with Blue, but she had to light the lamp for the girls.

Still she didn't immediately step inside. "Thank you for taking us to see the deer. That was special."

He caught her hand and pulled her so close the cold air was shut out. She breathed in the smell of wool and wood smoke, leather and oak shavings. Every time she caught a whiff of any of them in the future, she would think of this moment and all the others she had shared with Blue.

He dipped his head to hers. "I enjoyed the evening, too."

She turned her face upward, shamelessly inviting the kiss she'd been longing for all day.

He responded immediately. She couldn't say whether it was because of her begging or his own reasons. And it didn't matter.

His lips met hers, and she clung to him, her arms slipping about his waist, pressing to his back. His lips were warm and possessive and, at the same time, tender and full of promise. Or was that only her own heart's cry?

"Mama," Libby called. "Can Eleanor light the lamp?"

She jerked back. "I'll be right there."

Blue didn't immediately release her. "Clara."

She waited, wondering what he meant to say.

He lowered his arms and stepped back, leaving her alone and cold. "Have a good sleep."

"You, too." She stepped into the shack, closed the door and went to the table to light the lamp.

"What were you doing, Mama?" Libby asked. "You and Mr. Blue."

"I was thanking him for taking us to see the deer."

Eleanor watched Clara, but when Clara turned to her, the child shifted away. What was going on in her little mind?

"Deer are scared," Eleanor said.

So that was it. Back to running from danger. "If they weren't, they'd get shot."

"No one is going to shoot us."

"Thank goodness for that." Though that wasn't the only danger they needed to run from. She guessed Eleanor understood that. And didn't like it.

She finally got the girls to bed, and she settled into her own bedding.

She'd enjoyed the evening more than she had a right to, knowing it couldn't last. The image of Blue's smile lingered in her thoughts.

Blue smiled as he took care of the fire, prepared for bed and lay on his bedroll. A few minutes later he decided it wasn't possible to fall asleep with his mouth constantly smiling.

He cupped his hands behind his head and stared up at the ceiling. The evening had been like walking into the sunset, the dark shadows behind him. Tonight, for as long as possible, he'd keep his face turned to the sun and forget his past. Or at least not let it be the direction he faced.

A thought surfaced, begged for attention. Sunsets lasted but a short while.

He pushed the warning behind him. He'd deal with reality when he must. He would have told Clara of his plans to follow her to Fort Calgary or wherever she went, but he figured she'd protest and he didn't want to spoil the evening.

The next morning he still had not decided if he should inform her.

The girls were talkative during breakfast. Several times, he slipped his gaze toward Clara. When their eyes connected, hers full of softness, his heart lurched against his ribs.

The four of them went to the church.

He looked about. The pile of wood that had been on one side of the room was gone, cut into shapes for pews. "We're all done sawing pieces."

"The pews are almost finished." Did she sound as regretful as he felt? This work had given them the opportunity and the excuse to spend time together. Once they were done, what would they do?

"It will still take a few hours to assemble them all." He held an end piece in position. She knew what to do and steadied the piece.

Her hand slid across the edge and rested against his.

Whether or not the touch was purposeful, he couldn't say, but his heart rushed up his throat in a response that was both primitive and surprising. When had he ever had such a powerful response to a simple touch? Never. Not even with Alice, though he'd loved her as fully as he could.

A stunning truth flared through his mind. His love for Alice had lacked a degree of depth he'd been incapable of back then. The sorrow he'd lived through had given him a deeper capacity for emotions.

He sought Clara's gaze.

When his eyes met hers, he realized she'd been watching him and was aware of his reaction. Her blue eyes were liquid with answering emotion. Her lips parted slightly. They were temptingly kissable.

At the sound of the girls playing across the room, he cleared his throat and forced his attention back to work. "Eleanor and Libby, do you want to help assemble this pew?"

They rushed over, always eager to be of assistance.

Over their heads, his gaze locked with Clara's. Time ceased as their look went on and on. Hers burning into his, silently claiming places in his heart that had never before been occupied. Places that had, until this moment, been hidden, curled like a flower bud waiting for her smile before they bloomed.

"Mr. Blue, is this where you want it?" Eleanor's question jerked him back to the here and now.

And the realities of his world.

He needed to keep his mind on his task, his emotions contained to what was possible and his heart firmly under control.

Throughout the day, he repeated that warning to himself often, but every time he and Clara touched, whenever their gazes brushed, he forgot it for minutes at a time.

Late in the afternoon, he stood back, Clara at his side. "They are all put together." The pews were crowded together against one wall. "Soon they'll be arranged for church." There was still work to be done—shellac to be applied, the pulpit to be built and the walls to be finished, but others had volunteered for those tasks.

"Even more importantly, they'll hold people who come to worship."

Did her voice contain a wistful note, as if she wanted to be among those worshippers?

"Are we done?" Libby asked. "Now what?"

He didn't have the materials for putting on the finish. Didn't know if Macpherson had what he needed. "Tomorrow I'll clean the tools, sweep the floor and generally tidy up."

"Can we help?" Eleanor asked.

He squeezed her shoulder. "I never turn down help."

"You're right." Clara studied the pews.

"What am I right about?" Dare he hope she'd changed her mind about leaving?

"There's a great deal of satisfaction in knowing I had a hand in making those."

He reached for her hands, examined the back of each

then turned them over and examined the palms. "These hands did a fine job." His voice had grown husky.

If the girls weren't watching them, he would have placed a kiss on each palm. Would have followed it up with a kiss to her lips.

"Then we're going to be done?" Libby didn't sound pleased about it.

"Yup," Blue answered.

"You'll go back to the ranch, won't you?" She faced him, anger and disappointment twisting her face.

"Maybe not. Why not wait and see?" He needed to tell them he meant to go wherever they went, but, fearing it might bring on an argument from Clara, he kept his plans to himself.

"Let's go for supper." He held a hand out and took a girl on either side. His smile included Clara. "Unfortunately, I don't have a third hand."

She laughed. "I'd say that was fortunate for you." She walked at Eleanor's side.

As the meal drew to a close, he faced the same quandary as the night before. How to avoid returning to his own empty quarters.

Bonnie and Clara, with the girls helping, began the task of cleaning up.

"I've been working on a quilt," Bonnie said. "I can't quite work out the colors for the pattern. Clara, maybe you could help me?"

"I know nothing about quilting, but I can have a look."

Blue swallowed back disappointment. This wasn't a project he could participate in. He edged his chair back.

Claude grabbed a handful of newspapers from the nearby shelf. "Maybe you'd like to read these. They're old newspapers. In fact, Eddie gave them to me, so perhaps you've seen them already."

"No, I've not." He took one of the offered papers, pushed his chair back from the table and began to read. His position gave him plenty of opportunity to glance up from the page and watch Clara as she washed dishes and then helped Bonnie lay out bright pieces of fabric on the table.

Bonnie explained the pattern.

"It's like a giant jigsaw puzzle." Clara sounded pleased. "What fun. Look, if you place this color here and then this one…"

Bonnie clapped her hands. "That's it. Why couldn't I figure it out?" She grinned at Clara. "You sure you haven't quilted before?"

"No, but it looks like fun. Maybe someday I'll learn how."

"I'd be glad to show you."

Blue lowered the page to watch Clara's reaction. She drew her mouth back as if disappointed. An almost imperceptible sigh passed her teeth. "That's very generous of you. However, I don't know if I'll be—" She paused. "Here." She slid her attention toward Blue, stalled there when their gazes connected.

Did he see regret? Longing? Or was he only wishing things could be different?

"The invitation is open anytime."

The women bent over the quilt pieces for the next half hour as the girls watched.

All too soon, Clara said she must take the girls to bed.

"I'll see you over." Blue folded the paper and handed it back to Claude with thanks, then joined them.

It was only a few yards to the shack. He could wish it was several blocks, but wishing didn't change anything, and he should remember that.

Wishing wouldn't make the evening last, or make Clara safe. Wishing would not change who either of them were.

He brushed her arm. Afraid if he lingered, he'd forget what was possible and what wasn't, he hurried away and didn't look back.

The next morning, the four of them swept and dusted. It took far less time than he'd have liked. The work was finished by midmorning.

"Now what?" Libby demanded.

"Now we are done."

"I know, but what are we going to do now?"

He shrugged. He gave Clara a helpless look, but she wore the same demanding, questioning look as her daughter. In fact, all three stared at him, waiting for him to tell them what was next.

How could he?

Besides, what did they truly want?

What did he truly want?

Now was the time to decide. Only he wasn't sure.

"I have something to take care of, so I'm going for a ride this afternoon."

"When will you be back?" Eleanor asked, her trembling voice revealing her worry that he'd ride away without a backward look.

"Later this afternoon." He cupped her head. "But I will come back. I promise. Okay?"

She nodded.

He went to the Mortons' for dinner, then saddled his horse and rode from town. Ignoring the trail, he rode directly north. He didn't care to meet anyone. He needed to think.

His gaze swept the landscape before him. To his left were the mountains, the rolling hills that were covered with lush grass during the summer. To his right the hills flattened toward the prairie, good for raising horses and cows. From the cabins he saw, it seemed it was also good for homesteaders who came in steadily increasing numbers. The railway would soon cross the country, joining the eastern provinces with British Columbia and bringing even more settlers.

It was good country.

After a couple of miles, he settled back in the saddle and let his mind examine the bothersome thoughts he'd been avoiding.

He didn't want to go to Fort Calgary. He knew no one there. He wanted to settle down among people he'd grown to love and trust.

All the weeks and months he'd been trying not to think past the moment in which he lived, his brain had been hoping and planning, and now a fully developed dream made itself known.

Often, as he had been taking care of Eddie's cows, he'd come across a pretty little valley. A small stream ran through it. Lush grass covered the rolling hills.

He'd gone out of his way to pass the same valley.

In his mind he pictured the place, a house on the plain next to the stream, a barn and other outbuildings to one side, cattle grazing contentedly on the hills.

That's what he wanted. What he'd always wanted.

A place of his own. A home of his own and a family.

Now those pictures in his mind sharpened, grew more detailed. A woman stepped from the house and waved, her golden hair bright in the sunshine. Two girls stood by her side. Clara, Eleanor and Libby.

That's what he wanted.

Not just to make sure they were safe but to make them part of his life. To love and cherish them as long as he was alive. The words of the psalm filled his heart. *He restoreth my soul.*

It might be possible if they grew to love him, too.

But would Clara ever stop running? Ever settle down and forget her past?

What would it take? Assurance that she was safe. That her father wouldn't send someone after her. That he wouldn't—couldn't—take the girls away.

He reined to his left. If that dark stranger was still camping in the same spot, he'd reach the place in a few miles.

And he'd demand to know the man's purpose. Perhaps he could eliminate one fear from Clara's life.

As he neared the area, he slowed down, alert to any sign of the stranger. Blue did not want to ride into a trap or startle the man and get himself shot.

"Hello?" he called as he drew closer. "Anyone about?" He slowed as he saw evidence of a recent campfire and a pot nearby.

He peered into the shadows. "Could a man get a drink of coffee?" he shouted. He stopped but stayed in his saddle lest he need to ride away in a hurry.

In a moment his persistence paid off. The man stepped into view. "You again?"

"Yup. Had such a nice welcome last time, I didn't think you'd object."

The man grunted and threw a piece of wood on the coals. "Coffee's cold." He set the pot over the flames.

Blue swung to the ground but kept the reins of the horse in his fist. His only defense, should the man turn ugly, was escape.

"You've been hanging around a few days," he observed as if it didn't matter and he only made idle observation.

The man straightened and faced him. "It's a free country last time I checked."

Blue nodded. "Was last time I checked, too."

They stared at the coffeepot until coffee sputtered through the spout.

The man grabbed a glove and pulled aside the pot, poured the dark liquid into two tin mugs and handed one to Blue.

"Thanks," Blue said. "Don't think I caught your name."

"Don't think I threw it."

"You looking for someone?" *Like a woman and two little girls.*

The stranger turned to face him, eyes dark and challenging. "You planning to write a book?"

"Hadn't thought to." He took a gulp of the scalding coffee. Then he decided to get direct. "But here's my problem. I care about some people who think you might be looking for them. It has them upset and worried. I'd like to fix that."

"Them?"

"That's right." He sent a swift prayer that he hadn't revealed more than was safe for Clara and the girls.

The man drained his cup without flinching though the drink steamed, convincing Blue he had a throat of iron.

"I can see you're curious." The stranger dropped his

cup to the ground, crossed his arms over his chest and balanced on the balls of his feet. "You going to keep bothering me until you learn my business?"

Blue shrugged. "Wouldn't bother you at all if I knew you didn't pose a threat to people I care about."

The man rocked back and forth, his expression as hard as the rocks around the fire pit.

Blue held his cup before him. He would outwait this man. He wouldn't leave until he got a satisfactory answer.

He wasn't riding away until he could be assured Clara and the girls were safe.

Chapter Eighteen

Clara stood inside the little shack while the girls played outside, promising to stay nearby.

Alone and lonely, she rubbed her hands up and down her arms. Blue had ridden away without explanation. Not that he owed her one, but still. Couldn't he have said more than he'd be back? When? And then what? Was he planning to return to the ranch now that his job at the church was done? The ache inside her heart clawed up her throat.

She shook her head. Enough feeling sorry for herself. She'd grown careless about putting the girls' clothes in their bag and she took a few minutes to fold each item carefully and put it away.

For a moment she let herself miss the pretty dresses they'd once owned. But that was in the past. It wasn't pretty clothes that mattered. It was staying together.

The boxes had somehow shifted during their stay, and she carefully arranged them into neater piles. One box tumbled over, and she gathered up the contents— a winter coat with one sleeve torn, a worn hat, a dress that was no more than a rag, a worn sweater and some old newspapers. Seems the Mortons didn't throw things out. They stored them. She put everything back in the box and finished tidying, then swept the floor carefully.

It only took a few minutes and then she stood in the middle of the small space.

Bonnie had told her how Cassie had started the business the Mortons now ran. Though she meant to be independent, Roper wasn't happy about leaving her in town. When he found the children they had eventually adopted, he struck a deal with Cassie. He'd help her build her house if she helped take care of the children. This tiny shack had been temporary quarters for Cassie and the children while Roper built the house the Mortons now occupied.

Clara smiled. Seemed she and Cassie had much in common. They both lived in this tiny shack and had a man in their lives who objected to their independence.

Her smile disappeared into a choked sob.

Cassie's story had ended differently than Clara's would.

Enough of that. She had two children who meant more than the world to her. Their murmured voices came from the sunny side of the shack.

The rattle of a harness, the thud of horse hooves and the creaking of wood signaled the approach of a heavy wagon.

Her heart stilled. Was it the stagecoach? Finally?

"Whoa. Whoa."

She opened the door and stepped outside so she could see. Perhaps it was only another farm wagon. But no, it was the stagecoach pulling to a stop before Macpherson's store.

This was what she'd been waiting for. She should

feel relief. Not this clogging tightness in her chest. Not the sudden drop of her heart.

She pressed her palm to her chest as if she could still the turmoil within.

She recognized the emotion for what it was. Anxiety. She didn't want to leave. But—

Her thoughts were cut short when the stagecoach door opened and a man in city wear stepped out.

Her heart lodged in her throat.

She must be mistaken. *Oh, God, please let me be mistaken.*

The man brushed off his coat, adjusted his hat and turned to consider the tiny, dusty town.

Clara pressed back against the shack. *Father.* He'd found her. Her knees folded. She forced them to straighten as her thoughts raced. *Run. Leave. Get away.* She looked around. *Where? How?*

First things first.

She backed out of sight and turned to face the girls, who played at the side of the shack. "Stay right there. Do not move. Do not make a sound. Do you hear?"

Eleanor's eyes widened at the intensity of Clara's instructions.

Libby looked curious. "Why, Mama?" she whispered.

"Don't ask questions, and do not move. Okay?"

Eleanor nodded and grabbed Libby's hand. "We'll stay right here."

Clara hated seeing the fear in her daughters' eyes, but she couldn't risk them bringing Father's attention in their direction.

She clung to the walls as she edged back into the shack. She slipped inside and leaned over her knees, struggling to catch her breath. After a moment she gained control and looked about. *Think. Think. What are you going to do*?

Her gaze lit on the box she'd recently repacked. An idea began to form. She grabbed a pencil and paper from her bag and scribbled a note explaining to Bonnie that she'd borrowed a few things. She took some items from the box, gathered up their belongings and everything they'd need and slipped out to join the girls.

"Put this on." She handed Eleanor the hat she'd borrowed and pulled the worn sweater over Libby's coat, ignoring their questions. She put the heavy overcoat on top of her own clothes. "Take your bags and follow me without making a sound."

Eleanor nodded and held her fingers to her lips when Libby would ask why.

They slipped into the cover of the trees and followed the path to the river that edged past the town. She clung as close to the edge of the bank as possible, hoping and praying no one would see her.

When she estimated they had reached the far side of town, she told the girls to wait and climbed up the bank to peek over. Looked to be about the right place to cross the street without being seen. "Come along. Keep your heads down and your bag close to your body so no one will give us a second look."

She wanted to run, but wouldn't that draw attention when she wanted nothing more than to be invisible? By the time they reached the livery stable, her heart pounded so hard she feared people might hear it.

She pushed the girls into a corner near the door. "Wait here." She tiptoed forward, ready to run should anyone be inside. Not just anyone. Father. Her heart kicked into a furious pace.

There appeared to be no one at all inside the dusty barn.

"Can I help you, ma'am?" A man stepped from the shadows, sending alarm up and down her spine. She sucked in air and forced her nerves to calm. She didn't want the livery man—Rufus, was it?—to grow curious.

"I understand I can rent a wagon here." Blue had rented one to take them to the ranch on Sunday. Was that only three days ago? Seemed a lifetime.

"That's right." He stepped closer and eyed her up and down. "You know how to drive a wagon?"

"Seen it done plenty of times."

He harrumphed. "Where you going?"

"Not far."

"Not far where?"

What a persistent man. "Just want to take a ride in your beautiful country."

He studied her hard enough to make her eyes water, but she didn't budge and hopefully didn't reveal her fear.

"Need something a little more specific than that."

She leaned forward and spoke softly so the girls wouldn't hear her. "I'm going to visit Mrs. Gardiner at the Eden Valley Ranch."

"There. Was that so hard? I got something that might suit you."

She'd have to part with a few coins. But surely Petey would show her mercy when she came up short for the fare to Fort Calgary. Though that destination seemed but a faint hope now. It would be impossible to slip into the stagecoach without Father seeing them. She must leave town. Now.

She waited for Rufus, her back to the wall, hoping she would escape before Father started asking after a young woman and two girls.

Rufus brought a horse and hitched it to the wagon.

She willingly admitted she didn't know anything about horses, but this one looked like a sack of bones held together by saggy skin. "You sure she can pull the wagon?"

"You sure you know how to drive one?" When she didn't answer, he continued. "You won't need any experience to handle Old Sal. She knows what to do."

Well, that might be to her benefit.

"There you go." He stepped back and waited as she climbed up to the seat. "You say whoa and giddup. You pull the reins this way to turn her right and that way to turn her left. Even a greenhorn should be able to manage that."

"I'll do just fine." She called the girls to join her and quietly instructed them to stay low in the wagon box.

Going down the street, passing the store, meant exposing herself. No, she'd take the back way out of town.

"Giddup." The horse leaned into the task, and they rumbled forward. They reached the end of the lot and came to the trail on the back side of town.

"Right," she called, trying to remember how to guide the horse. She pulled at the reins, but the horse only continued straight ahead. They'd soon be in the middle of the open prairie, visible to everyone, if the horse didn't turn. "Right. Go right."

Old Sal stopped dead. Well, that wasn't much help, either.

"Like this, Mama." Eleanor pulled Clara's hand the correct way.

How did her child know what to do and she didn't? Clara knew the answer. Eleanor observed life carefully. Clara, too, had watched Blue's hands on the reins Saturday as they rode to the ranch. But her interest had been in studying his strong hands.

"Where we going, Mama?"

"Hush, Libby. No talking until we're out of town." She didn't want the sound of a child's voice to draw attention to them. *Please, God, let us be invisible.*

They passed businesses on their right, residences on their left without anyone seeing them. Her ribs hurt with every heartbeat. The air in her lungs felt heavy.

They passed a small log building with a prominent wooden sign on which was burned NWMP Detachment.

The North West Mounted Police had an office here? She'd never seen a Mountie. But then she'd gone out of her way to avoid meeting anyone in town.

They passed the church. Blue's horse was not back. Hadn't he said he'd take care of them? Instead, he'd left. It was for the best. Now she could prove she could manage on her own.

The open road lay ahead. But she couldn't relax yet. Maybe never.

"Can we talk now?" Libby whispered.

"It's okay now." Both girls would be curious and likely alarmed. "Thank you both for being obedient."

Libby let out a gust of air. "Mama, why'd we have to dress like this? I don't like this sweater. It stinks."

"It's to trick people. Right, Mama?" Eleanor said.

Clara wished there was a way to take care of the girls without teaching them to be sneaky. "Something like that." If Father saw them, he'd dismiss them as poor country folk and not give them a second look.

"Are we running from someone?" Eleanor tried to sound brave, but her voice caught.

Clara considered her answer and decided to be truthful with them…at least as much as she could be without alarming them. "I guess we are."

"Where we going?" Libby demanded.

Clara smiled. "Someplace I think you'll like."

Libby wriggled about with excitement. "We're going to have our own home again where we can have Christmas?"

Oh, how Clara wished she could say that was the case. "Maybe not for a while. Do you think you'd like to spend some time at the Eden Valley Ranch?"

"Oh, yes." Libby's eyes glowed with approval.

Clara turned to Eleanor. "What about you?"

"Will Mr. Blue be there?"

"I don't know." She didn't know where he'd gone or when he'd return.

"He'll be back," Eleanor said with utmost conviction. "He promised."

Clara hugged her. "That's right." *But then what?* He'd said he was ready to move on, stop living in the past.

A man approached on horseback. Clara ducked her head.

"Mama, the horse is turning in the middle of the road." Eleanor's squeaky voice jerked Clara's attention back to driving the animal. She must have accidently pulled on the reins.

"Whoa." At her cry, the horse stopped.

That wasn't what Clara meant for it to do. "Giddup. Go straight."

Old Sal pulled ahead, blocking the road entirely.

The rider pulled to a halt and watched.

Clara did not look at the man. She had her hands full trying to sort out the reins that she now held in a tangle.

"Ma'am, do you need help?"

"I'll figure it out. You could ride around." There was plenty of room. Thousands of acres. Couldn't the man simply ride on by?

"I could, but I'll make sure you get sorted out first."

She sent him a narrow-eyed look, hoping it conveyed determination and confidence. She was afraid it showed confusion and frustration. Not to mention a dozen other things she'd like to deny.

"Ma'am, allow me to introduce myself. Constable Allen of the North West Mounted Police at your service."

She gave him closer study. He wore a fur coat and fur hat. A belt on the outside of his great coat held his sidearm. He portrayed determination and fairness in every line.

"Ma'am, it would be my pleasure to get the wagon headed in the correct direction."

She considered his offer and sighed. "Thank you."

He dismounted. His horse obediently stayed where it had been left. Constable Allen climbed up beside Clara and took the reins. "Watch. I'll show you how it's done."

"Thank you." How many lessons would she need before she understood?

He instructed her on the proper use of the reins, and this time she hoped she got it.

"Ma'am, where are you going?"

She looked straight ahead, not willing to answer.

"It's my business to know." His tone was soft but left no doubt in her mind that he made sure he knew who was where.

"I'm headed for the Eden Valley Ranch."

"Oh, that makes sense."

She blinked at him.

"People who need help often turn there." He jumped down and returned to his horse, mounting it in one easy movement. "If I can help in any way, you can find me at my office in town for the next few days. And if I'm not there, I'll leave a message on the door saying where I am and when I'll be back."

She nodded and waited for him to ride on.

He studied her with unblinking forcefulness. "I've often helped people out of their troubles. I have the law behind me." Constable Allen lifted his hand in a farewell salute.

"Thank you." She urged Old Sal on.

The girls moved up beside her on the seat.

"Maybe he could help us like he says," Eleanor said.

"We'll be fine on our own."

As she successfully reined the horse westward, she glanced over her shoulder. Though the delay had cost her time, she saw no one but the disappearing Mountie. But for how long?

Her heart raced; her limbs shook. Her head felt ready to explode from fear and tension.

He leadeth me beside still waters.

Not into panicked flight.

He restoreth my soul.

How long had it been since her soul had been at real peace? She'd known a taste of it the past few days but always laced with the fear of her father showing up.

"Are we like the people in the Bible? You know, the ones in Exodus?"

Clara turned to Eleanor, uncertain what she meant. "Because we are leaving?"

"No, because we don't think God can help."

"Oh, Eleanor, my sweet child, that's not true. God has guided us and protected us every day."

"That's right," Libby said importantly. "Moses isn't still alive, so God sent Mr. Blue."

Clara stared from one girl to the other. Where did they get such profound ideas?

Was she like the children of Israel, refusing to trust God and follow His guidance? Had He brought her this far to show her something, teach her the things she needed to know to be strong and independent?

She'd told Blue she wanted to be able to choose. Then do it, he'd said.

"Mama, we're not moving," Eleanor pointed out helpfully.

"I know. I need to think." If only God would send a guiding light like he'd done for the Israelites.

Yea, though I walk through the valley of the shadow of death, I will fear no evil: for Thou art with me; Thy rod and Thy staff they comfort me.

Could she walk through the dark valley? She could if she knew God was at her side. If that was all she needed, she knew she had it. God was always with her, always ready to help.

"Girls, we're going back."

Libby jumped off the seat. "Really, Mama?" She faced Clara, her hands clasped in front of her.

"Yes. Now sit down before you fall."

"Oh, Mama," Eleanor said with such feeling it brought tears to Clara's eyes. "This is exactly what we should do."

"I'm glad you approve." She hugged the child.

"Mr. Blue will be glad," Libby added as she perched on the wagon seat again, her eyes beaming her pleasure.

Clara had no idea if he would or not. She hoped for the former. However, it had no bearing on her decision.

It took her a few minutes to get the wagon turned around and headed in the right direction. As they traveled, she made plans.

She turned to the trail on the back side of town. She pulled the wagon in beside the NWMP building. "Girls, come with me and be quiet. I need to talk to Constable Allen." The heels of her boots clicked on boards as she climbed the three steps and opened the door, the girls at her side.

"Constable Allen, I need your help."

Blue held out his hand to the stranger. "All the best in locating your brother."

Harv Winch squeezed Blue's hand hard. "Thanks."

Blue reached for his horse, then paused. "No need to camp out in the cold. You'd find a warm place to sleep at Eden Valley Ranch. Someone there might have seen or heard about your brother."

Harv stepped back, his arms folded across his chest. "I might pass by."

Blue nodded. Some people preferred to be alone. Not too long ago, he would have placed himself in that category. Now he couldn't wait to get back to town and assure Clara this man posed no threat to her.

As he rode toward Edendale, he tried to plan what he'd say and guess how she'd react. Would she agree to stay in the area?

He sucked in a deep breath. *One step at a time*, he reminded himself.

He reached the church, the first building on this side of Edendale, glanced through the windows at the empty room, then rode directly to the shed at the back of the lot and tended his horse. He took his hat off and swatted the dust and horsehair from his clothes before he trotted over to the shack.

At the door, he stopped and took three steadying breaths.

"Hello. It's me. Blue." When no one answered him, he knocked and called again and cocked his head to listen. Not a sound emanated from within. He edged the door open. The shack was empty. Disappointment filled his thoughts; then he turned toward the river and strained to hear little girls' voices that carried a great distance. Nothing. Maybe they were visiting Bonnie.

He covered the distance in long, hungry strides and knocked, then threw open the door. One look informed him they weren't there.

"Bonnie, have you see Clara and the girls? They aren't at the shack."

"I haven't. But then I've been working on this quilt so I wouldn't have seen them if they went down to the river. They seem to like being there."

"Thanks." He dashed back outside before she could ask why he was interested and jogged down to the river. He looked both ways, listened hard. Was it possible he wouldn't hear them if they were within shouting distance? It seemed unlikely.

He strained for any telltale sound but heard nothing.

No reason for concern, he assured himself, which did nothing to ease the sinking sensation in his stomach. He'd planned that he would give her his good news and she'd be so happy, so relieved she'd—

Well, he wasn't quite ready to decide what she'd do

but the thought of a grateful hug and kiss had entered his mind.

And now nothing. Where had she gone? He returned to the yard. Perhaps she'd gone to the store. He looked in that direction and saw the stagecoach. His throat closed so tight he couldn't swallow. In double-quick time he returned to the shack and stepped inside. All her things were gone. The bedding, Libby's dress that recently hung near the stove. The place had been swept clean and vacated.

She was leaving on the stage.

Not without him. He raced toward the store, up the steps and inside. He skidded to a halt at the surprised look on Macpherson's face and the annoyed one on the face of a stranger. A city fellow who glanced at Blue and then away again as if Blue was only a minor disturbance.

"Blue, this here is Mr. Creighton. Come all the way from Toronto." Macpherson tipped his head toward the city man.

Blue nodded a greeting.

Mr. Creighton managed to look offended. "It's been a long trip. If you could offer any assistance—"

Blue wondered how a carefully worded sentence could sound so much like an order meant to be obeyed with all due haste.

"By all means. Maybe Blue can help." Macpherson turned to Blue. "Mr. Creighton is looking for his daughter and grandchildren. Says the woman's name is Mrs. Westbury."

"She has two little girls," Mr. Creighton said. "She'd be needing help because she doesn't know how to take care of herself, let alone the girls."

This was Clara's father!

Shock scalded Blue's veins.

Macpherson continued to look at Blue. "I told this fine gentleman I haven't seen anyone fitting that description. Have you?" His look said far more than his words. What he meant was Clara didn't fit the description of helpless female.

Blue stilled his reaction. "Can't say I have." He hoped he sounded disinterested. It wasn't difficult to sound sincere. Clara wasn't a woman who needed help as her father said. She was strong and resourceful. "I'll take some peppermints."

Macpherson poured some into a bag. "Enough?"

"That'll do. Thanks." He tossed a few coins on the counter and popped a mint into his mouth as he strolled from the store, intending to give the impression he had not a care in the world.

As soon as he was out of sight of the store, he ducked down an alleyway and leaned against the wall of the nearest building to still his racing heart.

Her father had come in on the stage. No doubt she had seen him and run. How? Where? Rufus might know.

Blue wasn't used to running, but he would have won a footrace in the next few minutes as he made haste to the livery barn.

"Rufus. Where are you?"

The man moseyed from one of the pens. "Hold your horses, Blue. Ain't never seen you in such a lather about anything." He squinted at Blue. "How come now?"

"Never mind assessing me. Did you happen to see a woman and two girls this afternoon?"

"Seen 'em and rented 'em a wagon."

"You did?"

"Yeah. I was just as surprised as you. I wondered if she knew what she was doing, but she assured me she did. Spunky thing."

"Stubborn, too. She say where she was going?"

"Thought you'd know seeing as you took her there yourself."

"Would you mind refreshing my memory?"

"Why, to Eden Valley Ranch."

Thank goodness. She'd be safe there. "How long ago did she leave?"

Rufus scratched his chin and considered the position of the sun. "Can't rightly say, but I'd guess an hour ago, more or less."

Blue's breath whooshed out. She would be safely there by now, surrounded by Linette's care and the protection of everyone at the ranch.

He wouldn't be able to relax until he saw for himself. "Thanks, Rufus." He hurried from the barn.

"You make sure my horse and wagon get back here safe and sound."

"Will do," he called over his shoulder. Not wanting Mr. Creighton to see him riding away, he ran toward the river, then turned toward the church.

Within minutes he had his horse saddled again and hit the road out of town.

All the way to the ranch, he kept his eyes peeled for any sign of a wagon. Not that he expected to see one. She'd surely be there by now. He rode directly to the big house and jumped down to rap on the door.

Linette opened it. "Blue. I didn't expect to see you today."

"Is she here?"

Linette looked startled. "Who?"

"Clara and the girls. Are they here?"

"No. Is she supposed to be?"

His mind blanked. Not a thought. Then it exploded into hundreds of questions and scenarios. "Yes. No. I don't know." He swung back on his horse and raced out of the yard.

She wasn't at the ranch. She wasn't in town. He had seen no sign of her on the road. Where were they? The question wailed through his head and hammered at his eardrums.

Only one horrifying thought made sense. Harv Winch must have fed him a bunch of horse apples to distract him. There was no brother. He was here, hired by Mr. Creighton.

Blue's insides turned to steel. If Harv had Clara and the girls, he would regret his actions.

Blue galloped his horse to the man's campsite. "Harv. Harv Winch, show yourself."

The man unwound from the shadows. How did he manage to blend in to the landscape so completely? It sent shivers up and down Blue's spine.

"Thought I'd seen the last of you," Harv said.

"Where are they? What did you do with them?"

Harv's expression changed not at all. Just when Blue thought he wasn't going to answer his questions, Harv said, "Might this be the 'them' you were concerned about earlier?"

"You know it is."

"You're barking up the wrong tree."

Blue stared.

"Have a look around if you don't believe me."

Realizing he was wrong about the stranger, he shook his head, swallowing back his aggression. "There's no point." He knew the man was telling the truth. He reined away and galloped back to the trail.

Clara, where are you?

Had Rufus been mistaken? Or had Clara changed her mind? Why had he left her alone in town? If anything happened to her and the girls...

Pain stabbed every nerve ending, and he groaned. He should have never let himself care.

He snorted derisively and admitted he could no more not care about Clara than he could turn back time... something he didn't want to do. He would always love Alice and Nancy and Beau, but there was room in his heart for more...for a beautiful woman and two little girls.

A future he wanted to share with Clara and the girls beckoned. He loved her and wished to spend his life with her. He wanted to love those little girls until they glowed with joy.

If only he got a chance to tell her.

But where was she?

Oh, God, my good shepherd, lead me to her. Please keep her safe.

He knew only one place to look, and he galloped back to town. He barely reached the churchyard before he leaped from the saddle and rushed into the building.

"Clara?"

But no one was there. He hurried out the back door. His steps didn't slow until he reached the shack, and he paused only long enough to holler, "It's Blue," before he pushed the door open. But it was still empty. So, too, now was the Morton house.

Where was Clara? He asked the question over and over as he raced to the store. He clattered up the steps and grabbed the doorknob. It wouldn't turn. He tried again. Locked? In the middle of the day? "Macpherson," he roared as he banged on the door.

The only sound was his own voice.

Chapter Nineteen

Her whole life hung in the balance. If this failed, she'd be lost. Clara prayed as never before as she sat on one side of Constable Allen's desk.

The constable had agreed to help her. "You and the girls are safe under my protection. You stay here while I round up some of Edendale's citizens. You say you've been eating at the Mortons'?"

She'd nodded. "I rented the horse and wagon from Rufus."

"That's good. Did Macpherson meet you?"

"On the first day."

"Good." He'd left her and the girls alone. She'd alternately shivered with fear and paced as she told herself to be strong.

The Constable returned. "They'll soon be here."

Clara clenched her hands, tried to relax her jaw. This was the hardest thing she'd ever done.

The girls waited in the back room. She hoped they wouldn't be able to hear what went on.

"Mama, is Grandfather here?" Eleanor had whispered as Clara explained they must stay there and not make a sound.

"Don't worry, little one." The words caught in her throat as she realized she used the same endearment as Blue. "We don't need to be afraid anymore." *Please God, let it be so. Let me be correct in thinking this is what I need to do.*

Bonnie and Claude were the first to enter the room where Clara sat, trying not to let her nerves make her shake visibly. Bonnie hugged her. "We're on your side," she whispered. Claude squeezed her hand and nodded.

Then Rufus stepped inside. "My horse and wagon still in one piece?"

She managed a trembling smile. "They're out back."

He moved to stand beside Claude.

The door opened again. Macpherson entered and stepped aside to let Father in. When he saw her sitting by the Mountie, his nostrils flared and disapproval set his mouth into a grim line.

Inside, she shrank back from the criticism she knew he'd be speaking soon enough; outwardly she managed to remain calm. "Father," she acknowledged with a nod of her head.

"So I finally find you." He looked about. "Where are the girls?" He parted his lips in a gesture that was faintly feral. "Please tell me you haven't abandoned them."

If he thought his words would frighten her, cow her, he was wrong. They gave her the strength she needed to confront him. "I would never, will never ever, abandon them." *And I will never let you take them from me.*

"Mr. Creighton," Constable Allen began. "If you'll

have a seat." He indicated the chair on the other side of the desk from Clara.

The Mountie looked about him. "We are here to hear Clara's concerns, bear witness to them, and I will render a decision."

Father turned. "See here—I don't think you have that kind of authority."

Constable Allen gave him a quelling look. "I have the authority granted me by an Act of Parliament." He held Father's eyes tightly until Father shifted away.

The Mountie began to speak, but his words were interrupted when the door opened and Eddie stepped inside.

"There you are, Clara. Linette was worried about you."

Father snorted. "Good to know someone is."

"Good of you to join us," the Mountie said.

Clara smiled. She was grateful for the support she knew Eddie would give, but there was one person absent, the one person she wanted to be on her side more than any other.

Blue, where are you?

Eddie glanced around the room. "What's going on?"

Constable Allen explained, then motioned for Eddie to join the others along the wall. "Clara, we'll begin with you. Can you explain to us what your concern is?"

She'd run from her father all her life. This was her chance to stand up to him. But it took a lot of strength. She knew she had the courage needed so she sucked in air, cleared her throat and gathered her thoughts.

The door banged open, and Blue rushed in. "Constable Allen, I need your help." He saw Clara and froze. "You're here? You're okay?" He glanced about, took in the scene and backed away. "What's going on? Where are the girls?" The look he gave Clara's father reassured Clara. If she failed, Blue would do his best to protect Eleanor and Libby.

"They're safe," she said.

His breath whooshed out.

"This is a waste of precious time," Father protested, his neck reddening as he blustered. "I demand—"

The Mountie held up a hand to silence him, then turned to Clara. "Go ahead, ma'am."

Clara began, finding it easier to be strong and courageous with Blue in the room. "I only want to keep my girls and be able to raise them. Father doesn't think I'm capable. He said he'd take them from me."

Bonnie's gasp strengthened Clara. It was good to know she had people on her side.

The Mountie turned to Father. "Mr. Creighton, is this true?"

"Of course it is. My daughter doesn't know how to care for herself or her children. She's always had servants to care for her and a nanny for the children. She has no money, no means of support. She'll starve, and the girls will starve with her. I've come to get all of them and take them back home where I can take care of them."

Every word hammered at Clara's confidence, destroying it brick by brick until she met Blue's gaze. He silently reminded her that she was more than what her father thought. She smiled ever so slightly, strengthened by his presence.

"Thank you, Mr. Creighton." The Mountie turned to Claude to ask how he saw Clara's abilities.

Claude stepped forward. "I've seen Clara take care

of her girls. They are always clean and happy. I'd say she was a very good mother."

Bonnie spoke. "She's an excellent mother. No one can fault her. She doesn't accept charity but works for what she needs."

Rufus came forward when called. "That little lady is pretty independent. Why, she rented a horse and wagon. I could see she hadn't driven one before, but that didn't stop her. And by gum, she managed just fine." He turned to Clara. "You're a spunky thing, all right."

She smiled her thanks.

Eddie indicated he'd like to say something. "I haven't seen much of Clara, but I've seen enough to say she reminds me of my wife, who you all know can do just about anything she sets her mind to."

Those who knew Linette chuckled.

"Thank you," Clara whispered. She couldn't have asked for a better compliment.

Father banged his fist on the desk. "Why are you all protecting her? How can she manage on her own? She's not trained for anything. Doesn't even know how to cook a meal."

"But she does," Bonnie said. "I know because she's helped me."

Father scowled. "Are you prepared to give her a job?"

Bonnie nodded. "If she needs it."

Clara rose. "Father, I traveled across the country on my own. I worked at various jobs to provide myself and the girls with food and shelter. I can survive." She sat down again.

Blue stepped away from the wall. "It doesn't appear I need to add anything to this discussion. We've all seen how capable and determined Clara is. There is only one thing she needs." He faced the Mountie. "She needs to know no one can take the girls from her. Then she can settle down and build them a real home. That's what she needs." He leaned back against the wall.

She gave him a grateful smile, the back of her eyes stinging with unshed tears. His support and assurance that she could manage on her own meant everything to her.

The Mountie leaned forward. "I believe there is enough evidence for me to be confident that Clara can provide for her daughters. Mr. Creighton, I'm sure you are welcome to visit your daughter and granddaughters, but under no circumstances are you to consider removing the girls from her care. Do you understand me?"

Father pushed to his feet and stuck out his chest in a gesture Clara recognized as one that often made others bow before his wishes. "These proceedings are a farce."

Constable Allen rose and faced Clara's father. He showed not the least sign of being intimidated. "Be assured they are legal and binding."

With a dark look toward her, Father stormed out the door, slamming it shut behind him.

Every bone in her body turned to rubber, and she pressed her face to her palms.

Bonnie wrapped her arms around Clara's shoulders. "You're safe now. You'll always be safe in our community."

The men clustered around her and, one by one, patted her back.

"Okay, folks, time to move on." Constable Allen thanked each of them as they left.

The door closed, and blessed silence filled the room. Even Blue had gone. She tried to convince herself she didn't mind that he hadn't stayed behind. But did he believe what he'd said—that she could build the girls a home on her own? Did that mean he'd leave her to her own devices? Her heart deflated at the thought. But wasn't that exactly what she'd told him every time he offered help? She rubbed at her chest where an ache had suddenly developed.

She drew in a steadying breath and pulled her thoughts from Blue. Instead, she focused on her victory. She could keep her girls. Finally, after all the running, no one could take them from her.

Now to tell them. She hurried to the back room, where they waited patiently, and held out her arms to bring them to her.

"We are safe," she said. "We don't have to run anymore."

"Does that mean we can stay here?" Libby asked.

Clara laughed. "I don't know. I need time to make new plans." But she couldn't think of any place she'd rather be, surrounded by people who believed in her, living in a community that honored a woman's abilities. Building a home for the girls where they'd feel safe and valued.

She had no doubt she could do it on her own. But she could think of something she'd sooner do—build a new home and a new family with the man she had come to care about more than she believed she could ever care about a man. She hoped and prayed that, in time, Blue might be willing to entertain such a notion.

She straightened. "Girls, we have a life to build." But first things first. "Take off these old clothes." She helped Libby out of the sweater and smoothed her daughter's hair. "Your grandfather is here. I'm going to take you to see him."

Eleanor stepped out of reach. "He'll take us away. Just like Mary said."

"No, he won't. He can't. The Mountie won't allow it."

"You're sure?" Eleanor's voice quivered.

"Trust me. Would I allow you to be taken from me?"

Eleanor shook her head, and slowly the fear faded from her eyes.

"Where's Grandfather?" Libby asked.

"At Macpherson's store, I suppose." Where else would he go? No doubt he'd be inquiring about the returning stagecoach.

"Let's go say hello." She took the girls by their hands and marched over to the store.

When she stepped inside, several men stood around, but she saw only one. Father was but a few feet away, his expression hard as granite.

Eleanor gripped Clara's hand so hard her fingers hurt. "Hello, Grandfather," she said.

Father took a step forward.

For one brief second Clara shrank back. She thought to turn and drag the girls from the store, but she held her ground. She drew a deep breath and threw her shoulders back, stiffening her spine and her resolve. Never again would she be controlled by this man. Never again would she be controlled by her fear.

Father patted Eleanor's head.

Clara urged her younger daughter forward.

"Hello, Grandfather," Libby said hesitantly. Then she saw Blue in the corner of the store and ran to him. "Mr. Blue, you're back."

Clara sought Blue's eyes. Did her gaze reveal the

many things she felt, wondered, wished? She wanted to thank him for speaking on her behalf. More than anything, she wanted to know if he was going to be part of her future.

Petey, the stagecoach driver, had been lounging against the counter. "Missy, you still wanting to go to Fort Calgary?"

Did she? Did it still offer the best place to start over?

No. She'd already started over. Right here in Edendale.

Eddie spoke. "You're more than welcome to come to Eden Valley Ranch until you know what you want to do."

Clara nodded. "Thank you. I accept." She turned to Petey. "I don't believe I'll be wanting passage to Fort Calgary, after all."

"Fine. Then I'll take Mr. Creighton back to Fort Macleod. We leave first thing in the morning. Now, if you'll all excuse me, I'm going to have a chin-wag with Rufus." He strode from the store.

"I'll get a wagon," Eddie said and also left.

Father turned away without another word. "Where is the best hotel?" he asked the shopkeeper.

Macpherson chuckled. "We ain't got a best or worst hotel. In fact, we ain't got a hotel."

Father drew himself up. "That's unacceptable. Where's a man supposed to sleep?"

Macpherson shrugged. "Most men bunk down in my back room or sleep over in the livery barn."

Clara could almost laugh at the shock in Father's face. Instead, she looked at Blue. He had his hat on, making it difficult to see his eyes clearly, but she saw his mouth curved in a barely there smile. He nodded.

As if to say goodbye?

Her heart plummeted to the ground. Had she proved so thoroughly she could manage on her own that he didn't want to be part of the picture?

Blue. Blue. Let me explain.

At that moment, Eddie returned with the wagon. "Are you ready to go?"

No. She had to talk to Blue. Make him see that she'd only needed to prove she was capable of taking care of the girls.

She did not want to do it alone. Not now that she'd come to know Blue. Come to love him. She must explain.

But Eddie waited at the door, and the girls tugged at her hands.

"Goodbye, Father. I'll write."

She gave Blue one more pleading look, but he only lifted his finger to the brim of his hat in a goodbye salute.

Blue forced himself to remain in the store as Clara and the girls left, even though every nerve in his body longed to hurry after her. Follow her to the ranch. Ask Clara's permission to court her.

But she'd only just had assurances given that her girls could not be taken from her. Her plans had changed profoundly. She'd hopefully seen herself as others saw her—strong, capable, self-reliant.

She needed time to figure out who she was and what she wanted. He was prepared to give her that time.

He returned to the ranch later in the day when he was certain he wouldn't overtake them, and he slipped into the bunkhouse.

Over the next few days he watched her take the girls for walks, saw her visiting the other women in their various homes. He always made sure to stay out of sight, patiently waiting.

Until Sunday. Surely she'd had enough time to sort things out by then. Even if she hadn't, he could no longer stay away from her.

He was in the cookhouse, ready for the Sunday service, when she stepped in and saw him.

Her eyes flared with welcome. She didn't move. He wasn't sure she even breathed. Surely her reaction meant she was glad to see him, was as eager to spend time with him as he was with her. Then she curtained her feelings. He would not allow himself to think she'd planned a future without him.

The girls saw him and raced over.

"Where have you been, Mr. Blue?" Libby demanded as she clung to his hand.

"We missed you," Eleanor whispered. "All of us."

All of them? He tucked the words into his heart.

He'd saved room for them beside him and pulled Libby to one side and Eleanor to the other, then signaled for Clara to join them.

She hesitated but a heartbeat, then crossed to sit beside Libby.

He shifted the little girl to his knee so he and Clara sat with their elbows touching. For the first time in days, his world felt complete. His heart swelled with love, with hope she might love him in return.

Cookie led them in two hymns, and he sang but he couldn't remember what the hymns were…only the joy and pleasure of joining his voice to Clara's, having the girls' voices sing along.

Bertie rose to speak. "I hear Blue has finished making the pews."

"With Clara and the girls' help," Blue said.

"Thank you all. Soon we'll be meeting in our new church, worshiping with others from the town and nearby farms and ranches. It's good to move on. It's good to start something new and better. As it says in Psalm 118, verse twenty-three, 'This is the Lord's doing; it is marvelous in our eyes.' Don't ever be afraid of moving forward with God."

Blue was no longer afraid of the future. Only one thing concerned him. Would Clara want to share it with him?

As always, Cookie served coffee and cinnamon rolls after the service. Then Linette invited everyone up the hill for dinner.

The cowboys didn't go without invitation. "You, too, Blue," she added. "The girls have asked about you every day."

The women left immediately. He watched Clara follow the others, wished she'd turn and, if not wave goodbye, at least signal something with her eyes. But she kept her attention on whatever Jayne said to her.

The men visited a bit longer at the cookhouse, then went up the hill. Blue didn't object to sharing the meal with the others, but he needed to talk to Clara.

When the meal finally ended and the dishes done at no hurry, he asked Eddie if he could borrow a wagon.

Eddie grinned as if enjoying a secret. "Of course."

Blue didn't care if everyone stared at him when he approached Clara as the women came to the front room. "Clara, may I take you for a drive?"

He knew he saw a flare of pleasure in her eyes before she quenched it. "The girls?"

"Please leave them here," Linette said. "They're enjoying having lots of playmates."

Clara spoke to the girls where they played with the other children, and both nodded. She returned to Blue's side. "Very well. I'd very much enjoy a drive."

He jogged down the hill, harnessed a horse to the wagon and rattled back to the big house.

Clara stepped out before Blue reached the door.

He took her hand and helped her up to the seat before scrambling up beside her. "I've missed you," he said.

He hadn't meant to blurt that out; he'd meant to work up to it. But his heart couldn't contain the words any longer.

"I've been here every day since I left town," she replied.

Did she sound disappointed that he had made no attempt to speak to her? "I thought you needed some time to sort out all the changes in your life," he said as they rode from the yard.

"I had it sorted out before I left town."

Good to know. Now if she would say if she saw him in her plans...

"There's a spot I want you to see."

They rode in silence for a spell. Then he pointed out the landmarks. "It's a good country. A man would have to look hard to find any better. Of course, there are those unexpected snowstorms to contend with." For the past three weeks they'd enjoyed sunshine and mild winter temperatures.

"I have learned it's the people who make this a good country."

His breath stalled. Did she mean him?

"They are accepting and supportive," she added. "Something I've learned to appreciate. Even more, people here accept a woman as a valuable partner in life."

He fit into that pattern. But he'd not tell her just yet. Not until they reached the spot he wanted to show her.

A few moments later, he pulled the wagon to a stop in view of a field, empty but for crusted grass and ringed by trees and a flowing creek. "This is it."

She stared. "What am I supposed to see?"

He took her hand and pulled her close. "A new place. A little house right there." He pointed. "Over there a barn. A garden there. Children playing on the hill there. Cattle farther afield."

She laughed. "You have a vivid imagination."

He turned to face her. "It's what I want. But I don't want it by myself." He searched her eyes. Dare he believe he saw encouragement in them? "Clara, I want you to be part of my future. Do you suppose it would be possible for us to start over together?"

"Maybe."

Maybe? He wanted more than that. So much more. "Clara, I love you. I want you in my life. I want the girls in my life."

A smile filled her face. "You love me?"

He'd thought it so often the past few days he thought everyone could tell. "Let's go look at my house." He jumped to the ground and lifted her down, keeping her hand tucked around his arm as they walked down the hill to the spot where he envisioned the house. He stood behind her and pointed as he spoke. "Right here where we can see the seasons change along the creek, where we'll be protected from the winter winds and be able to see the sunset every evening."

She leaned against him. "Sounds like a nice place."

He wrapped his arms around her. "It will be a lonely place without you." He turned her to face him. "Clara, I love you like I never imagined a man could love a woman."

When she didn't speak, his heart lurched. Then she cupped her hands about his face. Her tenderness, her warmth, reached straight through his chest, cradling his questing heart.

He closed his eyes and lived the moment. He allowed nothing to rob him of a single sensation of her touch. Not worry, not doubts, nothing but the joy of this moment.

"Blue, you have taught me to value my strengths, helped me see how I can do whatever is necessary. You made me believe things I only hoped were possible."

His eyes opened to watch her.

She examined his every feature as if wanting to burn them deep into her memories.

"I can't imagine life without you." She brought her gaze to him, and his heart exploded at the love pouring from her blue eyes. "I love you like I never dreamed possible."

He caught her hands and brought them to his lips. "Clara, I want to spend the rest of my life loving you. Will you marry me?"

"I will love you to the ends of the earth and back, and, yes, I will marry you."

He tossed his hat in the air and whooped with joy, then swung her off her feet. "Mrs. Clara Lyons. Imagine that." He set her on her feet and tipped her head up. "I love you." He caught her lips in a gentle kiss, promising his heart and support for the rest of his life.

He meant to keep the kiss short and gentle, but she wrapped her arms about his waist, pressed one hand to his back and the other to his head and clung to him.

What could he do but kiss her with his whole heart?

Chapter Twenty

Blue led Clara from spot to spot, telling her of his plans. "A big garden here. Of course, I'll have to fence it. I'll put it close to the house so you can easily tend it. You do want a garden, don't you?" he asked, as if realizing she might have a say in the plans.

But she didn't care where he put the garden or anything else.

He loved her. She loved him. They were going to start over again. A new family. A new home.

"Show me again where the house will be."

He led her to the spot he'd chosen. "Do you like it here?"

"I like it fine. What kind of house will it be?"

He scrubbed at his chin. "Do you want one as big as the Gardiners'? I know it's what you're used to but—" He lifted his hands in a helpless gesture. "I'm not a rich man."

She pulled him to face her. "I've been rich and pampered. I didn't much care for it. I've been penniless and homeless over the past weeks. Worried about how I was going to take care of the girls. I didn't like that, either."

She wrapped her arms around his neck. "But I do have a dream." She pulled his head down and kissed him.

"Tell me," he said when she released him.

"Stop distracting me."

He laughed and kissed her nose. "Tell me about your dream."

She turned and leaned her back into his chest and pulled his arms about her. He rested his chin on the top of her head.

"I dream of a home where I make simple meals, where our children share our mealtimes and help with chores. I dream of a real family where each individual is valued and important."

He chuckled, his breath warm against her cheek. "And I thought you meant to tell me about the house you wanted."

"That's easy. Four walls and a roof that doesn't leak. A big kitchen, a cozy sitting room with books and dolls and wagons for the children. Two bedrooms…maybe more."

He turned her into his arms. "I can see we're going to be busy." His voice grew husky. He kissed her again, so tenderly her heart squeezed out pure, sweet joy.

He leaned back and sighed. "I won't be able to build a house here until spring."

"Spring? Why, that's months away. Must we wait until then to marry?"

He laughed at her eagerness, and heat rushed up her cheek. "Am I being presumptuous?"

"I'm pleased to know you're as eager as I to get married. But we need a house."

"Blue, I've lived in a little half-canvas shack and

would do it again if it meant we could be together. I don't need much. Only you and the girls."

"I don't want to wait, either. You know, there is a small house in town that is empty. Perhaps we could rent it for the winter."

She hugged him. "That sounds fine to me. Now let's go tell the girls."

He hesitated. "Do you think they'll approve?"

She laughed. "I'm quite sure they will. They've been cross at me because I said I wasn't going to stay and keep Mr. Blue in their lives."

He grinned. "I love those girls of yours."

"From now on, they're ours."

"I like that."

She cuddled close to him as they made the return trip. Oh, how she loved this man. "When we arrived in Edendale, I assured the girls that God would lead us to where we were meant to be. I thought it was Fort Calgary. But He has guided us to a far better outcome than I could have ever asked or dreamed."

Snow began to fall. Great fluffy flakes that plopped to her face and clung on her lashes. She caught some on her tongue and laughed. "I need not fear the winter for the good shepherd has led me to a safe place."

He pulled her close and kissed the snow from her lashes. "God blessed us with our love."

When they reached the ranch, he pointed to the big house. "Look."

The two little girls had their faces pressed to the glass of the window overlooking the ranch. Eleanor was pointing toward them, and Libby jumped up and down.

Clara turned to him. "A kiss for their benefit?"

He chuckled. "Not only for theirs, I trust." He lowered his head and caught her lips in a kiss full of promise and possibility.

They broke apart, and she turned toward the house.

Eleanor and Libby could not have looked more pleased.

"God has answered all our prayers," she whispered and pressed her head to Blue's shoulder.

The future beckoned…a future filled with love and trust and things she couldn't even imagine at this moment.

Her heart was full to overflowing.

Blue and Clara took the girls into the library so they could talk to them privately.

Blue pulled them each to sit on his knees. "Is it okay with you if I marry your mama?"

Eleanor nodded, her eyes brimming with joy.

Libby patted Blue's cheek. "I always knowed it."

Clara laughed. "I think they saw you as a permanent part of our lives from the beginning."

Eleanor nodded. "We did."

Libby squirmed about on Blue's knee and leaned over to whisper in Eleanor's ear. "Can I tell now?"

Eleanor shushed her sister. "Not yet." She turned to her mama. "When will you and Mr. Blue get married?"

"I don't know. We haven't made plans." Clara looked at him for answer.

He shrugged. He'd get married this moment if she agreed, but perhaps she needed time to make plans.

Clara turned back to Eleanor. "Why do you ask?"

Eleanor and Libby shared a secretive look.

"Can you get married before Christmas?" Eleanor asked.

Blue studied the three females who were about to become his family. He sensed the girls had a wish.

"I'm agreeable if your mama is."

Clara smiled, warmth and love and a hundred promises brimming from her eyes. "I'm most agreeable. No need for rush but no need for delay, either."

He knew his eyes must surely speak from the overflow of a grateful, happy heart.

"Will we have our own home for Christmas?" Eleanor asked, her voice revealing a mixture of caution and hope. Then she shook her head. "It doesn't matter. We can stay in the shack."

Blue smiled. "We already have a home picked out. Did you notice the house near the river behind the store?" He wasn't sure they would know which one he meant.

"Is that where we're going to live?" Eleanor didn't wait for an answer. "Can we put up a Christmas tree?" Eleanor seemed to think it was important they do so.

Considering the abundance of pine and spruce to the west, Blue thought a Christmas tree would be a simple thing to find and said so.

"Good. Now we can tell." Libby bounced up and down so hard Blue could hardly hold her. "We asked God to send us a special Christmas present."

Eleanor nodded and slid in a few words as Libby paused to catch her breath. "We asked for a new papa for Christmas."

"And a new family," Libby added.

"And we got Mr. Blue." The girls spoke the words in unison and turned to wrap their arms around his neck.

Blue felt the tears gather in his eyes, but he didn't bother to hide them. He had never thought to know such love and joy. He signaled for Clara to join them. She sat beside him and pressed her head to his shoulder.

He kissed the top of her head, then pressed a kiss atop each girl's head.

"I am a very blessed man."

"God has led us together, and I will never cease to be grateful." Clara sounded as if she was close to tears.

"This is going to be the best Christmas ever," Libby crowed. Unable to sit still, she leaped to her feet, grabbed her sister's hands and the pair swung about in joyful abandon. "The best Christmas ever," they sang over and over.

Clara tipped her face to Blue.

"It will be a Christmas to remember," he said before he kissed her lips gently.

* * * * *

Dear Reader,

I love Christmas. I love sharing it with family. When I think of those who are alone at this time of year, I want to draw my family closer and hold them tight. I thank God for each of them. They fill my life with joy. So it saddened me to think of two little girls longing for a new daddy. I like to think, too, that they were far less interested in material gifts than in the joy of finding a papa who loved them. Even that pales in comparison to the greatest gift of all—God's holy son coming to earth to redeem fallen mankind. Jesus is the reason for the season. May you enjoy the season and celebrate the reason.

I love to hear from my readers. You can contact me at *www.lindaford.org* where you'll find my email address and where you can find out more about me and my books.

Blessings,

Linda Ford

REQUEST YOUR FREE BOOKS!

2 FREE INSPIRATIONAL NOVELS
PLUS 2 *FREE* MYSTERY GIFTS

Love Inspired® HISTORICAL

LIHI5

SPECIAL EXCERPT FROM

Love Inspired HISTORICAL

A marriage of convenience to rancher Shane McCoy is the only solution to Tessa Spencer's predicament. He needs a mother for his twins, and she needs a fresh start.

Can two pint-size matchmakers help them open their guarded hearts in time for Christmas?

Read on for a sneak preview of
THE RANCHER'S CHRISTMAS PROPOSAL
by **Sherri Shackelford,**
available in November 2015 from Love Inspired Historical!

"We could make a list." Tessa's voice quivered. "Of all the reasons for and against the marriage."

She had the look of a wide-eyed doe, softly innocent, ready to flee at the least disturbance. She'd been strong and brave since the moment he'd met her, and he'd never considered how much energy that courage cost her. For a woman on her own, harassment from men like Dead Eye Dan Fulton must be all too familiar. He felt her desperation as though her plea had taken on a physical presence. If he refused, if he turned her away, where would she turn to next?

A fierce need to shelter her from harm welled up inside him, and he stalled for time. "It's not a bad idea. Unexpected, sure. But not crazy."

These past days without the children had been a nightmare. Being together again was right and good, the way things were supposed to be. He hadn't felt this at peace since he'd held Alyce and Owen in his arms that first time nearly two years ago.

"We don't need a list." Her hesitant uncertainty spurred him into action. "After thinking things through, getting married is the best solution."

"Are you certain?" Tessa asked softly, a heartbreaking note of doubt in her voice.

"I'd ask you the same. It's a hard life. Be sure you know the bargain you're making. I don't want you making a mistake you can't take back."

"You're not a mistake, Mr. McCoy."

"Shane," he said, his throat working. "Call me Shane."

The last time he'd plunged into a marriage, he'd been confident that friendship would turn into love. Never again. He'd go about things differently this time. With this marriage, he'd keep his distance, treat the relationship as a partnership in the business. He'd give her space instead of stifling her.

She was more than he deserved. Her affection for the children had obviously instigated her precipitous suggestion. Though he lauded her compassion, someday Owen and Alyce would be grown and gone, and there'd be only the two of them. What then? Would they have enough in common after the years to survive the loss of what had brought them together in the first place?

"You're certain?" he asked.

Her chin came up a notch. "There's one thing you should know about me. Once I make up my mind, I don't change it. I'll feel the same in a day, a week, a month and a year. There's no reason to wait."

Don't miss
THE RANCHER'S CHRISTMAS PROPOSAL
by Sherri Shackelford,
available November 2015 wherever
Love Inspired® Historical books and ebooks are sold.

SPECIAL EXCERPT FROM

Love Inspired®

*When an Amish bachelor suddenly must care for a baby,
will his beautiful next-door neighbor rush to his aid?*

*Read on for a sneak preview of
THE AMISH MIDWIFE,
the final book in the brand-new trilogy
LANCASTER COURTSHIPS*

"I know I can't raise a baby. I can't! You know what to do. You take her! You raise her." Joseph thrust Leah toward Anne. The baby started crying.

"Don't say that. She is your niece, your blood. You will find the strength you need to care for her."

"She needs more than my strength. She needs a mother's love. I can't give her that."

Joseph had no idea what a precious gift he was trying to give away. He didn't understand the grief he would feel when his panic subsided. She had to make him see that.

Anne stared into his eyes. "I can help you, Joseph, but I can't raise Leah for you. Your sister Fannie has wounded you deeply, but she must have enormous faith in you. Think about it. She could have given her child away. She didn't. She wanted Leah to be raised by you, in our Amish ways. Don't you see that?"

He rubbed a hand over his face. "I don't know what to think."

"You haven't had much sleep in the past four days. If you truly feel you can't raise Leah, you must go to Bishop Andy. He will know what to do."

"He will tell me it is my duty to raise her. Did you mean it when you said you would help me?" His voice held a desperate edge.

"Of course. Before you make any rash decisions, let's see if we can get this fussy child to eat something. Nothing wears on the nerves faster than a crying *bubbel* that can't be consoled."

She took the baby from him.

He raked his hands through his thick blond hair again. "I must milk my goats and get them fed."

"That's fine, Joseph. Go and do what you must. Leah can stay with me until you're done."

"*Danki*, Anne Stoltzfus. You have proven you are a good neighbor. Something I have not been to you." He went out the door with hunched shoulders, as if he carried the weight of the world upon them.

Anne looked down at little Leah with a smile. "He'd better come back for you. I know where he lives."

Don't miss
THE AMISH MIDWIFE
by USA TODAY bestselling author Patricia Davids.
Available November 2015 wherever
Love Inspired® books and ebooks are sold.

JUST CAN'T GET ENOUGH OF INSPIRATIONAL ROMANCE?

Love Inspired has all the inspirational romance you need including contemporary, suspenseful and historical.

Whatever your mood, we have a romance just for you!

Connect with us to find your next great read, special offers and more.

 www.Facebook.com/LoveInspiredBooks

www.Twitter.com/LoveInspiredBks

Harlequin.com/Community

ISBN-13:978-0-373-28330-9

Earn
FREE
REWARDS
Join
Today!

Cowboy to the Rescue

Summoned by two little girls to help their mother in distress,
Blue Lyons rushes to rescue widow Clara Weston. When the
cowboy discovers the fatherless family has nowhere to go,
he offers them food and shelter. But widower Blue won't get
too close to the needy trio. He's lost too many people he's
cared for, and he isn't about to set himself up for loss again.

For Clara, any dangers she may face on the frontier are
preferable to staying with her controlling father. Although
she's determined to keep her independence, Blue's kindness
and tenderness are hard to resist. Can two pint-size
matchmakers help Clara and Blue open their guarded
hearts in time for Christmas?

*Christmas
in
Eden Valley*

*Forging a future in
Canada's west country*

$5.99 U.S./$6.75 CAN.

ISBN-13: 978-0-373-28330-9

9 780373 283309

50599

CATEGORY
INSPIRATIONAL

HARLEQUIN®
LOVE INSPIRED®
HISTORICAL

harlequin.com